T0158198

Ordinary Harassment

Maria Madonna Martin
vs
Penn Area Vocational Technical School

DONNA M. HEINTZ

iUniverse, Inc.
Bloomington

Ordinary Harassment
Maria Madonna Martin vs Penn Area Vocational Technical School

iUniverse books may be ordered through booksellers or by contacting:

iUniverse
1663 Liberty Drive
Bloomington, IN 47403
www.iuniverse.com
1-800-Authors (1-800-288-4677)

ISBN: 978-1-4759-4578-2 (sc)
ISBN: 978-1-4759-4579-9 (hc)
ISBN: 978-1-4759-4580-5 (e)

Library of Congress Control Number: 2012914939

Printed in the United States of America

iUniverse rev. date: 9/4/2012

For those who deal with workplace harassment
and the people who helped them survive

Special thanks to

Jean Borsodi
who gave me guidance

Alexandria Maria Madonna Heintz-Smith
who gave me purpose

Marc Nebraski
who helped me find strength

Frank and Kathy Korona
who demonstrated the true meaning of friendship through their actions

Foreword

Life is filled with lessons. Sometimes we learn from mistakes we have made, sometimes we learn from things that were done to us and sometimes we learn from watching how someone has handled what has happened to them.

Maria Martin is my mother; a small woman, with a big heart and a strong mind. She is a great teacher, and an idealist who looks for the good in all people. It was gut wrenching to watch as she went through her journey with bullying and harassment at the school where she teaches but it taught me four very important lessons.

Lesson One
No matter how much you want to believe there is good in everyone, sometimes you are just wrong. There are people in this world who are just mean and get great pleasure from bullying others. They may feel you are weaker or think they have power over you; especially if they are your boss. It is difficult to understand why a bully will choose you as their target.

Lesson Two
When you run into these people maintain your poise. No matter how hard it is, do not let someone provoke you into lowering your standards. Scream all you want at home into a pillow, but in public always hold your head up high and hold onto your dignity. It is not easy but you will be the better person in the long run.

Lesson Three

And this is the most important lesson to remember; you can find the strength you need to get through anything. It is not always easy but the key to survival is to reach inside for just enough strength to get through the day. Tomorrow is a new day and you can reach for more strength to get through that day. Many days will be difficult, but you will always find strength if you reach down inside yourself deep enough.

Lesson Four

Keep a diary. My mother always kept diaries to document different parts of her life. We would sit down every year on my birthday, look back over her diaries and relive memories of wonderful times we had together. It was one of my favorite times of the year. It was something that she had done with her parents and something I look forward to doing with my children.

When my mother began student teaching she had to keep a diary for school. Her professor said it could be a tool to analyze her behavior, her reaction to others and could help her become a better teacher. She continued the diary when she began working at Penn. Her diary turned into a key piece of evidence describing years of abuse. I was touched when she shared this part of her life with me. It was a part of her life she had always tried to shield me from. Reading her diary took me on a journey of fear, frustration, disillusionment, and above all, tremendous courage. I learned many things on the journey. Above all I learned what I already knew; there is no one else I would want as a mother.

Alonna

Maria's Story

I became a teacher to share my passion for learning. I never imagined myself teaching on a high school level but I immediately fell in love with the students. They were all unique in their own right; each struggling with the challenges that teenagers face today; each searching to find their own identity, their own voice. I became more than a teacher of coursework. I became a mentor, a sounding board, and a guide to help students become self advocates. I developed a deep respect for this group of young adults and I was honored that the respect was reciprocated.

Life was good and fulfilling then suddenly I became the victim of bullying and harassment by a male co-worker. Was he jealous of my relationship with the students? Was he angered that I had rebuffed his advances? Was he threatened that yet another strong-minded woman had entered the revered good ol'e boys club of the Pennsylvania tech school? I doubt that I will ever know. Sometimes a bully is just a bully. It is one of the uglier sides of work that few people dare to talk about. It can leave the strongest of women weak and frustrated and even afraid. It is even uglier when your boss joins forces with the bully.

My work diary started out as a way to record events in hopes that it would help me become a better teacher, a better role model, a better person. How ironic that it also helped to record the heartless, malicious behavior of my tormentors. This diary became a key piece of evidence in the legal battle that would ensue from my life with what the school attorneys described as ordinary harassment. It is sad they don't understand there is nothing ordinary about harassment of any kind. It does damage beyond measure. It can chip away at your strength and destroy your self confidence. Ordinary harassment can turn you into a shell of the woman who you once were. It takes tremendous energy to hang on to your identity and not become a victim for life. The diary helped me do that. And on a very bright note; it turns out that writing is not just good therapy, it is good evidence.

The Beginning

JUNE 23, 2000

Everyone has that one really important job interview that comes along at some point in their life. Mine was tonight. I spent the past four years working, going to school full time, and devoting every minute in between to Alonna, my daughter. I even served for three years as president of her elementary PTA. I graduated with honors in May and surprised myself with how well I did on the National Teacher Exams, but in Gallatin County teaching jobs are very hard to come by. You can spend years on the substitute teaching list unless you know someone on the school board or are related to them. I don't know anyone on any of the local school boards so when I was called for an interview at The Penn Area Vocational Technical School I was a nervous wreck for days. There are four teaching jobs open at Penn; two instructional and two shop jobs. I qualify for the instructional jobs. I almost feel like my nerves are going to pop through my skin! If I am hired I can stay in Pennsylvania. I don't want Alonna to go through what I did when I was growing up. We were constantly moving and just when I started to make friends and feel a little comfortable, we would move again. It was unbelievably hard even though I had two parents, a brother and a sister to help me.

Life is different for me and Alonna. She has been my greatest joy for the past nine years but it isn't easy raising a child on your own. I want to stay in Pennsylvania. I don't want to have to move away. I want Alonna to continue to grow up around her grandmother and aunts, uncles and cousins. Life is so much easier when you have the love of a strong family around you. All I could do at this point was pray.

I waited for half an hour in the front hall of Penn for my interview. I had never been to an interview where they didn't have at least a chair to sit on while you waited for the interview to begin. It was uncomfortable and a little unsettling. Finally a large, stocky man came out of the conference room to get me. His suit was a size too small, he was sweating profusely and he looked more nervous than I was. He didn't introduce himself so I had no way of knowing he was actually Mr. Bart, the school's director. Other than calling my name he didn't say a word as we walked down the long hallway. He opened the door and pointed toward an open seat at the head of the table.

Ten out of the twelve school board members were at the interview. I didn't expect to see that many people there to interview me but I have learned to be prepared for anything. Thank goodness because I was expecting a real interview and that's not what I got. Five board members were shuffling through piles of papers instead of listening to me and one woman actually got up as I was answering a question and placed a call on her cell phone. It was very distracting, not to mention extremely rude. I could understand answering the phone if you were expecting an important call, but to actually place a call was very disrespectful. The board members didn't seem to have much respect for Bart either. Every time he tried to ask me a question someone cut him off. He just sank back into his seat. I was quickly losing any respect that I might have had for this board.

As the interview was wrapping up, a male board member seated next to me patted my hand and told me that I had done a good job. He made me feel like I was ten, but deep inside I hoped he was right. I am not your typical new teacher. I am forty years old and it is a late age to enter the teaching field. I am competing with people who are vibrant twenty year olds. But I did inherit good genes — my father's dark hair and olive skin along with my mother's big brown eyes and petite frame. I don't know if I would consider myself vibrant, but I have always had a free spirit. Changing jobs every two years; always searching for my place in life. Things changed nine years ago though. My spirit found ground. Mac, the man I loved, walked out on me when I was five months pregnant. He talked a good game of civic duty and responsibility but that only applied when it involved public recognition for himself. His brother convinced him that the baby and I would just hold him back politically so he lost no time in packing his bags and heading out the door. Actually he ran to the door; he wanted that political prize more than anything in the world. I wanted to fall apart, but I didn't have that option. I had a baby on the way and she would need me to be her everything. I knew I would protect her and care for her with every breath in me. I don't know if it was right or wrong but I made the decision I wasn't going to play games with her heart so I made a deal with Mac; I got sole custody of Alonna and he was free and clear of any child support or us for that matter. He was free to pursue his quest for public acclaim. He jumped on the offer.

My decision meant life wasn't always easy. There were many tears and many fears but Alonna was worth every struggle. I was devoted to her. And now my ability to provide for her rested in the hands of a group of individuals who reminded me of Mac; craving power and praise without putting forth any effort to earn it. But since teaching positions in this area are hard to come by I just had to suck it up and smile. I smiled as big as I could for them even though I wanted to tell the cell phone woman how she could use a lesson in basic manners and how the rest of the group needed lessons in common courtesy and respect. I guess I will just have to wait and see what happens.

JUNE 27, 2000
Wow! I feel like I can finally breathe. I have a teaching job! It is what I have been working toward for the past four years. I was officially hired this evening as the Resource Instructor for Penn. It is Pennsylvania's first area vocational technical school. The fact that Penn is a historic school suits me. I am the descendant of George Ross the Signer, member of the First Continental Congress, Signer of The Declaration of Independence, uncle by marriage to Betsy Ross, and friend of George Washington. I like being part of something rich in history.

There is one unsettling aspect about taking the job at Penn. Legend has it there is a bad vibration in the school. Penn is closely located to Fort Liberty, a military fort where people sought refuge from Indian attacks in the 1700s and was a stop–over for Daniel Boone and his band of settlers on their way to Kentucky. There has been a lot of bloodshed over the centuries on the school's property. It is said there is a sense of unrest there and it can affect those who spend a lot of time on the property. More than a few deaths have also occurred in the building. Is it a connection or a coincidence? The thought of the history associated with the area is intriguing for a history buff like me, but it is also a little unnerving. Actually after all of these years, so is the thought of going back to high school. I just have to get through the rest of the summer and then I will have a real paycheck. Maybe we can even have a real Christmas this year. No more poster board painted Christmas trees hung on the wall and doll houses made from cardboard and wallpaper sample books.

AUGUST 24, 2000
School started today; actually there is a two day in-service for teachers before the students start on Monday. All those first day of school feelings still exist after all these years and this time it seems to be more intense. It reminds me of the first time I taught a graphics class at the community college; I almost threw up. The head of the graphics department told me that was a good thing though. He said it is that combination of adrenaline and nervous excitement that would keep me on my toes and make me a better teacher.

There are a few familiar faces from unexpected places; Samantha Hull who lives just down the road from me and Dave Sanders who I had classes with at Washington University. There are also a few new teachers starting with me; two other women and one man; Sam Waters, who was hired in at $7,000 more than the women. It would appear that male teachers are valued more than female teachers. How is that fair? He isn't any more qualified than any of the women. I guess this is my first back to school lesson. High school, even after all these years, still isn't fair. At this point I am just grateful for the job and the opportunity to provide a secure life for Alonna.

AUGUST 25, 2000
I am a quick study of people. Personalities fascinate me and there are an extraordinary number of strong personalities here. Most people think I am very quiet. I used to be surprised by that, but then I realized that although nothing much comes out of my mouth, my mind never shuts off. I listen to and analyze what is being said around me. It tells me a lot about the people I am dealing with. I learned a lot about the people I would be working with today. One of my favorite TV shows growing up was MASH and today Alan Pierce showed up in a Hawaiian print shirt. He's not in the medical field but I got the distinct feeling he thinks he's as cool as Hawkeye Pierce. He is tall, lean and scruffy. The major difference between the character

and this man as I see it right now is that Hawkeye was naturally cool and kind hearted. Alan Pierce appears to be neither. He is trying too hard to be cool. There is a definite arrogance about him and I must say an obvious mean streak. Hot Lips was also there and a woman who looked so nervous I thought she was going to jump out of her track shoes and bolt for the door. Will she make it through the year? Will I? I have to. This isn't about me anymore. It is about providing for Alonna.

I wondered if Chris, the man who sat next to me, made it to lunch without having a drink. He smelled like he had one before he got to school. The rest of the room was filled with a mixture of nurture/caretakers, skilled professionals and more than a few complainers all trying to make it through Mr. Bart's monotone speeches. Bart then had us put a puzzle together, but the pieces didn't match the picture on the outside of the box. Out of the corner of my eye I saw a woman send puzzle pieces flying across the room and storm out. What the hell just happened? Chris explained that he, unlike most women he knew, was not a gossip, but the woman's husband had left her for the next door neighbor's cousin who was visiting from London. The picture on her puzzle box was Big Ben; the clock, not the Steeler.

I left the day questioning many things I had been taught during the four years I worked on my education degree at Washington University and with one unyielding certainty; contrary to what some of my colleagues had adamantly expressed, the person you are as you begin high school is not a true measure of the person you are capable of becoming. I am proof of that. There is no ruler to measure one's potential. As teachers it is our duty to educate, motivate, and inspire our students to tap into the potential that lies within each of us. I guess I'll take it one inch at a time. Can I do this? Yes I can!

SEPTEMBER 1, 2000

I am not quite sure how I am feeling. Lost? Disillusioned? Many of the shop teachers don't seem to think too highly of my job which is basically to introduce technology to all of the students thru the use of computers. There are computer training programs for each of the shop programs and a wealth of information on the internet. Chris told me that of course he wouldn't gossip but most of the shop teachers thought of my position as more or less a babysitting service for their students a few times a week. I don't want to cast stones here but I studied for four years to become a teacher. I had to get my bachelor's degree and take six National Teachers' Exams to get my certification before I could walk into the classroom. Vocational shop teachers are different. They come in from industry. They start teaching immediately and take courses as they go along. I suppose I understand it on some level. There are not many jobs out there for shop teachers so vo-tech schools like Penn look for people highly skilled in their trade area to teach the program. But honestly some of them have a crazy attitude; they don't think you are important if you are not a shop teacher. I'll deal with it and I'm sure eventually they will see how helpful the resource program can be. I hope it doesn't take too long. Sometimes it is best not to take a preconceived attitude toward you personally. You just have to be yourself, do your best and let people get to know you. Honestly, I don't think it is going to be that easy. I also have to admit that my feelings are more than a little hurt. Did I make the right decision taking this job? Since there were no other job opening this year I guess the answer is yes.

SEPTEMBER 21, 2000
I am still trying to get familiar with the work that goes on in each shop so I decided to walk down to Pete's shop instead of calling him. As I was walking down the lower corridor, I noticed Jack Keffer standing outside the door to his shop. He seems to spend a lot of time standing in the hall instead of actually being in the shop. Bart would never notice because he spends all of his days locked inside his office. The students don't even know that Bart is the director. By the way, what are the students doing while Keffer is standing in the hall? Anyways. Keffer asked me where I was going. He said I shouldn't go down to the maximum security area alone. Was he serious? He seemed serious. I didn't quite get it. I know the shops at the lower end are considered to have a rougher rep, but if they had a bad reputation for security issues, then why didn't Bart do something about it? Is this really the good ol'e boys club that I've heard it is or could it be that Bart and the school board just don't care what happens here? I care and I want to feel safe anywhere within the school.

OCTOBER 31, 2000
It's Halloween. I chaperoned a Halloween dance at the school this past Friday night. I didn't wear a costume. I thought about it and I wanted to because I love Halloween. It is a night for dressing up and having fun but I'm still feeling my way at school and don't want to cross any boundaries between teacher and student. Kathy Crawler slow danced with a senior

and I almost couldn't get my jaw off of the floor. Was she nuts? She is only about ten years younger than me so she should have some sense of maturity but she seems to thrive on attention from the boys and being included in gossipy conversations with the girls. I think Kathy is walking a dangerous line. As much as you like the students you are not one of them. You can be friendly but not friends; and you most certainly should not slow dance with a teenage boy!

Teaching at Penn is so much different than what I thought it was going to be. In addition to the lack of direction from Bart there is one other huge thing that bothers me. School is a place where we are legally required to send our children. Aren't we morally, ethically, and legally bound to treat each and every student fairly? This doesn't happen at Penn. At this school two students can commit the same offense but one will get suspended and the other just needs to apologize because he was having a bad day. Boys get away with a lot more than the girls do here. That irritates me but there doesn't seem to be anyone I can talk to about my concerns.

Hopefully I can make the time I spend with the students meaningful for them and show them that there are people who will listen and not judge them before knowing the whole story. I am just overwhelmed with the number of students I need to see. Bart wants me to see every student in the building every week. That's a lot of students. We have over 400 students for the first semester and almost that many for the second semester. That's a lot of teenagers to deal with. How can I possibly do any good if I am trying to move these kids through like cattle?

NOVEMBER 3, 2000

On the first day of school we were told that one of the instructional teachers had called and said she accepted a job in Texas. At the October board meeting Charlotte Donavan was hired to replace her. She is now the fourth teacher in the instructional education department. The instructional education program includes enrichment programs like my resource program as well as programs that work with learning support students and do tutoring. I remember Charlotte from Washington University. She always had a smile on her face and had a bounce in her step. I don't know what her personal life is like but it seems like she doesn't have a care in the world. Boy do I envy that. I love my life but it is anything but carefree. I guess that comes from the responsibility of being both a mother and a father to Alonna. I think I am doing a good job at it. Several years ago

Alonna's kindergarten teacher told me that he couldn't even tell that she didn't have a father in her life. Hmmmm. I wasn't sure how to take that. She does have two uncles who treat her just like they treat their own children. Anyways. It will be good working with Charlotte. I can't help but feel motherly toward her. She was born the year I graduated from high school but our personalities seem to click. Maybe some of that carefree enthusiasm will rub off on me.

Geoffrey Edmonson was also hired at the October board meeting. He is my new immediate supervisor. Maybe the board wanted someone who would actually come out of the administrative office during the day. He has only been here a short amount of time but I get a very bad feeling from this guy. I don't know him at all but he talks to me in a very intimate manner and I don't like it. He is a small, thin, bony man; not much bigger than me so when he gets close to me he is literally right up in my face. He almost whispers when he talks like he is telling secrets and leans in close. I think it is just an excuse to get close and it makes me uncomfortable. I'm not sure what his background is but there are a lot of upset people around here because he was hired over two applicants from within the school.

It's my first year at Penn and I would like to try to avoid any drama but it seems to be everywhere in the building especially since Edmonson came on board. The union is already talking about fighting his hiring. Keffer, the union president claims Edmonson doesn't have the proper credentials for the position. It does sound a little suspicious; the board changed the job title from Assistant Director to *Assistant to the Director* at the board meeting and within minutes of the title change hired Edmonson without reposting the position with the changes. I'm not a legal expert but I don't think what happened was legal. At the very least it was unethical. Is this what we're supposed to teach the students? What kind of influence will Edmonson have in the building? My grandmother always seemed to be able to sense what was in a person's heart the moment she met them and looked into their eyes. She said I have her gift. I sense a lot of darkness in Edmonson. I hope his darkness doesn't start to seep into the school. With the dark vibrations still hanging around from the days of Fort Liberty I think it could be a very dangerous combination.

NOVEMBER 15, 2000
After eleven weeks I am finally started to feel comfortable with my job. I think I felt so unsettled because I was so unsure what was expected of

me. Bart told me to just do what I want to and work out a schedule with the shop teachers. I've never had a job before where my boss didn't give me any direction at all. Is it a trick or doesn't he care just as long as I don't bother him? The students need to be exposed to technology. We live in a semi rural part of the country and for some students this may be the only chance they have to use a computer. I will do my best with the time I have. By the way, why don't we have a library?

Edmonson makes me more uncomfortable every day. There is something very off and very, very creepy about him. He tries to flatter me every time I see him. He gets a quizzical look on his face like he really doesn't understand why I am not gushing all over him. It's like maple syrup is pouring out of his mouth. I don't like it. He also keeps touching me when he talks to me. I definitely don't like that! There is no reason for him to rest his hand on the small of my back or brush a hair away from my face when he talks to me. I have only know him for a little over a month and this past week he told me that he would like to move me to an administrative position. He doesn't have the authority to do that. Not to mention the fact that even if there was an administrative position open, I don't have the credentials. Does he think I am stupid or am just some naive woman who will just fall into his scrawny arms to move into administration? Neither thought is very pleasant. Skin covered bones caressing me are not a turn on and I didn't go into education to become an administrator; I went into education to work with the students as a teacher. I am going to have to be very cautious around him. That darkness I see in his heart tells me he could be a very vindictive man. I hope I don't actually vomit on his Italian shoes one day when he puts his hands on me.

December 5, 2000

It's my birthday! Oh ya, it's my birthday! Forty-one years old today. I love my birthday. Absolutely love my birthday! Every year gets better for me emotionally. When I turned thirty I finally felt like an adult and when I turned forty I felt like it was time for people to start taking me seriously, although I don't think that has really happened. I'm still working on it. Maybe it's because I have always had more of a free spirit or because I never like to say anything that is going to embarrass someone or hurt their feelings. I don't even like to watch TV shows where someone is purposely embarrassed or humiliated. It might be just a make believe story but it still makes my heart hurt. I just don't know how to be any other way. Some people misinterpret that for a sign of weakness or being a push over. I am not weak or a push over. I have a feeling I am going to have to learn to let my inner strength show more visibly. I have only been at Penn for a little over three months and I already know that if I don't start to speak up for myself some of the people here are going to try and devour me.

Anyways. I received some nice birthday presents from a few of the people I am closest with at the school. I also received a bouquet of flowers on my desk; no card attached. No good has ever come from mystery flowers. It does not get a woman all excited. It gives her the creeps! As mysterious flowers have been appearing for about a month now on my desk; two or three single carnations left on my desk several times a week I officially have the creeps! The horticulture shop sells carnations daily. I want to believe it is someone in the building just supporting the shop but I don't get that feeling and curiosity is starting to get the best of me. I think I'll ask Lonnie if she knows anything about it. I hope they are not from Edmonson.

DECEMBER 22, 2000
It is the last day before Christmas break; we got out an hour early. I'm not sure why the schools dismiss an hour early the day before a holiday but I'm not complaining! I just feel bad for all the parents who have to make arrangements for their children who are getting out of school early. That can really mess up a parent's work schedule.

Communication isn't very good between the staff. I didn't know that it was tradition to go somewhere after school for a holiday celebration. I don't really drink. Well, I haven't since before Alonna came along. One drink now makes me tired and two makes me a little loopy so I just don't do it. I will still go out with my friends on a rare occasion but I'll have a soda. I think whatever an individual does before they have children is their own business, but once you bring a child into the world your obligation is to your child. Alonna's last day of school was yesterday so she and my mother were picking me up to go out for our own celebratory lunch. If I had known about the staff going out before today I might have gone with them but there was no way I was going to call Alonna and cancel on her at the last minute. She is my priority. We had a wonderful lunch.

DECEMBER 27, 2000
Dave Sanders called me. He is not your typical math teacher. He is a ball of fire and has such a carefree attitude. You would think that a carefree

attitude and a free spirit are the same thing but they are not. Sanders has a carefree attitude. I have a free spirit. I still believe that rules and regulations are a good thing as long as they apply equally for everyone. David's carefree attitude means he doesn't care much for rules. For a math teacher there is nothing really logical about him. I guess he has a very abstract mathematical mind. He said I missed quite a gathering at the George House. Rene Peterson got completely smashed and threw up all over the table and landed in it face first. I must say, I never saw that one coming. She is so stern and uptight at school. There is nothing relaxed about her. I don't think I have ever seen her smile. Strange that she is a child care shop teacher. Sometimes you just never know about people and alcohol. I'm told there are pictures to document the occasion. I think I'll pass on the viewing. Just the thought of it is disgusting enough. Edmonson stopped in for a drink before the Peterson puking. He was overheard having a brief conversation with the owner. Apparently he didn't think he would be welcome there. The owner called him Geoffy and said that Geoffy's marriage to his sister happened a long time ago and she was finally able to put what he had done to her behind her and she was happy now. He said that Geoffy was just lucky she could run faster than him or he would have been at the bottom of the river. He also said that his money spent just the same as anyone's but not to make it a habit. Well, well, well. Edmonson told me that his wife was a flight attendant and she had died from cancer after they had been married for only nine months. That appears to be one big lie. If a person can lie about something that significant they are probably capable of lying about anything. I knew he was a person who couldn't be trusted. Hmmm. I wonder what Edmonson did to his wife. Would he have hurt her if he had been able to run faster? Up until now I don't think I would have felt that he was capable of physically hurting someone but I guess there are ways to hurt someone without using your own strength; guns, knives…I wonder what his preferences would be. I wonder if I need to be more cautious around him.

FEBRUARY 5, 2001

The second semester of the school year has been in effect for a few weeks. This is kind of cool. We have a whole new group of students in the school. It is like two mini years within one school year. I think it's going to make the year go faster. We are one of the few vo-techs in Pennsylvania that operates on a semester-about system. We have one group of students all day for a semester and then they go back to their home schools for a semester of academics. It's a good system. The students are able to go out into the community and do service projects that benefit the community and they are able to get real on–the–job experience.

Edmonson did take the time this week to tell me that *people* were upset with two of the instructional education teachers and math teachers. He said *they* felt it wasn't fair that we were just having one big party every day and taking a couple of hours to have lunch. Of course I was upset by this accusation but I was even more upset because he wouldn't tell me who *they* were and he didn't defend our professionalism. He told them he would check into it and get back to them. If he believed their accusations were true why didn't he come down to check and see if we were actually working or having a party?

Edmondson knows that we would love to start classes right away at the beginning of each semester. We have talked to him about the problems we have getting information from the home schools. The math department has to figure out who needs math and make a schedule. Then a new resource schedule needs made that works with the math department and other people in the instructional department. We've all been working on scheduling together. Even with 20 shops and four lunches to schedule, it takes way more time than it should. I am not placing blame on any one person here. There are many good people who we deal with at the sending schools, but everything we need should be provided for us *before* the first day of classes. We shouldn't have to beg for information and try to figure out what the kids need, then try to cram in everything twice as fast. The home schools have their schedules figured out before the students arrive on the first day. We should be able to do the same thing. We are an elective for the students. If the home schools can provide a roster to their foreign language teacher, then shouldn't they be able to provide us with a roster as well? Shouldn't Bart demand this? I don't think Bart has a clue how to deal with people. I wonder how he made it this far up the administrative ladder.

I am confused about my feelings where Edmonson is concerned. I don't know if I am more furious, frustrated or fearful. I just want to come to school and do the work I was hired to do. I don't need to walk through the front doors wondering if today he is going to try to goad me into an argument, ignore my concerns or hit on me. I like and respect straight forward, up front people. He likes veiled illusions, threats and secrecy. I think he acts the way he does because he likes to watch the drama ensue. He is just a dramalama. I try my hardest to avoid him but he is always calling me to the office to talk to me about things that have nothing to do with my job. He goes on and on about his vision for the school or how much money he has or how many condos he has; none of which I care about. He really likes to hear himself talk.

FEBRUARY 14, 2001

Valentine's Day. The flowers have been continuing to show up on my desk more often but they are a mystery no longer. Lonnie told me that Pierce purchases the flowers from the horticulture students when they sell flowers shop to shop every day. He pays them extra to place the flowers on my desk when I am not around and without saying who they are from. That in itself is amazing; not that Pierce would do it but that the kids actually kept their mouths shut. Teenagers have a tendency to talk. I guess they did tell Lonnie.

Now what? Do I have to say anything? Do I ask him to stop? I have to get this stopped. I don't do well hiding my head in the sand. That always just makes an awkward situation more awkward. I'll have to give this one some thought; he is a man without a conscious. He is married but quite the player from what I've heard. He comes to school and tells the male shop teachers of his most recent sexual exploits. Personally I don't want to know about them and I most certainly don't want to be part of them. Maybe it would be best if I just stuck my head in the sand this one time.

I made little valentines for some of my staff friends. I have a graphics background and was just playing around on the computer the other night. Of course I didn't give one to Pierce. There is no way I would do anything to lead him on. As bad luck would have it though Edmonson walked up when I was giving one to Brian. He gushed all over it and stood there for a minute like he was waiting for me to give him one. When he was gushing over the heart I realized who he reminds me of—Slick Willy, the stereotypical used car salesman; big on overkill and big on false flattery. When I didn't offer him one he just ripped the one out of Brian's hand and walked away. We all just stood there dumbfounded. I saw it later that day sitting propped up on his desk. Oh how I hope he doesn't spin this into me making him a special Valentine's Day card. The thought of that creeps me out. I almost pulled it off of his desk when he wasn't' looking but I was afraid I would get caught. I always get caught when I do things I shouldn't. I probably should have taken it anyway.

On another note, big news for the day—David Sanders is going to run for Marion Township Supervisor. He just doesn't feel his heart is in teaching. I wonder if his heart isn't in teaching or if it is just the bullshit that goes on at Penn. Maybe teaching really isn't his passion because although I think he is a great guy he can get away with anything he wants to at Penn. Is it because he is a man or is it because Edmonson thinks that David has money.

David asked me if I'd help him with his campaign. Of course I said yes. I like doing stuff like that. It's going to be fun to get into designing and marketing again. It will be a nice change of pace from teaching without actually changing jobs again. The primary is in May and the general election in November. If he wins he'll start in January of 2002. He would be the youngest Township Supervisor in Pennsylvania history. Pretty cool. I think he has a really good shot at it. It is something he really wants to do and is willing to go out and campaign hard and get his message out there. I wonder what his message is. Better find that out before the campaign starts.

MARCH 16, 2001
Something weird has happened. Pierce and Keffer—who I thought were extremely good friends—had a falling out. Pierce resigned as Vice-President of the Union. It was all very hush, hush. It's extremely odd how people try to stay so tight mouthed about union issues. Some think our little union is a very powerful tool. I don't get it. There are 30 people in the union and maybe half of that number comes to union meetings. Why is everything so secretive? Seems to be a lot of secrets around this place and a lot of whispering. I don't like the secrecy. What is there to hide?

Thank goodness for the students around here. They keep me grounded. I have seen kids with problems bigger than I could have ever dreamed of dealing with at their age. There is hunger, and a lack of appropriate clothing for the weather—no jackets or good shoes—parents that have walked out on them leaving them in an apartment alone with no money for food or clothes. There is pregnancy from a lack of sexual education and more than a fair share of bullies. They are troubled but they are trying their best. There are also some of the brightest, talented and optimistic young adults I have ever known. They are filled with joy and hope for the future. I can feel each and every one of these kids helping me to become a better person. I wonder what would happen if all of the staff just opened themselves up to becoming a learner as well as a teacher. Wouldn't that make for a fabulous school?

APRIL 30, 2001

There was a union election this month. A few people asked me to run for secretary. I wasn't sure if I should since I have only been at Penn for less than one full school year, but I ran and I won—probably because no one else wanted the job. Samantha Hull is the new treasurer. Tyler Smith is vice and quite unexpectedly, Pierce beat Jake Keffer for president. It was a pretty close election. I hope I can do some good for the union and the school. I was able to help get a lot of things done at Alonna's elementary school through the PTA. I was the only person in the history of the elementary school to be elected as president for three consecutive years. We worked well as a team and always put the needs of the students first. I wonder what this will be like. I hope there are no power trips with the union or administration. I'm not holding my breath on the whole power trip thing. I am not a genius. I admit it and I am not ashamed about it. I am average. I have an IQ of 110. It has never bothered me because I live by the principle of the seven intelligences. Okay, it does unnerve me a little bit to know that Alonna has an IQ 24 points higher than mine. Did she inherit it? Did I help through proper prenatal care, music to my belly, and pumping up her brain after she was born with reflexology techniques? I have two degrees and by the time I have opened the box and taken out the instruction manual for the new cell phone she has programmed every feature on the phone. She is phenomenal at an IQ of 134. In the past ten years she and I have not changed our digits. We have changed our address, our phone number, our height and weight. We have, however, not changed our IQ. Pierce on the other hand goes beyond measure. In the short time I have known him; his IQ—by his own admission—has risen from 160 to 220. Freakin' amazing! What is he doing teaching in a small vocational school? He should be running his own country. I think he is either trying to get practice for when he has to deal with his people in his own little kingdom or he is just on a major power trip. He has already started referring to the staff as "my teachers." We are not his teachers. We are his co-workers and he just happens to be the local union leader. I am already second guessing myself about having run for union office. Pierce and Edmonson do nothing but bounce back and forth between degrading me and hitting on me and now as a union officer I have put myself deeper into the hot zone. Stupid, stupid, stupid. What have I done?

May 16, 2001

Thank God this school year will soon be coming to an end. I need some time away from Pierce and Edmonson. Before the year ends though the teachers hold an annual Student Awards Banquet. It is a wonderful event. This was the 16th year for the event. One of the things that make it special is that it is an event completely sponsored by and paid for by the teaching staff. I wrote a letter to the local paper about the event and they printed it in the Letters to the Editor. A good portion of the community thinks that only bad students attend classes at Penn. We are not an alternative school. We are a vocational school. People should hear more about the quality of students we have. Some of the teachers and students thanked me but neither Bart nor Edmonson said one word about the letter. I think they were ticked that I didn't run it by them first. I don't think they have ever heard the concept, catch them being good and praise them, or even just thanking someone for putting in a good day's work. You really do get better results from people when you praise rather than criticize continually.

June 10, 2001

Well, I survived my first year of teaching. I now understand why summer break is still three months; it's not because students are needed to work the farms, although this area has a lot of agriculture industry. It's because teachers would burn out way too quickly if there wasn't time away from the school. Is it too much to hope for that Pierce and Edmonson will change professions and be gone when we come back in August?

August 29, 2001

Damn! Year two and it has begun already. Kathy Crawler resigned on the second day of school without notice. Edmonson said they didn't care she was leaving because she was just trouble. He said she had cashed a $700 check made out to the school and kept the money although they didn't prosecute. He also said a student had walked in on Kathy and Pierce in the downstairs bathroom engaged in a sexual activity at the end of the previous school year. That was a vision I really did not need to have put in my head first thing in the morning; especially one that involved the downstairs bathroom. It is dark and dank and is filled with the stench of day old urine. Edmonson said they both could have been fired and that if Pierce's wife knew what happened, she would probably divorce him. He told me this in the front hallway; which is where he typically spreads gossip. He then just walked away without ever saying why nothing was done to reprimand either one. Surely stealing $700 is a crime and having sex at school has to be breaking some kind of rule. Talking with Edmonson in the front hall always leaves you feeling like you've just been involved in a hit-and-run. It really isn't talking. He talks, you try to get a word in, he ignores you and then he quickly scurries away with a satisfied look on his face; the look that a gossip has when they spread vicious tales.

I don't want to judge and I don't really care to see anyone get in trouble, even Pierce, but what was the point of telling me about last year's sexcapades? Shouldn't he have done something if it was true and he knew about it? Maybe that's why Kathy left. Maybe Edmonson did force her out; threaten to prosecute her for the check and fire her for having sex with Pierce if she didn't quit. It is definitely his style to protect the men and boys while being extremely harsh on the women and the girls, except of course the women who fawn all over him. I know Kathy was very upset that Edmonson was hired. She had applied for the job but she didn't have the credentials. She left her transcripts in the copier one day last year and I found them. She had many, many, *many* incompletes in her graduate coursework. Keffer also applied. He told me he had the credentials for the job but I don't know what to believe. I don't know why the board would pass him over if he had the credentials and Edmonson didn't. Does it have anything to do with politics or favors or payoffs? Keffer says he has proof that Edmondson doesn't have the credentials. If this is true why would he just sit on it? I wouldn't.

SEPTEMBER 11, 2001

What can you say about a day like today? It is tragic beyond belief. Miranda, our guidance counselor, ran into my room and told us about a plane crashing into the Twin Towers. I thought she meant a small aircraft. There is no way my brain could have envisioned what she was talking about. I asked her if anyone was hurt. She looked at me like I didn't understand a word of English. She said, *"A PLANE HIT THE TWIN TOWERS. THEY ARE DEAD!"* Everyone started scrambling to turn on TVs. New York is only about five hours away by car; the terror seemed way too close but even more frightening and confusing news came in less than two hours. All we knew at that point was that another hijacked plane had gone down. It was United Flight 93. We were only an hour away from where the plane went down. Phones started ringing off the hook and parents just started showing up to get their children. No one felt safe. I couldn't wait to get home and hold onto Alonna. Nothing is ever going to be the same. 911. A day that will never be forgotten.

OCTOBER 12, 2001

When Kathy resigned I requested a lateral bump from the Resource Room to Instructional Education Classroom Teacher. The job provides support for any student who needs extra help with their theory work in the shop. I would only have eight shops to deal with instead of twenty because the shops are divided between the instructional education teachers. I thought it would be a good move but Edmonson realigned the shops and gave me Pierce's shop. Charlotte said she would trade with me but Edmonson said absolutely not. Why? Why would he make me work with a man that I felt uncomfortable being around? I tried to explain to him why Charlotte and I were going to trade shops but he just dug his heels in and told me that he was the F'ing boss and what he said was how it was going to be. He refused to let me trade with Charlotte.

I am already feeling more and more uneasy with Pierce every day. Having to be the shop support teacher for his students is going to make things worse. I had hoped we were going to be able to work together professionally this year but he has already asked me to have dinner with him. I asked, "Aren't you married?" He just let out a very strange, creepy laugh, ran his hand across the back of my neck and asked, "Am I?"

Seriously! Was I supposed to giggle, say how flattered I was and jump into his arms? I wanted to call him a name that emphasized how vile I thought he was, but I couldn't think of anything bad enough so I just jerked away, said, "Yes you are married and absolutely not!"

I don't know how we are going to be able to continue to work together without it getting nasty. I have a feeling it won't be getting better any time soon. Pierce's ego is escalating. Samantha was standing right behind him when Pierce touched me and asked me out. Didn't he know or didn't he care? My money is on the fact that he is really just that bold and arrogant.

DECEMBER 5, 2001

Another year, another birthday. I should be happy. I am always happy on my birthday but my heart feels heavy from the turmoil at work. Pierce gets more aggressive with me every day. He doesn't ask me for help with his students or even tells me what they need in a civilized manner. He barks out orders and treats me like I am his servant. He never misses an opportunity to try and make me look like an idiot in front of my co-workers or the students. Edmonson sees it and just snickers. How can a place that is supposed to be safe make you feel so afraid? I don't know what to do. Is there anyone out there that can help me? I have worked so hard to become a teacher. I can't let two obnoxious men take that away from me.

DECEMBER 10, 2001

Edmonson and Bart are polar opposites. Bart doesn't want to talk to me about any problems at school with Pierce or Edmonson. I guess I said that wrong. The truth is that Bart won't talk to me. He is the director. He is supposed to help me but he just hides in his office.

Pierce's attitude since becoming union president has gotten way out of control. He is yelling more and going on little tirades during staff meetings and union meetings. He actually has started beating hard on his chest when he is ranting. That can't be a good sign of what's to come.

He calls the kids monkeys behind their backs but runs his shop like he is friends with the students rather than their teacher. I hear stories of smoking and snuff and lots of profanity. It is sickening. They are great kids capable of great things. I know this because when they are with me they are respectful and focused. They need a teacher who will show them how to be a professional, not a bully.

It is obvious that Bart is afraid to deal with people, especially with someone like Pierce. Edmonson isn't dealing with it either but in a different way; he rambles on in double speak. He tells me I should pray over things and if I am worthy than God will protect me. To make matters worse, he gets more and more touchy every day. I think he believes that if Pierce can get away with his behavior than as Assistant to the Director he is untouchable. Edmonson is always trying to grab my hand and always putting his hand on my arm or shoulder. Not just resting it there for a second—he lingers and then squeezes. Women know what I mean. It is a subtle come on; you can feel it in your gut but if you tell anyone they think you are just imagining things. A woman can tell a lot from a touch or a squeeze. Edmonson's touch sends a stomach-turning, nauseating feeling through my entire body. It would be so easy to grab his tiny, bony hands and break them but I think I would get fired. Wouldn't I? I have to think about Alonna. I am her provider. Do I just have to put up with this? It is winter and snowy and very cold and I find myself feeling more and more depressed and frustrated. Do other people cry on their way to work?

December 14, 2001

My mother came to school to have lunch with me today. That cheered me up. She always knows when I need a little cheering up. The culinary program operates a restaurant for the public. It's a wonderful restaurant and the students do a great job.

Edmonson came in while we were having lunch. He stopped by our table to say hello and he gushed all over my mother. He thought for sure that she was my sister not my mother. How lame! And then he went on and on about how he didn't know what the school would do without me because I am such a wonderful teacher. My mother has this special gift of making friends with complete strangers. She will know more about them in a brief conversation than people who have known them for years. She is wonderful at making people feel comfortable. It was quite amazing to watch my mother's reaction to Edmonson. She never spoke a word. She just stared at him not even attempting to fake a smile. She reads people even better than I do and she does not like false flattery. I was very proud of her. If I was in her shoes I would have felt that I would have had to say something to avoid an uncomfortable feeling but my mother is a very strong woman and there is nothing fake about her. She doesn't play games and she has a way of letting you know that she knows the game you are trying to play. My mother has the biggest brown eyes I have ever seen and I swear she can see right into a person's heart. She did not like what she saw in Edmonson's heart. I got the distinct feeling he knew what she was picking up on. It's the only explanation because he was in mid sentence and suddenly bolted out of the restaurant. I think her pure spirit frightened him. I was glad to see him go.

December 21, 2001

Christmas break is here! Edmonson approached me on my way out of the building. My arms were full of presents so I couldn't push him away as he got closer. I heard him mumble something about a holiday hug. He wrapped his arms around me and then I saw his mouth coming for me. I tried to turn my head so he wouldn't kiss me right on the mouth but it was all happening so fast and I wasn't quick enough and he caught part of my cheek and part of my lip. It was the most awkward kiss I have ever been a part of so to speak. I dropped the presents and my beautiful new Christmas snow globe broke and water leaked all over my beautiful new stationery. I heard him call me a bitch under his breath as he stormed off into the office.

I have repeatedly told Edmonson that I don't feel comfortable with him hugging me and touching me. I wanted to run after him and slap him but I'm a single mother and this job is very important to me. I don't have tenure yet and I need to provide for Alonna. I just want to work without any problems. What am I supposed to do?

I have asked to talk to Bart several times about the situation with both Edmonson and Pierce but he won't return any of the messages I have left him. He finally put a note in my mailbox that Edmonson is my immediate supervisor and I need to follow the chain of command. What is the chain of command when your problem is your immediate supervisor and your union president? Isn't Bart next on the chain of command? Is Bart really that stupid or he is just trying to blow me off? I won't think about it today. I'll think about it in two weeks. I am just going to try and enjoy Christmas with my baby girl.

JANUARY 4, 2002

David Sanders won the election in November. He is the new Marion Township Supervisor; he didn't come back to school after the Christmas break. Helping him with his campaign was a lot of fun and I am glad he won, but I am going to miss having him around the school. He always had such a good outlook on things. He doesn't seem to get upset over little things. I guess that's the advantage of having a carefree attitude. He also had a good sense of humor. He made me laugh on the tough days. There have been so many tough days. I am going to miss his laughter.

His absence is going to be hard for the kids. A lot of the students felt comfortable talking to him because he is on the younger side and he could relate to them. There are going to be substitutes in the room until someone permanent starts. I don't think any of the subs they have lined up have a math background. We have to wait until the January board meeting at the end of the month for a math teacher to be hired. You would have thought that the board would have hired someone in December but they didn't. I believe they are going to hire Andie Bradshaw. She used to teach math here but left to go to another school that had a better contract. As bad luck would have it; two days after she resigned, Penn finally signed a decent contract. I hear she's a very nice woman. Samantha likes her very much so we should all get along.

FEBRUARY 28, 2002

Things are getting worse at work since the Christmas kiss incident. You would think that Edmonson would stay away from me but he has progressed to being even more touchy and vocal. I didn't really think that was possible but he has gone from telling me how nice I look to how pretty I am and now he has started to actually ask me out on dates. At first when he asked me what I was doing over the weekend I thought he was just rambling again. He was talking about the many phone calls he had to return from people who wanted favors from him so I didn't pay much attention because I thought he was trying to impress me. But then he started to fidget a little and he got closer and ran his fingers through my hair and said he could pick me up around seven on Saturday. I must have looked like a deer caught in headlights. I wanted to say something but I was stunned and the words just seemed to be stuck in my throat. I jumped up out of the chair I was sitting in. Nothing was coming out of my mouth but my head was violently shaking no and his fingers were stuck in my hair. Why couldn't I talk? I felt so violated and so stupid and so weak. Finally I just could hear myself saying, "No, no, no, NO!" My whole body was shaking. He got very nervous and told me to think about it and he bolted out of his office. I thought I was going to throw up. I'm not sure if he was hurt or angry. Either way it is not a good idea to date your boss; especially when you are not attracted to him. I kept wondering what repercussions awaited me on Monday. I wanted to go home and cut my hair.

APRIL 3, 2002

April 3rd is always a bad day for me emotionally. April 3, 1993 was the day my father got the official diagnosis—inoperable cancer. There were no obvious signs that he had cancer. Only a week before the diagnosis the doctors said he just had a chest cold. Not only did he have cancer, it had spread to the brain. It could have been so horrific, but he had no pain. The medical staff couldn't explain it other than to say it was our miracle. There are no words to describe how much I miss him. I wish he was here. If I close my eyes I can still smell him; Old Spice. I have visions of my father having a talk with Pierce and Edmonson. He was a very strong, protective, loving family man. My father never laid a hand on us growing up but when we got a little too wound up he would roll up his newspaper and swat the coffee table. It didn't happen often but it certainly got our attention. I often picture my dad rolling up his newspaper and driving both Edmonson and Pierce into the ground with one good swat on the top of the head like a Warner Brothers cartoon. That makes me smile. Nothing else makes me smile about Pierce or Edmonson.

I have always been fascinated by people and I try to understand them so I have been trying hard to understand Edmonson and Pierce but how do you understand cold hearted egocentric bullies? Did I mention completely self absorbed? They refuse to hear anything other than what they want.

When a woman, or a man, says no the first time; it actually does mean no. Not only have the words come out of my mouth but I have also shaken my head so violently that I thought it was going to fly off. Surely if they didn't understand the words, they understood my meaning. I don't think this is about being attracted to me. I think this is about power. They want to show they have power over me. They don't. I may not have been able to stop them yet but I come from a lineage of strength and courage. God, please let me tap into my ancestors strength to put an end to this.

MAY 13, 2002

I attended my second Student Awards Banquet. I love to see the pride on the students' faces and their families. There are so many wonderful, hard working young people at the school that are deserving of being recognized. This night is supposed to be about them. But once again Edmonson wanted to steal the spotlight. He ordered a huge plaque for Bart and in front of nearly 200 people he presented the plaque for Outstanding Director to Bart on behalf of the teachers. We were all shocked. No one had a clue that Edmonson was going to do something like that. He had somehow snuck the plaque in and hid it under the front table. Bart accepted it so proudly and we all felt embarrassed for him because it was just a sham. It looked like most of the teaching staff was trying to slither down in their chairs to avoid eye contact with Bart. Edmonson on the other hand did what he does so well; stood there blowing smoke up Bart's ass. I wonder how Bart will feel when he finds out that it wasn't real. I wonder who paid for the plaque.

JUNE 14, 2002

It's Flag Day; just an observation, nothing special about the day other than I like thinking about my heritage. Elizabeth Grisom was married to James Ross, the nephew of my ancestor George Ross, signer of the Declaration of Independence. He wasn't afraid to let his voice be heard and sign his name to the Declaration of Independence.

After James died George Ross kept in touch with Elizabeth, better known as Betsy. He went with George Washington to talk to Betsy Ross about making a new flag for a new nation. I know it's by marriage, but I'll claim her as a relative! I think about them every day in school when we say the Pledge. The Ross blood runs through my veins. Does that mean I can find the same strength and courage that he had? I hope so. Most days I feel so drained from dealing with Pierce and Edmondson it is hard to find the energy to stay up past 8:00.

I'm glad school is finally over for the year. I feel like I will be able to breathe a little. I won't have to wonder if today will be a safe day at school or if Pierce or Edmonson are going to spend the day harassing me. Pierce never got it through his head that I was not interested in him. The flowers continued throughout the year and he kept asking me to go out with him. It worries me that right before school was over Pierce appeared out of nowhere as I was walking down the hallway. He got so close to me that his body was in full contact with mine and he pushed me up against the wall. Thank goodness someone walked out of a classroom and he moved away from me. How do I not be afraid when this is getting physical and it is happening inside the school? Is this a game to him or he is actually a predator? I find it hard to believe that I am the first woman he has ever done this to. He is too old for me to be his first terror attempt.

This was Guy Sanction's last year at school. We got along fairly well. Guy is ten years older than me but he always said I was too old for him. Like I was ever interested! What is it with the men here? Don't they know men and women can just be friends and work together? Guy made it clear to me that he liked his women younger than twenty-five. Several years ago a female student from his shop moved in with him and lived with him for several years. The week that she turned twenty-one she left him. I guess she figured that she could buy her own alcohol then.

I do feel bad for Guy. He's an admitted alcoholic. I know it's a disease that is hard to deal with. He came to school so many times hung over and sometimes I would say, drunk. I think he had so much alcohol in his system that just having one drink sent him back into a drunken state. He knew he had a problem but it's a very hard disease to conquer. He just didn't have the strength to overcome it.

What I don't understand is why administration didn't do anything about it until now. They could have gotten him into rehab or fired him but they let him resign at the end of the year. Pierce beat his chest at a union meeting and said Guy should have fought to keep his job. Pierce was just looking for an excuse to beat his chest. Guy couldn't have stayed under any circumstances. He never did anything about getting credits toward his Vocational II certification. There is a deadline for getting your Level II certification completed. If you don't have it done, you cannot stay; there is no grace period. Guy just acted like he could have stayed. I guess it's easier to feel you were forced out rather than to admit you didn't take care of business.

Sometimes separating the feelings you have for a person and the situation they are in can be very confusing. You really like someone as a person but they don't follow the rules and you know you shouldn't feel sorry for them but you do. Oh well, I wish him the best. Wonder what he will do now?

SEPTEMBER 18, 2002
We are back for another round of school. I went to a yearbook seminar today with a student and Chip Watson, the man who replaced Guy in Graphics. Edmonson wants Chip to be co-advisor for the yearbook. I drove to the seminar. Chip didn't want to take his truck. I had to take my own car; I wasn't permitted to take a school vehicle. Edmonson said it was too far to take the van. Funny how everyone else can use the school vehicles except me.

It was a long and silent drive to Johnstown. It takes about an hour and a half to get there from the school. I tried to make small talk with Chip and the girl but I might as well have been talking to a stone. I don't know if they are both that quiet or if Edmonson told Chip that I don't like him, which isn't true. I had talked to Bart about the graphics job when it came open but he blew me off. I love graphics and I was more than qualified than Chip. I have a degree in Graphic Communications, taught graphics courses at a local college for five years, was the marketing manager for a cable company and worked for two different newspapers in the advertising and pre-press departments. How could Bart just blow me off about bidding into the job? One of the women who work in the office told me that Bart and the board were working on some deal with one of the sending districts to give Chip the job. I hate to think that's true. Why is so much of education about favors? Is it like that everywhere or is it just a problem in our area? I don't hold it against Chip because I know how it feels to need a job but it still doesn't make it right. I am not implying in any way that Chip isn't creative or talented but his work is very distinctive. Visually too busy for my taste.

Chip wants to take the shop in a new direction; getting rid of the dark room and printing presses. It's just a new direction, not right or wrong, just different. Edmonson seems very excited about having Chip here. Chip is very muscular and works out a lot. Did I say he is very muscular! A lot of the teenage girls are drooling but his muscles are just not my cup of tea. Alright, I admit it. I hate to exercise. I believe in trying to stay healthy, but not to go to that extreme. It's just not for me. People have noticed that Edmonson seems to be drooling over Chip's muscles. Someone called it Chip envy. Wonder if other men in the building feel that way.

October 22, 2002
Tonight was a very rare evening. Even though Dave Sanders has moved on from teaching at Penn he paid for everyone to get together for dinner and drinks. It wasn't a special occasion, it was just an attempt to get everyone together outside of the building so we could talk and laugh. There is no time at school for everyone to get together and socialize. The only time we are all together is at staff meetings and those always end up with Edmonson telling bold face lies or trying to stir up trouble and Pierce beating on his chest. It would be nice to get together more often but I don't think that is going to happen. Life is just too busy.

October 30, 2002
On October 2nd, I chaperoned a student council field trip to the Flight 93 Memorial along with Diana, Samantha and Charlotte. Edmonson asked me to write a field trip report to be presented to the Operating Board. I

turned in the report, but he never presented to the board. Why do I bother to do all this paper work and reports? They never go any further than the corner of Edmonson's desk. It's a shame; it was a really good report. It was an amazing trip; the site where United Flight 93 went down is so powerful. There is such a strong vibration in the air. I can't explain it but I know the students felt it too because as talkative as they were on the ride up to Shanksville, as soon as we stepped off the bus they instantly became silent. The boys even removed their hats without anyone asking them to do so. There was a very solemn feeling in the air. We stayed for hours taking pictures, signing the benches, leaving items in honor of the Heroes of Flight 93, and talking to one of the Flight 93 Ambassadors who owns the farm next to the crash site. I don't think anyone who visits the site will ever lose the feeling they experience there.

When we got back on the bus the students realized how hungry they were; me too. We stopped at Burger King for a quick bite to eat. It was the very first food place we saw. What tremendous luck! We met two of the Que Creek Miners. It was an amazing experience. We had just left a place where a small group of people gave their lives on Flight 93 to save so many others and now we were meeting The Que Creek Miners. So many people gave of their time, energy and spirit for days to rescue nine men who were trapped 240 feet below the earth for more than three days. The miners, John Unger and Bob Pugh, were incredible. They posed for pictures with everyone and told us how to get to their rescue site. I'm so glad they all came out of it alive. I don't think I could ever work below ground. I would be so scared. Some days high school feels scary too; dissention, bullying, drugs, alcohol, sex, and politics are all a part of everyday life. I don't know if I would have become a teacher if I really knew how scary it was going to be. The sad thing is that it's not the students I am afraid of. It is sad that a few men are allowed to make life so unbearable. People who are in a position to stop the problems should not be allowed to let it go on. There should be consequences.

OCTOBER 31, 2002

Woo Hoo! There was an in-school Halloween dance today. This year I dressed up. The kids had a good time but in my opinion some of the girls' costumes revealed a little too much skin. Actually, way too much skin! Just because it's Halloween doesn't mean you still shouldn't be school appropriate. Edmonson just seemed to look the other way, or was he looking at them? In any event, no one said anything to the girls about their dress or made them cover up. Hormones seemed to be raging and there were lots of public displays of affections to deal with. I had a round with Edmonson about the situation. I talked to the kids over and over about too much touching and kissing, but kids are kids and like I said, their hormones were raging. Edmonson's solution to the problem was to remove the girls in question from the dance. I couldn't believe what was happening? His reasoning was that by sending the girls away the boys would be very upset and disappointed and not enjoy the dance so much. Seriously? Teenage boys? They might not like it but teenage boys are very adaptable and they would just hang with their friends. After arguing as strongly as I could without crossing the line, he agreed to let the girls come back. There was only ten minutes left in the dance; too little, too late. He just reinforced his message that he has no respect for the girls or the women in the building. He is just teaching another generation that it is perfectly acceptable to degrade females. He has no right to be in a school. I think his actions are deplorable!

NOVEMBER 28, 2002

There was a very nice article in the paper today about the Salvation Army Thanksgiving luncheon. Charlotte, Nikki, and I took a few student volunteers to serve during the two hour luncheon. There were over 300 people who turned out yesterday for the meal. It was open free of charge to anyone who needed some support. There are so many people who are going through hard times right now. It made me sad to think that there are so many people in need but I think it was a good experience for our students. They have to become aware of the needs of the community. I know they left the Salvation Army feeling good about what they had done yesterday. Hopefully it will inspire them to keep looking for ways to help the community.

DECEMBER 5, 2002

Yes, that's right, it's my birthday! And it's a snow day. Yay! I am feeling more than a little guilty about not having to go out in this weather like so many other people who are out there driving to work in this mess. My brother drives an hour and a half one way to provide for his family. I worry about him in this weather.

Teaching is a strange occupation. When you put your heart and soul into the job there can be a high burn out factor. The time off from the kids, even one day like today, is truly a necessary part of the job and I appreciate it very much. I hate it when I hear teachers complaining about how bad they have it. Leave the profession then. Get a real job. I know I have a real job. It's just a little jab I say to those who have the audacity to complain. I'm just going to hang out on the couch with my girl and be a couch potato and watch movies today. It is so nice being on the same schedule as Alonna. That is definitely the most wonderful thing about being a parent and a teacher. It's the perfect job for a parent. I wonder why Edmonson doesn't ever talk about his children. We all know he has children but they don't live with him. It is as they don't exist. They are real though because they are listed as dependents on his health insurance. Too bad he didn't include them as part of his life insurance. I think I talk too much sometimes about Alonna but she is such an incredible girl. She is my every day gift.

DECEMBER 10, 2002

A wonderful field trip to the Carnegie Science Center in Pittsburgh today with the horticulture shop! It is an extraordinary place. I cannot believe that I have never been there before. It is nice to get out of the building and interact more with the students on a fun level. Glad we had a two hour delay yesterday and not today or else the field trip would have been cancelled.

I need to get a lot more comfortable with getting around Pittsburgh by myself. It's so hard to drive in the city. There are probably hundreds of one way streets and the city streets are shaped like a triangle. I have driven in a lot of cities and Pittsburgh is truly one of the most difficult to navigate your way around if you don't know exactly where you are going. I suppose one could get used to anything if they had to do it enough. I just prefer driving in the country and through the mountains; except in the winter. I have a tendency to stay away from the mountains in the winter. I'm not a big fan of snow or cold.

We have a lot of students from The Mountain School District. There are a lot of students that live way up on top of the mountain. I feel so bad for them when it comes to the school commute. Some have told me that they actually catch the bus at 5:30 a.m. and are on the bus for almost two hours. No wonder when they get to school they look so tired and rumpled. They just get up and jump on the bus. I'd look rumpled too and it wouldn't make school a lot of fun. I wonder why there isn't a small high school up in the mountains. But on the other hand, the kids that live within the city limits have to walk to school. Some of them have a two or three mile walk to school everyday. Come rain or shine or snow. Why isn't there some money for bus service for the city students?

December 19, 2002

Watching schools waste money makes me crazy. Today we had a training session for a testing system called an Apticom Unit. Bart bought two of them for the school at a cost of $16,000.00. It was wicked crazy to try to learn and to make matters worse it takes a minimum of two hours to give the test and you can only do one student at a time. Wait! This is the part I love the most; the results. Yes, wait for it. It tells you that the student is hands on and should be at a vocational school. Genius. Pure genius! The students who are taking the test are already at a vocational school. Why couldn't we have spent the money elsewhere in a more useful manner? Do all schools waste like that? I wonder how many bus trips $16,000 could have been made for the students in the city.

December 29, 2002

There's no putting the Genie back in the bottle now. I don't remember exactly who made that remark during the evening, but it certainly was true. I thought the party with the Renee incident couldn't be topped but we have a new winner with this holiday staff party. Luckily I missed the Renee-orama, even the pictures, but I got to see this adventure in vivid Technicolor. As designated driver you get to see events unfold from a whole new perspective. Sometimes it is not a very pretty site.

The party started off rather on the dull side. We were pool side and it was cold but the décor was very festive. There was a small hotel room to the left side of the area set up as a hospitality room. We had sold lottery tickets several times over the last couple of months to raise money for the party but I kept forgetting to sell the damn tickets and ended up paying $80 for the tickets plus $14 for the dinner. I feel better believing I paid $94 for a live reality show because I don't think it really was a dinner. There were several tables of cheese cubes, crackers and raw veggies, and Swedish meatballs. It's not that I am anti Swedish meatball….okay, I am. Perhaps I never have had them prepared properly but they simply seem like little blobs of meat chunks dripping with a sauce that always lands on my shirt.

A pasta bar was also set up for dinner. It was a nice concept but picture this; it's a very cold winter's night and for some reason the pasta, the sauce, and the veggies are also very cold. The little sterno source is not kicking up a lot of heat so you have a long line of people waiting for the pasta dish to get hot, and the chef's assistant is getting nervous so he's just trying to dish it out as quickly as he can. Rachel Ray could have pumped out two 30 minute meals in the time it took for me to get a cold pasta dish. I would venture to say many people skipped the long pasta line and headed straight for the hospitality room.

I should or could, at the very least, be kind and say that the lack of food intake led to the drunken fest that took place next, but I think it would have happened anyway. Drunken and shocking behavior has become a staple of the American company Christmas party.

I desperately needed something to wash down the dinner so I headed to the hospitality room to get a soda or some water. There was no water in the room. Yes, a few bottles of soda (for mixers) but no ice. There was however lots and lots of alcohol and the majority of the staff. It was in this setting where I got to witness my first blow job. A blow job doesn't have anything to do with sex—until later I assume. It's a drink. Is a shot a drink? I'm not sure. Anyways; you fill a shot glass with Kaluha and Cream and then you top it off with a big dollop of whipped cream. What made this spectacle so fascinating is that there was only one shot glass for the entire room, and people took turns sucking down the blow job.

Did I mention exactly how this feat is performed? You place the shot glass on the bar, put your hands behind your back, bend over, wrap your mouth around the glass, lift the glass up, throw your head back, and suck down the shot.

Now, I've done my share of partaking with others over the years back in the day, but I've never seen anything like this; a definite over share. Nikki seemed to enjoy giving a little something extra for effect; a little shimmy as the shot went down, licking the glass clean, and then smacking her lips. Even if I had not been DD there would have been no way I would have wrapped my lips around that glass.

There was a band playing in the lounge that night. The lounge was close to the pool area and the music was loud and very inviting; inhibitions seemed to be set free. I danced from time to time when I was drug out onto the dance floor, but I mostly sat at the bar, sipping my ice water and watching my colleagues entertain the hotel guests.

Pierce was in rare form. I wondered what his wife would think about him lying on the dance floor on his back while Charlotte danced over him. I guess he wanted to reach out and touch someone because in the blink of an eye he was up and dancing behind Nikki. She was wearing a tight knit dress and had her arms wrapped tight around the neck of a random stranger who had wandered onto the dance floor. She swayed back and forth brushing across his body. Pierce moved in closer behind Nikki and pulled her away from the stranger. Soon his hands were wrapped around her front working their way across her breasts. Nikki did not flinch.

OMG. This type of behavior continued for hours. Did anyone realize what they were doing? Did anyone realize that this was a public place? It wasn't long before Pierce and Nikki put on their coats and said goodnight to everyone. Should we have believed that they were just leaving at the same time and walking out together? I think not. I believe everyone felt confident in the fact that they wouldn't be driving home that night. We were at a hotel. I don't think anyone needed to say *Get a Room*. I bet they did.

FEBRUARY 6, 2003
Edmonson sent me, Miranda and Peter Griffin to a student discipline seminar in Pittsburgh yesterday. It was a very long day. We had to be in Pittsburgh by 8:00 and it wasn't over until 5:00. There was one half hour lunch break because they were trying to cram three days worth of material into one day. I'm not sure exactly why he sent me; probably because he paid for three people and didn't feel like going himself. It was very complicated. It dealt a lot with legalities such as when you can search a student or their property, when you can drug test, and how you should defend yourself. Edmonson really should have gone instead of me. I don't think I have the authority to do any of the things they talked about. I just kept wondering what I was supposed to do with my new found knowledge other than notice even more things that Edmonson was doing wrong.

Today was an even longer and more difficult day. You would probably think that it was the worst day I have yet experienced, but there have been so many different levels of difficult days. A student decided that today would be the day he ended his life. Did he cry out for help before today or did he live with his fears, frustrations and demons in silence. I don't know. Did anyone? Did his torment happen at school? Is that why he decided he would end his life at Penn? Was there something going on with another student that I should have seen and put a stop to? Has my life here battling my own demons like Pierce and Edmonson blind me to what is going on around me with others?

Whatever he was dealing with must have hurt him deeper than words could express. I imagine this to be so because there were no words, no note, and no explanation as to why he wanted to do this. No explanation as to why he would choose a method that would be painful. He hung himself in the main hall bathroom; the bathroom directly across from the office. He used his belt. I still haven't figured out how the process worked. I don't want to think about it. Should I want to think about it? Should I want to understand it so I can be prepared for future events? Will there be any future events like this? God I hope not.

I heard that he was gone from his shop for twenty-five minutes before anyone looked for him. I understand that. The shops are big, and people are always moving around. Students in a vocational school don't spend their time sitting at a desk. That's why most of them like to come to Penn. What I don't understand, what's hard to imagine is that no one walked into the bathroom sooner. Would it have saved him? Was he hoping that someone would have found him before it was too late?

FEBRUARY 7, 2003
Edmonson picked today to ask me if I would go to Pittsburgh with him. I thought he was talking about another conference because of the tragedy that just occurred, but then he started talking about all the amazing cars that would be at the car show. I was very confused. I didn't understand what a car show had to do with a student who just committed suicide while at school. While I was trying to process what he was asking me he said he could pick me up at 4:00. I just stood there for a minute feeling dazed and bewildered. He wasn't asking me to go to another conference or workshop; he was asking me to go to a car show with him in Pittsburgh. Is he just planning on showing up at my house? How can I possibly make it any clearer to him that I don't want to go out with him? I fear that if I am any clearer he is going to become extremely vengeful. This is very frightening. I don't like the position this as put me in. I feel like I've been involved in a hit and run. It takes me a minute for my brain to process what is going

on because I am doing my best to be able to maintain a work relationship with him and then it starts to kick in that he is back on the personal relationship issue and I get this confused look on my face and before I can get thoughts formed into words he actually runs away. Those little feet can move! This just has to stop or my mind has to be able to process what he is saying faster. Bart still won't see me. I have left him many messages but he won't even give me the courtesy of returning my call.

February 11, 2003

Every January and February we bring over 1,000 eighth graders to Penn to tour the shops. Today we had one of the eighth grade glasses from The Unity District. Of course today could not go smoothly; Pierce threw one of the tour groups out of his shop. The kids were just excited and talking a little bit and he flipped out, beating on his chest, and cussing at them. He told them to get out and go wait in the hall. The group he threw out was the one Charlotte was leading. She was the group in front of me. I was so embarrassed. I didn't want to take my group in there but I had to. Pierce was very curt and he just glared at me as if he was daring me to say something to him. Someone told Edmonson what happened. He called me to the office and interrogated me about what happened. I wasn't in there when it happened. Why didn't he ask Charlotte? Edmonson wanted me to get the teachers from the visiting school to write a complaint letter. He said that I could get Pierce in a lot of trouble if I did that. That's not my style and it's certainly not my place. Why can't he just talk to Pierce? Is he really that afraid of Pierce that he can't do his job?

March 1, 2003

What the hell? Another training session today for another new project! Keys to Work—Reading, Math, and Locating Information. We are always starting something new before we have had time to perfect the last exciting project we were supposed to work with. The $16,000 Apticom Units are still just sitting there. We haven't used them once. There wasn't even enough time today to be properly trained in this new program. I am not clear if this new project is in addition to the others we have started or if this is supposed to replace them. There has to be a better way of spending tax payer dollars. I have to admit I didn't do very well on the test. I hate standardized tests. They are too broad. Plus I feel like there is too much pressure that comes with the tests. I did surprise myself with all of the National Teacher Exams though, I kicked ass on those tests. I was comfortable with the information though. I feel so sorry for students today. We are testing them to no end. Every time you turn around there is a different kind of test they have to take and the pressure is unbelievable. I think we should just get back to the basics and stop worrying about these state mandated tests so much. But funding is tied in with testing so I know that is never going to happen. I often wonder if any of the state higher ups could pass the tests that we make the students take. I don't think they could.

MARCH 4, 2003

Nikki made a guest appearance to the lower level. She showed up in Charlotte's room to talk to me, Samantha and Charlotte. She said she felt the women at Penn had not been adequately represented in the building. She is right about that. She discussed encouraging women to run for union office. Nikki said that she was interested in running for vice-president and she suggested that I run for president, Charlotte for secretary and Samantha again for treasurer. I really wasn't sure about it at first but Nikki presented quite a good case. It is time for strong, smart women to have an important role in the boy's club. Is this a way of actually getting someone to take a serious look at the problems in the building? This would mean running against Pierce but it looks like we are all going to do it. It's campaign time. Nominations for offices are March 26th. Maybe this is actually a way to force Bart to talk to me.

APRIL 16, 2003

Hank, our co-op coordinator and his wife Katy are two of the most genuine people I have ever met. Katy is a strong, amazing woman. She is battling cancer and doing very well so far. She was at Penn today and saw Edmonson; of course in the front hall. Out of the blue he said to her, "You know I have cancer too."

When Katy told me that tonight my heart started to hurt for him. But then she finished the story. He turned something as horrific as being a cancer victim into one big lie! He is nothing but a pathological liar. He told Katy that he is currently going through cancer treatments in Pittsburgh. He swore that he goes two or three times a week for treatment *before* school and is still able to make it back to Penn before the first bus arrives. PLEASE! Pittsburgh is well over an hour away. We sign in at 7:30 a.m. so where is there a middle of the night cancer treatment center in Pittsburgh?

I do not know his medical history so I don't know if he had cancer in the past or has cancer now; but the cancer treatment story, without a doubt, is an incredible lie. My father lost his battle with cancer in 1993. It was too advanced by the time we found out what was wrong with him. A week before he was diagnosed with stage four cancer he was told that he had a cold. Some cold. Anyways. I took my father to some of his cancer treatments and even though we went to a local facility and he was only having radiation, not chemo, the whole daily process was very time consuming and one of the most emotionally gut wrenching things I have ever done in my life. He had always been the one taking care of me and our family. Now I was doing my best to take care of him but do it in a way that allowed him to maintain his dignity. That balancing act was not easy but I would do it all again in a heartbeat. I wouldn't have missed spending one minute with him and I would have taken him anywhere on the planet; even to an all night cancer treatment center in Pittsburgh if such a thing actually existed. Standing by my father as we went our battle with cancer and knowing what Katy is going through, leaves me feeling completely disgusted by the ridiculous tale that Edmonson has told. I can't imagine how Katy must feel. Watch out for karma. As Evelyn said in The Mummy, "Nasty little men always get their cumupins. Always." How long will it take for that day to come?

APRIL 28, 2003

This union election business is one of the craziest things I have ever been a part of. It's like a high power; control the world, 1970s Watergate kind of thing; dirty tricks and all. Pierce demanded to talk to me a couple of weeks ago and when I didn't go down to his shop immediately he showed up in my classroom blocking the doorway so I couldn't get out. The situation was very frightening. He wanted me to know that he was going to CRUSH me during the election. He didn't say it light heartedly at all. He was glaring at me like it was a stare down before a boxing match. He was definitely trying to intimidate me. I don't like being alone with him. He seems to be wound very tight. I was lucky that I had a phone in my room. Charlotte's room is right next to mine but she was at a meeting so I dialed Andie's extension and told her I needed her right away; she could hear Pierce ranting in the background. She didn't hesitate. She left her class and came racing over. She passed Pierce in the hall. She said he was pounding the walls with his fist. Was that from rage or was he trying to intimidate Andie?

I have the feeling Pierce has enlisted help on his destruction mission from Nikki. A few Sundays ago I got a call from her in the afternoon; she said she was calling from her cell phone at the grocery store. She has never called me at home before. She sounded very strange; like someone was listening to her and coaching her. We talked for a long time. She told me that she was concerned about me running for president. She said there could be all kinds of trouble stirred up if I continued the campaign. She wanted me to drop out of the election. I told her not to worry. It was simply a school union election. I go to school, do my job, come home and take care of Alonna Jean. How could there be trouble from that? As we were talking though a very strong feeling came over me. It was more like a knowing. I felt that she was with Pierce. Was it a feeling, a knowing or was I just picking up on little things I have seen at school? Over the past month Pierce has been whispering a lot in Nikki's ear. Is he trying to seduce her just to win a little union election?

I tried to be very calm. I told her that this wasn't my first rodeo; I had run for various offices before. I had won some and lost others. I told her I wasn't worried about the election and she should not worry either. I guess I did not understand how seriously Pierce would take being challenged by a woman. He hired a campaign manager and he stole marketing materials I had put out, ripped down flyers and signs and put up a picture of me in the lounge with a line crossed through my face. There is a very disturbing feeling that comes over a person when you see your face disfigured. Is it just a woman thing? I don't know but it bothered me tremendously.

Patty told me that Pierce was visiting all of the teachers telling them that he was worried about me because I didn't have tenure, which is a lie. He professed that he was worried if I won the election, administration would make life really bad for me. He said that if they voted for him they would actually be protecting me. How do I deal with this? Pierce, my harasser is trying to show the school that he is actually my protector. How do I now deal with Nikki? Has she been conning me the whole time I have known her? Several people have told me not to trust her, especially Hank and he is one of the best judges of character I know. I feel very stupid and betrayed. I really did trust her. I thought she was a friend.

Pierce's behavior is getting beyond sinister. Does he think he is back in Viet Nam on some kind of secret op? One of the custodians told me that they found Pierce going through my garbage the other day. What did he think he would find? Since the behavior was happening at school I demanded to talk to Bart about the things Pierce has said and done. I left a message for Bart and told him that I was going to wait in the office and not move until he agreed to see me. After I left the message I went straight to the office and sat down in the waiting room. Bart caved. He finally agreed to see me but he had Edmonson with him. Their reaction was not what I expected. They already knew about everything that had been going on with Pierce and thought it was amusing. They made jokes about it in front of me. I didn't think it was the least bit funny. My heart sank. There doesn't seem to be anyone at Penn who is willing to help me. Should I just quit? Realistically in my situation as a single parent, that isn't an option. Where will I get another job? I have to think about Alonna. I have a steady pay check, medical insurance and my work schedule is basically the same as her school schedule. I guess we'll see what happens Wednesday with the election.

MAY 1, 2003

This past month has been horrific. Pierce seems to have become severely unglued and antagonistic about the fact that I ran against him even though he won the election. He seems to have taken it as a personal attack on his manhood. Yes I lost. He won by a handful of votes; five I think. He took the ballots to two women in LPN personally and waited for them to fill out the ballots. He also took a ballot to Keffer who is out sick. Jim Daniels told me that he really didn't want to get into it but he thought it was terrible all the dirty things Pierce had done to me during the election. I asked him to elaborate but he said he didn't feel comfortable getting into it especially since the election was over. What is it with people half telling me things? I'd rather they didn't tell me anything at all. I know most of what he did though because he did it to me. It's probably better that I don't know the rest.

I got a call from Jake Keffer at home. He confirmed what I already knew; that Pierce had personally taken a ballot to him at home because he was ill and waited while he filled it out. That goes against our election guidelines. I have no intention of challenging it though. I think an election challenge would push Pierce over the edge. Why is Pierce making this seem like it was such a personal attack on him? We are not talking about controlling the United Mine Workers. We are talking about being the representative voice for thirty people. I don't believe there would be any way that Pierce could lead the UMW. I met Rich Trumka on several occasions; once at a conference and once at a casual summer evening's party of a mutual friend. Trumka was very down to earth and chill. He actually smiled and laughed and talked to people and showed respect. Not once did I see Trumka beating on his chest proclaiming his power.

The phone call from Keffer also confirmed my suspicions that Nikki, Pierce and Keffer are definitely talking about me. It wasn't hard to figure out. We had gotten word at school that Hank had a heart attack. I was very upset about it because I like Hank and Katy so much and we weren't sure how serious the heart attack was. Just after I found out about Hank, Nikki came downstairs to talk to me about the election. It was obvious that I was upset about something and she just assumed that I was upset about the election. I told her I was upset about Hank but she kept saying that I shouldn't be so upset over the election. She was kind of pissing me off. Were her ears clogged? I got a little bit loud and told her that I didn't give a rat's ass about the election, I was concerned about Hank. I don't know where that phrase came from. I have never used that phrase once in my life. Honestly, I don't know how those words managed to come out of my mouth. Anyways, she is the only person I said that to and when Keffer called me he said that he thought I was really upset deep down inside about the election and that I actually did give a rat's ass about it. There is only one way he would have known I said that; Nikki or Pierce. I am sure Nikki ran to Pierce and Pierce told Keffer. I suspect Pierce told him because Keffer said he had an argument with Pierce after the election and he should never have voted for him. Pierce told him that if Keffer helped him win the election then Nikki would step down as vice-president and Pierce would appoint Keffer. Pierce decided to back out of his deal. Big surprise there; Pierce is such an honorable man! Keffer also told me that Nikki voted for Pierce. I had already figured that one out on my own too. Usually when you are sleeping with someone, you vote for them. Nikki has changed dramatically over the past two years. She used to dress stylish but not trashy. Now most days her clothes are so tight I wonder how she got them on. Not to mention that she leaves her shirt unbuttoned almost down to her navel. How is that school appropriate? Nikki loves that some people are calling her Hillary; except she doesn't dress like Hillary. I think she gave herself that nickname. It's so stupid. Pierce and Nikki are acting so smug, like they actually won the White House.

MAY 15, 2003

I got a letter from the regional Pennsylvania State Education Association in the mail at home. It was a copy sent to all Penn union members. The letter was addressed to Pierce. It said they were responding to concerns from members about the representation they have been receiving from the regional PSEA. The letter didn't say who complained. The letter talked about how PSEA knows and has known that Edmonson does not possess the time or experience in vocational work to be properly certified. The letter stated that an unfair labor practice charge was filed and that the regional PSEA attorney was ready to go to the hearing but the local leader decided to pull the charge at the last minute. It has been rumored for a few years that Edmonson and Bart have something incriminating on Pierce and told him they would leave him alone if he kept things in the union on the quiet side. It seems there are a lot of unanswered questions about this issue.

I'm fairly certain that at the time the charge was pulled Pierce was president. Since Keffer wanted Edmonson's job my money would be on complaints coming from Keffer and Kathy Krawler. Not to mention that it would be more Pierce's style to make a decision on his own instead of talking to the membership. The whole thing is so shady. It's sad that this is how our educational system is working. I guess we can add blackmail to the list of skills that are taught at Penn.

MAY 22, 2003

Last night the Student Award's Banquet was held at the Holiday Inn. It was such a nice evening. This is the second year I have been on the banquet committee. It's a nice function and turned out very well if I do say so myself. Bart was looking at the favors on the tables. They were mini candy bars wrapped with the Penn logo and the date of the banquet. The back listed all of the shops. Bart said he thought we spent too much on something like that even though they were very nice. He wanted to know where we got them and how much they cost and why would we spend money on something like that. He looked dumbfounded when I told him that I made them. I do have a graphics background and there were only 200 of them. It cost less than $30 for all of them. They were very simple to make. Bart and Edmonson spend money on outrageous things for the office but they question the cost of banquet favors. The school didn't pay for them. The banquet is a teacher funded event. The favors make more sense to me than the plaque Edmonson presented to Bart last year.

MAY 26, 2003

This year cannot end soon enough! Pierce came down to Miranda's office about two weeks ago. Actually he stormed down the hall and beat on her door. I would not have opened the door for him at that point. While he was with Miranda he was yelling and screaming at the tops of his lungs. He could be heard out in the hallways. Charlotte was fearful that Miranda was in physical danger. God bless her. Even though she is a tiny woman her first instinct was to help someone she thought was in trouble. She ran back to Miranda's office to check on her. Miranda's door was locked. It automatically locks when it shuts so people can't just walk in on her when she is in a counseling session with a student. Charlotte couldn't get in and was pulling and banging on the door. Pierce pushed the door open and almost knocked Charlotte over. He was still yelling at Miranda and then he started yelling at Charlotte and pounding on his chest. He was screaming, "I am the president. The people elected me." Charlotte just responded, "So what?" Wow; a gusty young woman. Should she have been afraid? I was afraid for her. Pierce looked like he wanted to knock her across the room.

People started coming in to see what was going on. Pierce took off down the hall. He did stop long enough to get up in my face and scream at me for a moment right in front of everyone. He was so loud and I felt absolutely frozen. Spit was flying everywhere. It was gross! I have no idea what he was screaming about. Something about the fact that he couldn't do anything with my group because we were a hot pocket of resistance. I didn't know I had a group. Wow. I never had one before. Maybe we should get jackets. Sometimes I think if I don't try to joke about the situation I will go absolutely out of my mind. I have done nothing to this man. I cannot understand where his rage is coming from. Is there something so wrong with his life that he feels he would be nothing without being president of our little union?

JUNE 2, 2003

Edmonson heard about Pierce's ranting and he used it for an opportunity to stir up some trouble. Like I need any more trouble! He made an announcement over the school intercom for Maria and her group to report to the lounge right after lunch for a brief meeting. I could just feel Pierce seething. What is wrong with Edmonson? Does he want to see Pierce go off the deep end and physically hurt me? At the meeting I told Edmonson I had concerns about being assaulted. He told me if I was worried about something like that I should pray over it. Why in the world would he tell me to pray instead of helping me? I wonder how Edmonson hears about all the things that are said at school. People are worried that he has the school bugged. It would explain a lot.

AUGUST 31, 2003

I adore living in this part of the country. Sometimes I go to school early just to sit in my room and look out the back window. I have the most fantastic view of the mountains with the Jumonville Cross shining in the morning light. This area is so rich in history. I can look out my window and catch a glimpse of the area where the French and Indian War began. I can bask in the remembrance of lying with Alonna on a blanket on the grounds of Fort Necessity listening to the Pittsburgh Symphony give an extraordinary performance.

The French and Indian War, the birthplace of the Big Mac and the pilot site for fiber optic technology in the late 1980s are also part of this area's legacy. I was involved with the fiber optics program when I was the marketing manager for the local cable company and it was quite impressive. I can pass on these tid bits of knowledge to our youth while I teach at the home of Pennsylvania's first area vocational technical school. There are always two sides to every coin though and the other side to our claim to fame is not so nice. We were the pilot site for the national food stamp program and although not known in vast numbers, we have an active Klu Klux Klan chapter which has a very strong hold on some of the people around here. It sickens me that this mentality exists and that it was thrown through my front door last night.

Over the weekend Alonna stayed with her cousins. I love being with her, but last night was mine. I could clean, and read, and watch old movies, and not be responsible for anyone but myself. And that's how it was until midnight. There was a banging on my front door. My initial thought was there must be something wrong with someone in the family so I opened the door. In hindsight that was probably a stupid thing to do. Six scared teenagers burst through my front door. I recognized three of them. There were three girls and three boys: a brother and sister, a male neighbor and three of their friends. Five of the teens were white and one boy was bi-racial. They were cut up, shaking and out of breath.

One of the boys was a techer, and two of the girls went to school with Alonna. They had *sort of* snuck out for a late night walk. Was it sneaking out if you left the house after your parents had gone to sleep and you didn't want to wake them to ask permission? I would say yes.

While they were walking down our country road, a car drove by them several times. The car kept turning around and driving past them. This set the element of fear into play. The kids couldn't tell who was in the car as it was a cloudy, starless night. It was very dark. There are no street lights in the country.

After a few passes, the car stopped. It was a little car with a bad exhaust. The car was very loud. Two voices came out of the car, a man and a woman. The man made a few racial comments. He told the kids to get down on the ground; except for Jimmy. He wanted Jimmy to get into the car. He told the teens that he had a gun.

The kids did a brave thing. They didn't give in. They didn't get down on the ground. They grabbed Jimmy and ran into a field in the opposite direction of the car. They said they kept running, never looking back. They ran through thickets and brush and tried to stay along tree lines. They were headed home, but they were getting tired, and they were bleeding. They saw the light on in my house. They ran as fast as they could and began banging on my door.

When I told them we had to call the police and their parents they became even more frightened. I assured them it was the right thing to do. When you live in the country the police situation presents a dilemma however. We don't have a local police force. We have to rely on the Pennsylvania State Police. I called 911 and they transferred the call to the barracks. I explained the situation and was told that the police were very busy that night, and the closest unit was twenty miles away on another call. It would take approximately forty-five minutes for the police to get to my home. They told me to keep the kids at my house until the police got there.

I made the kids call the parents of the family where they were spending the night. They called but there was no answer. We would have to try again in a little while. Some people are just sound sleepers. So I sat with six scared teenagers watching MTV and sneaking a peak out the window every time a loud car cruised down the road. Was this maniac looking for the kids? Would he come here? When in the world were the police going to arrive?

Two hours later I called 911 again. I was once again transferred to the police barracks. The unit was delayed, but I was assured they would get there eventually. They told me to just keep holding onto the kids.

It was 3:30 a.m. before two troopers arrived. I had to explain again what happened. The troopers wanted to know which children were mine. I explained again; none of the kids were mine.

A report was taken and the police gave the kids a safety talk. They said the car was probably gone, but in any event, walking down a country road late at night was not a good idea. It is very dark and dangerous. Street lights on country roads don't exist and there are crazy people out there with guns in loud cars. Hmmm. I think they figured that out on their own. I thought about talking to the police officers about Pierce and Edmonson but it is a long story and I was really exhausted. I decided the best thing for me to do was go to sleep as soon as the troopers left.

The police still needed to talk to the parents. They would take the kids home. Finally! They walked out the front door and I started to close it. Before the door shut a hand came back in. There were six kids, two state troopers and only one police car. Could I help transport the kids to their home? I got my keys at 4:45 a.m.; almost five hours after I had made the first 911 call. When I got home I went to sleep with mixed emotions; my heart ached for Jimmy, and my blood boiled that it took hours for the police to arrive. Would they have come sooner if the gun had gone off and one of the kids was wounded or dead?

There would be other nights for reading and watching old movies. I was afraid there would also be other nights for Jimmy to face the ugly side of life.

OCTOBER 13, 2003

I am a techer teacher, and that in itself carries a bit of a stigma in this county. We are people who need to hold their own with other county teachers, students, parents, and the community. Techer teachers don't intimidate easily. Since we are a relatively small group, we tend to bond closely. You can always count on your true tech friends to laugh at you.

I have heard the saying Slippery When Wet. I can't help thinking of Bon Jovi when I hear that saying. It was a great album. I had occasion though to find out that things can be even more slippery when dry.

I am fortunate if my classroom at school gets a lick and a promise by the custodial staff. Sometimes we will let a deceased insect lie in its resting place to see how long it will be before he is swept away. One particular day, unknown to me, there was a substitute custodian. Who would have thought he would have swept my floor, let alone waxed it? And boy did he wax it.

It would have been alright; except my phone was located on the other side of the classroom and it only rings four times before it goes into voice mail. I was standing by the copier outside of my room when the phone rang. I took off in between a sprint and a run to answer it because I was expecting an important call from a parent whose son was having problems in his shop. Suddenly I felt my feet taking on a life of their own. My body was connected to them, but they were doing their own little dance. And the dance threw me into the corner of the table which housed a TV/VCR. I managed to push the TV back as I was headed for the floor.

God bless my friends. They heard the ruckus and came running to see what had happened. They came, they looked, and they laughed. And then they laughed some more. I imagine it was quite a site. The laughter was contagious. I even had to laugh at myself amid the bruises and contusions, and the skid marks on the floor that outlined my descent.

Edmonson didn't quite see the humor when I called and told him I needed to go to the Emergency Room. As I explained what had happened his response was simple, "Can this wait until school is over?" Of course it can, I'm a techer teacher. I'm tough. I wish I could be this tough when it comes to dealing with Pierce!

OCTOBER 23, 2003

It's been a difficult month, especially this week. My cousin Bobby, only forty years old, has died from cancer and I've been involved with helping with the funeral arrangements. I thought Bart and Edmonson were nice to me when they allowed me to take a half a personal day this week to meet my cousin Barb, Bob's twin, at the funeral home to make funeral arrangements. But truth be told they couldn't just be nice this once without wanting something in return. We're having an in-service on November 4th and they want me to handle the agenda and all the details. It was not a request, it was an order. Oh well. It will have to wait until Monday. Bob's funeral is tomorrow and I'm going to do the eulogy. I've got to pull myself together so I can give him the tribute he deserves. I'll put together the in-service agenda next week. I may have to put in a good bit of time after school but that isn't anything new.

November 7, 2003

I did a presentation on the special education process for the staff during in-service. Pierce sat there, put his feet up on the chair next to him, put a rub in and read the paper. He would occasionally make a smart remark about something I said. He complains a lot about the number of special needs kids he has in his shop but he doesn't want to learn anything that may help him. Rick says that Pierce is a master teacher. I guess the master knows it all. I seriously don't need his bullshit right now. I think about how we just buried my cousin who was a good man and here sits a person who is his own little version of Hitler.

I mentioned the spit cup to Bart and Edmonson. They would have seen the spit cup for themselves if they had bothered to come in to the presentation I was giving. To top things off they didn't reprimand Pierce for using tobacco inside the building. They did, however, refer the matter to our security guard, Peter Griffin. Peter told me that there was nothing that could be done because the building is smoke free and Pierce wasn't smoking, he was using smokeless tobacco. You have got to be joking. So if I walk around all day with an unlit cigarette hanging out of my mouth would that be okay?

Of course Edmonson couldn't wait to tell Pierce I had complained. What they didn't know was during the presentation I had already told Pierce he wasn't allowed to have a rub in. Pierce just stared at me and spit into his cup. Maybe I shouldn't have said anything about Pierce having a rub in but it irritates me that he gets away with everything. Rubbing snuff, cussing at students, having sex in the bathroom, and who knows what else. Not to mention all the yelling and screaming and threatening he has done with me.

Anytime I point out something to administration that needs corrected they run to the staff and say that I've complained; funny though how Edmonson will never tell me who has complained about me. I'm glad I learned from my family never to say anything behind someone's back that you wouldn't say to their face. Still there was no need to say anything to Pierce since they weren't going to do anything about his behavior. Edmonson seems to lay in wait always looking for ways to fuel Pierce's irrational behavior. He knows that Pierce continues to bully me daily and he refuses to do anything to help me. Not helping me is bad. I think throwing fuel on the fire is reprehensible.

JANUARY 9, 2004

Some days I feel like I am going to lose my ever lovin' mind. Besides the daily bullying from Pierce I've still got to deal with Edmonson. He is like a freakin' yo-yo. One day he is trying to throw me under the bus any way he can and the next day he is stopping me in the hall to hit on me. Today he wanted to know if I would go to a game with him. I don't know what kind of game he was talking about but my mind was working faster and I started to shake my head and say no as soon as he started talking. Before I could get a full sentence out he ran away; in the literal sense of the word. Those little feet seem to get faster all the time. It is so frustrating. Edmonson always tries to tell everyone what a smart man he is. I don't think he is all that smart. I think he is shady and sneaky. I also heard he actually bought his degrees. He has a friend who works at a local, prestigious university. Rumor has it that Edmonson paid for the classes and just got the grades and the degree.

Whatever he is, wouldn't you think he would be embarrassed after being rejected so many times and stop hitting on me. It's more than pursuit of a personal relationship. What he is doing to me is out and out harassment. Who has the power to stop this?

MARCH 27, 2004

Today would have been my father's birthday. I miss him more than I could ever put into words. He had the most gentle, strong hands I have ever seen. He would put his hand on my head and it felt like there was an umbrella of strength and protection covering me. If he was here I wouldn't be going through everything I am with Edmonson and Pierce. He would have made a visit a long time ago to have a man to man with Pierce and Edmonson.

My father would have been the only man there though; I don't really know what to call those other two.

APRIL 18, 2004

Bart called me at home today. I wrote a letter to the editor of the local paper about how teachers should treat students with more decency and respect. I didn't necessarily write it about Penn because there are issues with the way Alonna has been treated at her school but Bart called because he said that someone called him at home to tell him I was publicly trashing Penn. Of course he wouldn't tell me who called him. It was that infamous someone. Gee, I wonder who it could have been. Nikki has been very, very chummy with Bart lately. My money is on her. I wonder how Pierce feels about Nikki flirting with Bart. Maybe he doesn't care because he is married or maybe he doesn't care because he is using Nikki to gather information from administration. Another secret op.

The newspaper turned my letter into a guest commentary. I'm pretty proud of that. I guess I will give Bart a copy of it tomorrow. I should make him find his own copy, but what the heck. I am proud of what I wrote. Maybe someone is just upset because what I wrote hit a little too close to home.

I cut out the article from the paper. So proud of it!

Guest Commentary by Maria Martin

TEACHER WILL NO LONGER REMAIN SILENT

My mother came across an anonymous quote one afternoon, some years ago in a publication she was reading. The quote was simple but quite profound; it said, "What you permit, you promote."

I have found myself pondering the meaning of this statement more and more as my life progresses and I mature. I am now part of the generation whose youth is fading and the time for seriousness is at hand. I scrutinize society more, and more diligently, I scrutinize the people who are part of society.

I believe that we, as human beings, are a very rich and diversified group of individuals. I am not someone who believes we can find good in everyone and in every situation. Sometimes, for whatever reason, the good just is not there. And sometimes, for whatever reason, there are individuals out there who we just do not care for.

Sociopaths and people who commit crimes should be dealt with within the reigns of the law. We elect individuals to write laws, and we hire people to enforce those laws. This matter seems pretty well cut and dry.

There is another matter that seems to be a gray area. It is the matter of dealing with the individual who seems to be living within the legal arena of the law, but is walking a fine line when it comes to interacting with other individuals. I have known these people all of my life. They are for the most part, to put it simplistically; mean. The range of their meanness can run the gamut. They can be daily, openly void of kindness, or sometimes can seem caring and nurturing, and then pounce when you least expect it. I have a great distaste for both.

Years ago I worked with a man who was mean. He was elderly and was mean with a capital M. I was put off by his lack of respect toward his coworkers.

While I was never rude, I did not smile at him or laugh forgivingly at his spiteful comments. A coworker asked me one day why I didn't care for this man. I said that I thought he was mean. I was counseled that I should overlook his manner because he was old. I didn't buy it then, and I don't buy it now. Old mean people are just young mean people who got old. Aging does not give you license to be rude.

One of my life's regrets is that I never said anything to the man about how I felt about his behavior. I would say I promoted his behavior because I permitted it. I am not going to do that any longer. I am no longer going to promote mean-spirited behavior. I will call people on it, and I am going to start with the people in my profession, the educators of the world.

I am a public school teacher. I am very proud to be a teacher. I have worked extremely hard to earn the right to teach. I chose this profession. I chose to work with children and young adults of all backgrounds and behaviors. I have seen firsthand, too many students who have been dealt a bad hand in life. For some of these students, school is the only place that is a stable factor.

School should absolutely be a safe haven for all who enter. It should be the place where we help to shape the individuals who will become our future. It yields a wonderful opportunity to teach respect, and values and discipline.

There should of course, be clear cut rules and consequences for breaking those rules. There should also be fairness in how the rules and consequences are governed.

Sometimes, as human nature dictates, you run across students, who are loud, or have a style unto your liking, or for whatever reason you just do not care for. This goes with the territory of teaching, and it is an opportunity for you to grow as a teacher. This is the student who is entitled to the same fairness and respect as the quietest, most demur student in your classroom. This student may turn out to be the next face you see on the post office wall, or this student may turn out to be the next great talent of our time.

It is an abomination for anyone in the field of education to think other than the best thoughts for our students. If we treat any one student differently than we would another, than we have in truth become the bully that we as educators should be protecting our students from. I have seen it happen too often, and it saddens me.

When I was in high school, I was denied admittance into the National Honor Society. My grades were high and I was active in extra-curricular activities. I met the so-called criteria for acceptance in every way. I was told that the reason I was denied admittance was because although I exhibited great leadership qualities, it was the wrong kind of leadership. It was a very hurtful time, but it was maybe one of my greatest life lessons. I would not grow up and try to impose my personality ideals on others.

We are not working with monkeys. We are working with the future of our society. It is not our place to predict what our students will become, or what they will accomplish as they grow. If we let feelings of disdain or skepticism show, if we foster disbelief in our students who we doubt, then we are perhaps denying our future society of Einsteins, and Disneys and Picassos. Educators must be held to a higher standard in the treatment of our youth.

It is our job, not just to pass on knowledge, it is our duty to inspire and motivate. As an educator, if you do not believe this, if you are not willing to do this, if you are one of the teacher/bullies who promote ill-advised behavior through permission, then just maybe it is time for you to call it a day and make room for someone who can imagine the potential in all students.

APRIL 19, 2004
Edmonson emailed me. He said he read the article with interest and laughter. Did he think it was about Penn? If he did, why doesn't anyone do anything about educating our staff on proper student interaction?

APRIL 28, 2004
Kelly, who is seventeen and pregnant, is green today. She has uber morning sickness, but she is here. I am proud of her for coming to school. She realizes the importance of an education. I was lucky in the fact that I never felt healthier in my life than I did when I was pregnant. I never experienced one day of morning sickness. My hair and my nails were to die for. I glowed. I slept a lot, took my vitamins, and never let caffeine enter my body. I felt great, but life was hard. Going through pregnancy as a future single parent is not easy. I don't know if Mac thought he was just walking out of me but he was also walking out on the precious baby growing inside of me. The stress from his actions could have caused all kinds of health problems for my baby. It actually did. I went into premature labor and Alonna almost died after an emergency C-section. But Mac's brother was the mayor and because he didn't like me he promised Mac his dream job if he would get out of the relationship. I was too much of a free spirit and I wasn't politically important. He told Mac that being with me would not help either one of their careers. It was not a tough choice for him. Mac bolted. At thirty years old reality soon set in. I was pregnant and completely on my own. Pregnancy is like being in some type of foreign, alien body prison. I woke up one morning and couldn't see my feet, let alone tie my shoes. I got stuck in a restaurant restroom stall and couldn't get up from the floor unless I climbed up the side of a couch or chair. Money choices

came down to simple basics as whether to buy that Big Mac I really wanted or undergarments that I needed for my daily changing, expanding body. Oh, how I remember REALLY wanting that Big Mac. I think it was a connection to my youth. I could go to the place where the Big Mac was created. That was so cool. I had access to that famous location any day of the year. That's why I worked there when I was seventeen. That's why I wanted a Big Mac when I was pregnant. But the choice was a Big Mac or underwear. I needed bra and panties.

I should tell Kelly there are some programs available to assist with formula when the baby comes, but they only provide so much assistance. You are allotted one can of formula a day when the baby comes. My baby, as she grew drank one and a half cans of formula a day. Money; it was a daily issue.

Life became about sterilizing bottles and changing diapers and trying to figure out how and when to get a shower in. Life is hard enough and it goes by so quickly. I think that teen pregnancy robs individuals of a time that is meant to be, and should be, light and carefree. Kelly is going to have a long and difficult road ahead of her. I hope she has enough strength to get thru it. I think today I will go and have a Big Mac.

MAY 14, 2004

Amy, Charlotte and I had a department meeting scheduled with Edmonson first thing this morning. He knew we were scheduled to have a very busy morning, but he said the meeting would only last about ten minutes. We went to the office and waited for him and waited and waited. We waited for twenty-five minutes in the outer office until Amy and Charlotte both had to leave for IEP meetings at the home schools. I left when they did because I didn't want to go into a meeting alone with him and since the meeting was supposed to be with the three of us I just figured he would reschedule.

I stopped by a shop on the way back to my room. When I got to my room I had a phone message waiting. It was from Edmonson. He said he was more than a little upset, in fact quite pissed, that we had blown him off for our scheduled meeting. He reminded me in no uncertain terms that he was our boss and when he scheduled a meeting we were mandated to be there. I called him but he was quite curt with me; he told me that I was responsible for my group's actions and I had better think of a way to make this embarrassment up to him and we could discuss it over dinner Saturday night. Then he slammed the phone down in my ear. What the hell is he thinking? This has to stop. I sound like a broken record. I am not having dinner with him on Saturday or any other night. I also don't have a group!!!

Since he did not give me a chance to say anything on the phone, I called him back right away. As soon as he answered the phone I talked as fast as I could without letting him get a word in. I explained how long we waited in the outer office. I also told him I did not have a group; I was only responsible for my actions. I told him that I was not available to have dinner with him on Saturday or any other evening. I told him that I felt him telling me that I had better think of a way to make things up to him sounded like a threat to me and that our relationship had to be strictly a working relationship. I had more to say but he slammed the phone down in my ear without acknowledging anything I had said. I didn't hear back from him until the end of the day when I was summoned for a meeting with him by myself. Edmonson did the little power thing again. He likes to keep people waiting for an audience; the wait can go on forever. I sat there wondering if I was going to get suspended or fired.

I left the meeting wondering if he has any idea or cares what is legal. He acted like this morning never happened and just started into a new situation. A girl should have and could have graduated this year but she's in the foster system and if she graduated she has to leave the foster system, which the girl didn't want to happen. She has been receiving her education at home from the district because of her anxiety. A higher up in the Mountain District knows the foster mom and this man's daughter did the home bound schooling for her. She was not a special needs student so they decided to come up with a way for her to stay in the system. An IEP was going to be created so she could stay in the system. But there's nothing for her to do at the high school so she's going to be coming to Penn every semester for the next three semesters. I thought administration should handle something like this but Edmonson told me that I have to handle everything on our end. Is this legal? I don't really know. I don't think it is. Does Edmonson want me to handle this so his name doesn't appear on any of the paperwork? That's where I would bet my money. Is this payback for not having dinner with him?

MAY 20, 2004

Steve Courson, former Pittsburgh Steeler Guard from 1978 to 1983 was the guest speaker at the Student Awards Banquet tonight. In his defense I will say that he does get paid for speaking engagements and appearances but he came to speak to our students and their families for free. On the flip side he forgot about us because he was an hour late. He only showed up when we called to check on his whereabouts. When he arrived he was wearing sunglasses, a lot of bling and a tight silver sequined t-shirt that actually smelled like he had just pulled it out of the hamper. On the plus side he sat next to Edmonson which was amusing because Edmonson cannot tolerate anything that has the slightest hint of an unpleasant odor. Watching Edmonson be torn between muscle envy and looking like he was going to vomit was priceless.

Miranda, Samantha, Charlotte, Lonnie and I were sitting at a table with Brian. We were talking and laughing about all kinds of things; one of which included how uncomfortable Edmonson looked. Never did we imagine when Brian got up to do his introduction for Steve Courson that he would point to our table and say that our table was laughing at him. He said it as part of a joke, but it did not quite come out like that and who wants to have a massive pro football player mad at them? Can we outrun Courson? I hope I don't have to find out. We might; Courson didn't look very happy.

JULY 29, 2004

In addition to my teaching duties I am the Perkins Federal Funds Grant Coordinator. I spoke with Edmonson several times during this week on the phone to take care of some grant issues. Typically I would have gone into the school but I was busy taking Alonna back and forth from Penn State University's Space Camp for girls where she is volunteering as an assistant. I love that about her; she wants to be involved in the community and help whenever she can. Honestly, I could have gone into the school. I just didn't want to be alone with Edmonson. I didn't want to hear him tell me how tan I was or how good I smelled. And I didn't want to take a chance on him trying to touch me again. We would have been working alone together. Touching someone is a very personal thing and every time he touches me it makes my skin crawl. So I chose to call him instead of going to the school.

I tried to be matter of fact and just give him information about the status of the grant. He then told me that I had to go to a meeting at the Mountain District. Several students had failed their program at Penn but The Mountain District superintendent wanted them to return to us in the fall. I told Edmonson he should be going to this meeting. I did not feel comfortable going to the meeting because I don't have the authority as a teacher to be making administrative decisions. He then asked me to join him on his upcoming vacation to Florida. He said that I could get out of the meeting and he could send someone else if I went to Florida with him. Seriously? Are we back to this already?

What was going through his mind? Why would he think that I would say yes to go on vacation with him just because I didn't feel I should be the one attending the meeting? What kind of a person does he think I am? What kind of a person is he? Is he smart enough or devious enough to keep asking me out when there are no witnesses? This was it. I had reached my breaking point with him. There was just no way for this refusal to come out politely. I knew it was time to just be more than frank and tell him in no uncertain terms to stop asking me out. He had to be very clear that NO meant NO, but before I got more than a handful of words out he slammed down the phone in my ear. Did he just hang up on me because I wasn't there in person to watch him run away? I was fed up and determined to make sure he knew how I felt. I am not interested in dating him at all. No means no. Leave me alone unless it has something to do with work.

I immediately called the school back and dialed his extension. I got his voice mail. Did he know it would be me on the other end of the phone? I redialed the school, let it go through to the receptionist and was told that Edmonson wasn't there. What did they mean he wasn't there? I had just talked to him less than sixty seconds ago. Did he hang up the phone and run out the door? Wow! Is he that angry or that cowardly to hide from me? Can he really move that fast? Did he really just hang up, run out the door and drive away?

He has what I consider to be a cowardly/passive aggressive personality. Is there such a thing? What I mean is that you know he is seething on the inside but the Slick Whilly salesman façade comes out to hide his cowardice and he starts with the false flattery. Then he sticks a knife in your back when you are walking away. I wonder how far his reach goes. I have a bad feeling I am going to be finding out.

AUGUST 3, 2004

I met with Jamie Tucker, the sending district's teacher to review the guidelines for a student who has failed a shop at Penn. We are the student's elective. The shop credit is worth 3.5 credits for one semester. So if a student fails the shop it puts them almost four classes behind on graduation credits. Should they be able to come back or should they stay at the home school to get the credits they need to graduate? I guess it all depends on how they are with the core subjects and if they have any kind of wiggle room with credits.

I think Jamie and I both kind of got caught in the cross fire of the system; we both try to abide by the rules we know that have been set by the state, but ultimately things are out of our control. I keep seeing things done at Penn that I know are wrong and probably illegal. I am also beginning to believe that I am being blamed for a lot of what the districts don't like. I think Edmonson does things behind our back and then blames our instructional education teachers and the shop instructors for following the rules he has set up. I guess it's the same in any job situation—but when you are dealing with special education students you have got to follow the law!

AUGUST 9, 2004

There was a special meeting this evening with some of the board members and the superintendents. Bart wasn't there. I got the feeling that Edmonson set up the meeting and didn't tell Bart about it so he would look bad. Edmonson called me a few hours before the meeting and asked me to come and explain to the board how the communication works between the Penn Instructional Education Department and the districts. I think he asked me to come because he just didn't have a clue what we really do so he couldn't explain it to them.

At the meeting I was told by Edmonson that the districts had concerns that the Penn instructional education teachers weren't doing their jobs and weren't giving information to the high schools about the support students who were at Penn. I explained to the board that all of the instructional education teachers at Penn had developed an excellent rapport with the special education teachers/case managers and guidance counselors at the home schools and that we communicated individually with the teachers and guidance counselors about the students. I explained that we just all took care of what needed to be done and did not talk to administration about every single communication we had about the students unless there was some type of problem that would need the attention of an administrator. The board just stared at me with blank expressions on their faces not saying a word.

Edmonson dismissed me at that point and I never heard what happened after I left. In my opinion this is a big on-going problem at tech; there is never any follow-up information given to anyone. A big question in my mind is why did Edmonson not defend our staff from the beginning? And why didn't he bring up the fact that while we know the home school staffs are busy we should not have to beg for needed information on the students they are sending to us. We should have all the information we need on a student before they come to Penn so we can be properly prepared to meet all the mandated accommodations for the student if they have an IEP.

If Bart or Edmonson paid attention to what we did then they would know that we did our jobs and that we did them well. I think the districts are upset about decisions Penn administration makes that causes paperwork trouble for them, but Edmonson blames us. In my opinion, he never mans up and takes responsibility for his own actions. Bart is just as bad. How do you just not show up for this meeting when you are the director? Is Edmonson trying to stab Bart in the back and worm his way into being director? Sounds plausible. Very bad words were running thru my mind as I drove home.

SEPTEMBER 2, 2004

We got a notice from The Mountain District superintendent about a Corrective Action Meeting. The superintendent said it was a directive from the state based on complaints that had come in about Penn. Really? Who were the complaints from? Oh yes, those unnamed sources again. Or was this coming from things Edmonson told the board after I was dismissed from the August meeting? Did it back fire on him? It looks like a lot of special education connected people from the districts will be there. The notice was also sent to Bart and Edmonson. It said that the meeting is mandatory. They don't seem to like the fact that someone who they consider to be their equal is telling them what they must do. Edmonson has made some remarks like "Who does Kurt think he is? He is not my superior. He cannot order me around. I don't know if we're going to go to this." We've been told that we are not going to attend. Are we playing chicken? This should be interesting. How do you play chicken with a man who thinks the hierarchy of life goes like this: Kurt - - - - God - - - - - - everyone else.

September 8, 2004

Ha! Who is chicken; Edmonson or Bart? We went to the meeting! It was, without a doubt, a slam the vo-tech staff meeting. I know they are looking for someone to take the fall for what they see as thorns in their side. It was ridiculous. I know that there are some individual problems here and there but what school doesn't have problems. Why don't they just address those problems? It's not the fault of the instructional education teachers. This meeting just seemed like a production to show which blow hard yielded more power. Bart didn't say anything, he just cowered in a corner and Edmonson turned very red and looked very angry, but he didn't say anything either. Penn came off looking very weak and incompetent. I don't think this meeting helped anything at all. It is obvious that the problems are at the top and filter their way down. I wonder how Edmonson will spin this. I have a feeling Edmonson plans on making the instructional education staff at Penn his sacrificial lambs.

September 21, 2004

There has been an ongoing battle at school for the past several years. Edmonson is trying to create an internal divide within the staff. What good does that do for anyone?

This is my feeling on the situation; everyone at Penn is very busy. I don't know what the instructors do minute by minute in their shops. I believe they are doing the work they are supposed to be doing. I also believe that Edmonson has been spreading lies trying to stir up trouble. Patty said Edmonson told the shop teachers we just want information about what their lesson plans are for the week are to track what they are doing and to look for ways to get them in trouble. I can hear him doing it. He is doing his best to split the staff. How can any one person love to create so much drama? And how can Bart let him get away with it? The unrest and tension in the building is getting worse. Is it man made or does it have something to do with the history of the land. Whatever it is, it is very bad. Every muscle aches in my body by the time I leave the school at the end of the day. I think it is from me carrying that tension around. I need a good massage. Actually, I need for a couple of people to pack their bags and move on.

SEPTEMBER 23, 2004

I got a message from The Drug and Alcohol Commission. They had given a donation for the May Student Awards Banquet and they needed receipts as to how the money was spent. Diana Ringold was the chair for the banquet this past school year, but my name and Samantha's name is on the checking account so we are responsible for an accounting of the money. I left a message for Diana to see what happened to the box of receipts, check book, etc. It should have stayed at school but she left us at the end of the school year to take a job closer to her home. I'm sure she left it in a safe place. The office probably has it. I should have had my name removed from the checking account when Diana took over as Chair. Just one more thing to worry about. If we don't come up with the receipts we will have to pay that money back. I will have to call Diana.

OCTOBER 4, 2004

Another double standard! The men who teach at Penn wear jeans and some wear flannel shirts all the time. We don't have a dress code in our contract so people can wear what they want. Whenever I have to go to a meeting or if I'm going to be seeing a parent or something important is going on then I dress very professionally. If I'm working in a shop or working in my room, sometimes I wear jeans. A vocational school is different than your average high school. We work with trade areas like auto mechanics and building construction and horticulture. I don't wear jeans on a daily basis but I don't see the problem when I choose to do so. Edmonson approached Liv a few days ago, then he approached me, the other instructional education teachers and the math teachers; he told us all that we were not allowed to wear jeans to school. Liv went to see Pierce. She wanted to file a grievance. Pierce told her that she should just let it go as there were more important things to worry about. If it doesn't affect Pierce then he doesn't really care. A union president needs to deal with issues that affect all of the members. He cannot pick and choose which issues he feels is worth his attention. I plan on wearing jeans whenever I want; no more than usual, but just like I always do.

Edmonson wants all the women in the building to look like Fortune 500 cover women. He has made very rude comments about the way many of the women in the building dress; including myself. I am not about to wear a $500 dress to school if I am working in one of the shops. He however can wear his $700 suits because he doesn't go into any of the shops. Who does he think he is to judge people by what they wear? Style over substance; that's his creed. If he wants to work around short skirted, leggy, blonde women, who he obviously prefers, then he should go start his own school and hire his own femme fatale blonde staff. He is a judgmental snob. He is also probably one of the cheapest men I have ever known. There have been numerous occasions that we have run out to pick up lunch and Edmonson would stop us on the way out the door and ask us to pick him up something. When we gave him his lunch order he would hand us two dollars and ask if that was enough. What do you say to your boss? No you cheap bastard, why would you possibly believe lunch would cost two dollars? I guess that's one way to keep all of his money. I guess he needs his money for all of those evenings when he takes his female groupies out for drinks after work. I wonder if he even pays for that.

I heard from Diana Ringold. She had turned the box of information over to the office when she resigned over the summer. Edmonson gave the box to Nikki. Why? I don't know. She didn't have anything to do with the banquet. I asked Nikki for the banquet information but she refused to give it to me. Seriously? She didn't have anything to do with the banquet. My name is on the account. Who does she think she is? Oh yes. She thinks she is Hillary and yields such great power. She told me that she had taken the banquet box home and if I let her know exactly what I wanted from it she would make me copies.

I needed to go through the receipts and either Samantha or I should have had the banquet box as our names are on the checking account. I just left a note in Pierce's mailbox that I couldn't complete the request from Drug and Alcohol and that Nikki would have to do it because she took the box home and refused to give it to me. It would have been so simple for Nikki to give me the box and I could have completed the information. It's just another one of their little power games. I'm not playing this one. At this point I don't care if she gives them the receipts or if we have to pay the money back. Nikki is a vile witch and I am beginning to think that she and Pierce make the perfect couple. Life would be so much better if the two of them just ran off together and ruled the underworld.

OCTOBER 13, 2004

In the world of special education there are a lot of rules and regulations. It is a blend of state laws and federal laws. You always have to go with the rule that protects the needs of the students more completely. We constantly receive updates from the Department of Education and it really is the job of our instructional education staff to inform the shop teachers of special education rules and regulations so they can make sure they don't do anything they are not supposed to do. We don't want to see them innocently do something that will get them into hot water. I sent out a memo to the entire staff on discipline for special education students. Pierce sent it back to me with a written note on it -

"There will be no outside interference in my methods of **dicipline** based on 25 years of success."

Doesn't he care about the law? He obviously doesn't care that much about the issue of discipline if he can't even spell it.

I gave a copy of Pierce's response to Edmonson and Bart. I told them how bothered I was by his reaction just in receiving information from me. I asked that they talk to him. I don't want to get into a confrontation with Pierce but the law is the law. It shouldn't matter if the information comes from me or someone else.

They told me I was over reacting and it was just Pierce being Pierce. Edmonson told me I should pray over the situation and he was sure that if it was meant to be that God would move his spirit and make him more agreeable. I am praying that Edmonson and Bart both either get a backbone or pick up and get the heck out of this school. It's so sad. I don't think it's going to happen because the board doesn't seem to give a care what they do as long as no one bothers them. Our board only seems to care what kind of soup and snacks the culinary program is going to prepare for their meetings. The culinary program does prepare some pretty incredible food for the board meetings.

OCTOBER 25, 2004

My latest encounter with Pierce has me sick. It's not my job to prepare study guides for tests for Pierce's class. I am supposed to support the special needs students so I choose to make study guides for them. I also want to see the whole class do well on the tests so I make copies of the study guides for the entire class. It is exactly what the name implies; it is a guide. It's not the actual questions that will be on the test but if they study the guide they will be able to pass the test. There is nothing on the guide that won't be on the test.

I work with his kids on their theory assignments; help them study for the tests and I read the tests to the kids if their IEP says to have the test read. On Friday I read a test to seven students. They just had to fill in a bubble answer sheet. Basic rules; no talking, wait to the end and I'll go over whatever questions you want. Blah, blah, bah. Everything seemed to go very smoothly.

Today at 7:30 in the morning I was on my way to my room when Edmonson stopped me, in the front hall of course, to talk. That was bad enough but then Pierce stepped right in front of me almost knocking me over and stood right in front of Edmonson who said nothing about Pierce's rude behavior. Pierce cut Edmonson off which I didn't care about because he was just rambling on about nothing but it was what came out of his mouth that made me so angry I was shaking. Pierce started yelling in an extremely loud voice that he needed to talk to Edmonson. There were students and teachers coming in and he started yelling louder and louder. I think he was trying to draw an audience around him.

Right in front of me and everyone in the front hall, Pierce screamed that I had given his boys a test and I had ALLOWED them to cheat. He beat his chest and screamed that he knew this was true because two of the boys received the same score, missing the same questions. HE COULD NOT ALLOW ME TO LET HIS STUDENTS CHEAT! I interrupted at that point and said that in no way did I allow his students to cheat. Pierce said I needed to learn how to administer a test. Again, Edmonson said nothing! He just stood there in a zombie like stance. My heart was pumping fast but my brain kicked in and told me to shut up and remove myself from the situation. I'm not going to get into a brawl in the front hall. I think that is exactly what Pierce wanted me to do. I am sure he wanted me to start shouting and becoming hysterical and act like a crazy woman. No such luck Pierce. I would never lower myself to your standards.

Around 8:30 Edmonson called me to his office. Pierce had written a disciplinary referral for both of the students who he said I had allowed to cheat on the test. One of the students said he had not cheated at all, and had not let anyone look off of his paper. The other student admitted that he was sitting next to the other boy and very slyly would strain to look at the other student's paper, and did in fact copy his answers.

As teachers we try to prevent cheating as much as possible, but it is a fact of life; there will always be cheaters. Some will get away with it and some will get caught. It is not the fault of the teacher. Your eyes simply cannot be on every student all of the time, especially when you are reading a test to them. Now granted I would notice if a student fell asleep while I was testing, but how can you possibly keep your eyes on seven sets of eyes while you are looking at a test and reading it?

Edmonson said Pierce wanted me to retest the boys using the same test. I was upset that we were having this conversation in front of the students. I said that I did not believe retesting should be done. The boy who had not cheated should retain his grade and the other boy should get an F. It was that simple. Why were we making such an issue out of this?

Edmonson jumped up, lunged toward the students and told the boys he wanted them to apologize to me. He said it in a very condescending way. He pointed his finger at me in a very animated manner and said that the boys could just look at me and see how upset I was. Bingo! I was upset, but I was upset with Pierce and Edmonson and I did not want to talk about it in front of students. It is never a good idea to say what you really are thinking about your boss in front of students.

Pierce called me later and asked me when I was going to retest. I told him the same thing I told Edmonson; just give the boy who cheated an F. Pierce said that if I didn't retest the boys, the boy who had cheated was in danger of failing. I said I thought he should fail if that was the grade he deserved. Obviously failing one test should not put him in danger of failing the program. There must be other issues in the shop. I look at it this way; having an IEP does not give you a free pass or the right to cheat. The accommodations are there to help level the academic playing field for you. As I tried to explain this, Pierce started screaming at me. I was glad we were on the phone instead of face to face. He said he was holding me accountable for the failure of this student. I told him I disagreed with everything he was saying. The more calm I was the more irate Pierce became. I told him as far as the test was concerned I disagreed about that too but since it was his student, if he wanted the boy retested I would read the test to him to comply with the IEP. He gave the student the test and he brought it up. I read it to him. I don't know if he passed or failed.

I don't know how to describe what I was feeling. I was humiliated, and infuriated that Pierce would use the front hall in the morning rush to mar my professional reputation. I was even more upset Edmonson allowed it to happen. I spoke to Edmonson about it, but he just made some kind of remark like, Oh you know how he is. That's just his personality. He told me if I felt strongly about it I should pray harder. That is just so completely unacceptable. The tension is getting worse and worse as each day goes by. It is a wonder I get the respect I do from the kids; Pierce rants like this in front of them and Edmonson calls me Maria in front of them. On the days I wonder why I am still there I just keep reminding myself that I am there for the students and to provide for Alonna. That thought helps me make it through the days but it is getting harder to stay positive.

NOVEMBER 4, 2004
Miranda was extremely upset today. She went into Pierce's shop to see a student. The student had a rub in his mouth and had just spit on the floor. Miranda took him over to Pierce and said, "Mr. Pierce, do you permit your students to chew tobacco and spit on the floor?" She thought he would have sense enough to say he didn't know anything about it and that he would not permit that to happen. Instead he said, "Yes. And if you don't want to see it then stay the hell out of my shop." He pointed toward the door. It was an absolutely disgraceful way to treat a co-worker, especially in front of students! He is an arrogant, egotistical bully. Miranda saw the student at lunch time. She said that he should not consider himself off the hook just because of Pierce. She was going to write him up on her own. And she did.

To make matters more confusing right now is that no one is quite sure who is in charge of the building at the moment. Bart is out of the building at least three days a week doing some medical study and Edmonson passed out at work on October 29th after having some kind of an episode. He was taken away in an ambulance. I just happened to be walking down the front hall on my way to a shop and got to see him being taken away. The paramedics had cut off his $200 Italian silk shirt. I heard he threw a fit about that. I don't understand; a $200 shirt versus someone trying to save your life. You would think he should be grateful. I bet he sends them a bill for his shirt.

I have tried to get the image of his shirtless body out of my head. I hope it goes away soon. I never want to see that again; EVER. Like I have said before, I'm not a big muscle fan but I guess I understand now why he has Chip envy. His body is really just skin covered bones.

NOVEMBER 10, 2004

Edmonson asked me to come and see him today. He is back from his medical leave. He is not saying what happened to him. It's all very hush-hush. I think that's the way it should be. You have an absolute right to medical privacy. Anyways. He wanted to talk to me about the situation between Miranda and Pierce. Why me? Things are volatile enough. Why drag me into this? But I'm not going to lie. I wasn't there but I confirmed that Miranda had told me about what happened and I have always known Miranda to be a very upfront and truthful person. I told him I believed it was just another example of how Pierce's behavior was getting out of control. He just shrugged his shoulders. I also told him some of the students told me that Pierce was laughing about how he threw Miranda out of his shop and how he keeps the door locked now to keep her out. Edmonson didn't seem to care. He seemed more interested in telling me how hurt he was that I didn't come and see him while he was off work. Why would that man think I would ever come and visit him under any conditions? Quite frankly, I'm not sure I would even go to his funeral.

DECEMBER 2, 2004

Pierce has an unusual background; a psychology degree, turned tradesman, turned soldier attached to an intelligence team in Viet Nam, turned trades teacher. I think he uses part of his background to try and mess with me mentally. He sent me a vocabulary worksheet today. I guess there is a quiz coming up in his shop. That's fine but he just can't seem to resist the urge to be a smart ass about it. There was a note attached: "Support Person – Student will demonstrate mastery of vocabulary words by scoring 90% on a quiz of those words." Please! I have a name. And while I provide theory support to his special needs students, to address me as Support Person is insulting. And he might want to take a lesson on how to write an educational objective. Oh, but I guess he doesn't need any additional education because he is the master teacher.

DECEMBER 27, 2004

The Christmas holiday is a time to spend with the family and I have been enjoying every minute of it except I got a gift certificate in the mail for a massage at a local spa. The card just was signed "G." Gee, I wonder who it could be from. I am going to pass on the massage. I don't want a thought of Geoffrey Edmonson popping into my head during a massage. It would undo all the benefits of the massage. But overall just being with my family has been great. I have been blessed by an extraordinarily large extended family. My heart feels so bad however that there are so many people in the world right now who are afraid and without hope. There are hundreds of thousands of people who are dead due to the tsunami in Southeast Asia. I never thought I would see such devastation in my lifetime. It makes me want to grab my daughter and hold on tight to her.

JANUARY 4, 2005

Back to school and another drive by hall stop by Edmonson today. Maybe he should just move his desk out into the hallway. He's always there—just standing and watching the monitors. There are eighteen cameras placed throughout the building. He also had some secret cameras hidden in the teacher's lounge but the union found out about it and threatened to file charges so they were removed. Or were they? The reason Edmonson stopped me was to tell me Bart was laughing at me. Apparently Nikki went to see Bart and said that she really put me in my place. When; in her dreams? This has got to stop. I'm going to try going through the union with the Professional Rights Committee. It appears that Nikki's tirade stemmed from a conference that Edmonson sent Nikki and Pierce to. Let's just call it was it really was; basically it was just a four day get away for the two of them. Someone who was there from another school told me about it but I didn't say anything to anyone in the building. What do I care what they do? I figure if Pierce is involved with Nikki that maybe at some point he will just leave me alone. I did say to the person who told me that I don't think it is right that administration knows these two have a relationship going on and they keep sending them on trips together. Nikki and Pierce don't even pretend to have learned anything. They never come back with any information or feedback on the workshops. But they do come back with smirks on their faces like they just pulled a fast one. It is absurd that they think none of the teachers or students know what is going on between the two of them.

Everyone thinks the building is bugged because too much information gets around. Maybe it is. Nikki asked to talk to me about a student so I stopped by her shop. She lied. Big surprise. She said she heard that I had been talking about her and Pierce. I told her what happened; someone came to me and told me about their behavior at the conference. I said as far as her personal life is concerned, I really don't care what she does just as long as it doesn't involve me. I did tell her that I don't think she and Pierce should be flaunting their relationship in front of the kids however. She didn't know what to say to me. Of course she denied any relationship with Pierce but the students are very observant and students talk. Nikki and Pierce aren't fooling anyone but themselves. I guess she thought she would get back at me by running to Bart and putting a spin on our conversation by telling him that she put me in my place. What a crock.

JANUARY 19, 2005

The union committee met with me today and asked if they could call Nikki down to discuss the situation. Of course; I will never say anything behind your back that I won't say to your face. I learned that from my Uncle. It's a great way to live your life.

Nikki was livid when she got there. She started to turn and walk out when she saw me but Liv stopped her and asked her to just sit down so we could talk this out. Nikki denied talking to Bart about me. Liv suggested that there was an easy way to clear this up—call Bart and ask him to join us. Nikki jumped up and said no; she would personally go to his office to talk to him. She started walking very quickly. I jumped up and was right behind her. There was no way I was going to let her get to Bart and try to get him to cover for her. Bart cracked like a dried heel in the winter. He tried to come up with lame excuses about how my name just happened to come up in a casual conversation when he and Nikki were discussing his daughter's wedding. He realized at this point he was cornered because I don't know his daughter and I didn't know she was getting married so why would my name come up in that conversation? He then said his big mistake was talking to Edmonson about it. No apologizes. But I don't care. They both know that I am not going to let things like that slide. It also gave me a better insight into the level of help I can expect from administration. And that level of help seems to be less than zero. I don't know how bad things are going to get, but I guess I'm on my own.

MARCH 25, 2005

It feels good to be off. It is Easter break. There's a full moon out tonight and it seems like people's behavior at school takes a major turn for the worse when the moon is full so I'm going to enjoy the few days we have off. It has been a busy two months. Alonna had abdominal exploratory surgery. She has been having severe pain on her side for two years now. They have done every test imaginable and come up with nothing. Children's Hospital in Pittsburgh told us that she may just have to learn to live with the pain. A doctor in Morgantown, West Virginia sent us to a pediatric surgeon at West Virginia University's Ruby Memorial Hospital. He did a few tests and decided to go in and do the surgery to see what they could find. She was filled with scar tissue from her colon to her ovary. They scraped it all out. Hopefully the pain will stop. There are no answers at this point as to how the scar tissue got there as she has never had a surgery before or was involved in a major trauma. I just want her to be pain free. Watching my child go through that kind of pain has been one of the hardest things I have experienced. It has been twice as stressful having to deal her health issues and everything going on at work simultaneously. Her health issues are a big part of why I stay at Penn. I have very good health insurance and I am thankful for that. Alonna wouldn't be able to get the medical treatment she needs without it. It's kind of ironic—my being at Penn is helping Alonna to get well and it's making me sick.

It's also union nomination month. Pierce is running for president again and Daniels is running against him. Pierce has been asking people what the *girls* are planning on doing. What a condescending jerk. I don't know what anyone else is planning on doing but I know what I'm going to do. It is not that I necessarily think Daniels is a strong leader but I know he really wants to do the right thing. Pierce or Daniels. It's a no-brainer. I'm not out on the campaign trail for Daniels but when people ask me what I think I tell them.

April 28, 2005

Yesterday was the union election. Daniels beat Pierce by a fairly large number. Pierce is furious and he is blaming me. He is the most ungracious loser I have ever seen. How is his loss my fault? I cast my own little vote. I didn't mark ballots for anyone else or take ballots to people who were out sick. Maybe the members just opened up their eyes and decided they don't want a bully running the union anymore; especially one who seems to be in cahoots with administration whenever it suits him. Daniels will take over the presidency at the union meeting in May. Nikki seems to be beside herself. She almost looked like she was going into shock. She is still vice-president and she will be serving with Daniels. Nikki demanded a recount of the ballots with her standing there watching. It isn't going to change anything. Pierce lost.

MAY 4, 2005

Man! Today was so out of my league. I should not have been made to go to this meeting alone. I should not be making decisions of this magnitude. Edmonson would not go to a meeting with me for a student who had made a hit list. I bet he was afraid. Was the student serious about the hit list? I don't know. It included students and teachers. I did find out that I wasn't on the list but what about the people who were on the list? Could they be in danger? Personally, I've always gotten along with this student but I try my best to treat everyone with respect. What happened to him? What is going to happen to him? Will he end up being another one of our students who I read about in the paper? I have asked Edmonson to go to other meetings with me when I felt an administrator was needed. He never goes with me to those kinds of meetings. It puts me in a very bad position. The home school expects that an administrator will attend and when they ask me where he is what do I say, "Oh, I'm sorry. He is afraid to be in a meeting that he can't control." Or "He didn't want to come." And I don't like to lie for anyone so I just say that he sent me. Let them figure it out on their own. It's not that I don't know what I'm doing. I know my job and the law very well. I just don't have the authority to make decisions that affect students' lives. I guess I am supposed to do it whether I have the authority or not.

MAY 5, 2005

Our Head of Maintenance has been relieved of his duties and is under criminal investigation by the FBI for child pornography and for contacting some of our female students. You would think that I would feel some sense of shock but after the hit list meeting yesterday I don't think there is much that can shock me. I am appalled though. And disgusted! There was a big segment on the Pittsburgh news and in the local paper. Edmonson held a teacher's meeting and pounded his fist on the podium and said that Ted was going to be prosecuted to the fullest extent of the law and no deals were being made. HA! By the end of the day he told me that Ted was permitted to resign instead of being fired so he would be able to keep his retirement. Edmonson said that Ted was a good guy but he just had a few problems and he needed our prayers, not prison. I wanted to scream. There is no doubt that he needs help. He has been scaring females for years. He used to get to so close to Charlotte and say such inappropriate things to her it made her skin crawl. Charlotte and I have become close friends even though I am old enough to be her mother and she came to me about the situation with Ted. It was making her very nervous. The mother vibe kicked in and I went immediately to see Ted after she told me what he had been doing to her. I told him that he was not to have any contact with Charlotte or I would make sure that he was reported and that I would push the issue. I didn't know about the pornography issue but I must have hit too close to home because he never bothered Charlotte again. He didn't speak to me for a year but what the heck did I care? I am not a judge or jury but what about the protection of our children and women in general? Shouldn't he go to prison for what he has done? I know the answer to that. At Penn the protection of our men comes first no matter what they have done. Sick. Oh my stars, a thought just ran through my mind. Why can I so forcefully stand up to someone like Ted when I am protecting someone else but I can't forcefully stand up for myself like that? Is it because I didn't see Ted as dangerous? But he is dangerous. He is a predator. How can our board let him resign? Don't they have a responsibility to our community? Aren't we supposed to be teaching our students about morals and values as well as their trade? How is it morally right to let this man resign instead of being fired?

MAY 6, 2005

The first year I was at Penn the student council held a car show as a fund raiser. The kids had a good time and they managed to make a little bit of money for charity. Since that time Edmonson has scheduled a car show every year, sometimes twice a year and has expected all of us to show up and work the event without any kind of compensation. Cars are his thing; the flashier the better. His brother buys and sells cars on EBay. Edmonson shows up to school every week with a different kind of sports cars. He is all about the façade.

Nobody minds volunteering for events when they are worthwhile but there is just no value to the school with the car show. It is completely an ego thing for Edmonson. Parents can't talk to teachers because we're working game booths or the concession stand and the community can't see the school because the school is shut down except for the front hall bathroom. It's not a student council event anymore and if there is any money being made from the event no one has said where it's going; although from the money being spent on unnecessary things for the car show, the school is probably going in the red.

In any event, the majority of the staff has had enough. Last fall was the breaking point I think. It was frustrating to be working hard and watching some people, like Nikki and Pierce just spend the evening walking around arm in arm. Edmonson saw them that night but of course he just turned a blind eye of indifference to it. There were parents and students there for goodness sake. It's too damn bad if the car show interrupted their date night, they should have just stayed home.

Edmonson has already scheduled another car show. There is no legal way he can make us organize it and show up to work but people are worried about retaliation from him if we don't do it. So the union came up with a solution; trade all of our after school meetings in the month of May for the teachers helping to organize and hold the car show. Since there is a definite lack of trust with Edmonson the union members said that we would agree to this only if it was put in writing by him. Pierce said, while pounding his fist on the table, that he would have the written agreement the next morning. But that never happened. What we did get was a memo from Pierce:

To: Membership, Penn AVTS EA

From: A. Pierce, EA President

It has come to my attention that there is a small group of what I will call union associates complaining about the after school sessions. I will no longer be your leader after this month so I feel I should leave you with some final words of guidance. Including the day of the car show we will have been released from eight after school sessions in this year. Eight sessions equal one month.

There are things that must be done in a timely manner, like calling parents that a good teacher does without complaint. At a time when jobs are at stake we have teachers splitting hairs over a 45-minute period. The Administration often lets teachers leave early at the end of the day when they have a personal errand to take care of. This courtesy is not mandated by the contract. Does no one appreciate that? Myself, I am not concerned and I appreciate the times I am permitted to leave early to attend to personal matters. People should start worrying about how to be good teacher and not worry about getting time off in exchange for helping to promote our school with the car show which could potentially bring in students to our programs.

Yes, there was a motion and a vote to get the agreement in writing. I chose not to. There are always people ready to try to make the Association President do things they don't have the guts to do. These are the same people that in a fit of anger may voice their displeasure to the Administration then having cooled down crawl into the office to apologize. I was your official leader for four years and I will always be available to guide you and lead you if needed but I am no ones patsy. If there are complaints be man or even woman enough to see me.

MAY 11, 2005
Sometimes you just have to stand up and defend people you work with. I did what Pierce suggested. It was wrong of him to slam the professionalism of the staff so I answered his memo and copied the members of the union. The copies were in sealed, individually addressed envelopes.

Pierce:

My grievance is not with administration. It is with you relative to this particular matter.

There was a motion made as follows: "We the Penn AVTS Education Association agree to organize and hold a car show on Wednesday, May 18, 2005, in exchange for the elimination of all after school meetings during the month of May, 2005. We agree to this only if the agreement is given in written form by administration." There was a motion, a second and the motion unanimously passed. You, Pierce, then said, "I will have the written agreement for you tomorrow."

You have stated that you chose not to get the agreement in writing. It was, at the very least, unfair of you to make that decision without letting the EA know of your choice. Asking to be the Association President, but believing that selectively following the rules makes you not a patsy, but from how I see it, a want to be dictator.

Additionally, your statement produced on May 6th gives the impression that the faculty at Penn counts minutes and does nothing outside of the school day. I truly believe that the faculty gives generously of their time outside of the school day by preparing lesson plans, study guides, grading tests, talking to parents. And they do all of this without asking for recognition. They do not complain about the extra time given. It goes with the job. They put forth their best effort for our students out of respect for the students and the profession. As you have stated you chose which by-laws and rules to follow, I believe it is in the best interest of everyone concerned for you to stop down effective immediately from the office you hold.

I got a note back on the letter from Pierce. He said, "Maria, thanks! I have received job offers from several South American countries and one in Central America. They are looking for good dictators down there. Pierce."

I thought that maybe since he was no longer going to be president he was finally going to try to put all of this behind us and his joke about the dictator job offers was his was of sending out an olive branch so I sent him a return email: "Pierce, It's nice to know that we can each voice our opinions and still have a good sense of humor around here. Maria."

After all these years it would be nice to be able to come to work without having to worry about Pierce's bullying behavior.

MAY 13, 2005

Looks like I'm in hot water again with Edmonson. A student has been bullied and it has been going on for quite a while. There is no doubt that this student appears troubled and can act out but there is no excuse for the things that has been done to him. The boy's father wants a meeting. His son was duct taped in class, had things hung on him like he was a Christmas tree and was made to stand on a box. The boys who did it had to say they were sorry but we all know they weren't sincere. Why didn't Edmonson do something meaningful? Because he didn't like the boy who was bullied? That's what my gut tells me. But he claims he didn't know about everything that had gone on in the shop. That is just plain hogwash. Some of the students in that shop gave me a copy of the list of shop rules. There are over one hundred rules in addition to the rules that are listed in the student handbook. One of the shop rules includes the issue of *flatulence.* "There shall be no passing of gas in the shop." How can that possibly be an enforceable rule? It is a bodily function.

The boy's father called me for help. I could hear the pain in his voice. Technically I don't have the power to help, but I can guide him. It makes me absolutely crazy when a student is bullied. School should be the one place where everyone who enters through the doors is safe and secure. What is the matter with this world? What is the matter with us at this school? We need to demand nothing less than safety for all. This should be a no brainer. Why do I have to have this fight with administration? I have to stand up for the students. It is my moral obligation but it always comes at a cost. Edmonson has a tendency to make it his mission to make my life as much of a living hell as he can for several weeks following such a situation. I guess that is the price I will have to pay. I can't sit back and do nothing. I would never be able to live with myself if this boy did something to harm himself and I just watched it happen because I was afraid that Edmonson was going to be mean to me.

MAY 14, 2005

Each year the Chamber of Commerce gives an Educator of the Year Award. There are categories for each of the districts and the IA/Vo-Tech. Selection is based on nominations submitted to the Chamber. The Educator of the Year is asked to select someone to present the award to them. It is typically someone who has nominated them. A couple of years ago I presented the award to Samantha. She is a great teacher, goes above and beyond for her students and was quite deserving of the award. This year none of the Penn staff received nominations forms. They are sent to administration by the Chamber to be distributed. I guess Bart and Edmonson forgot to distribute them.

Pierce was awarded Educator of the Year. The teachers and staff at school were stunned when we heard. Bart presented the award to Pierce and gave a glowing presentation. I wonder if both Bart and Edmonson wrote recommendation letters for Pierce. How could they recommend him for such an important award? They have just made a mockery of the Educator of the Year Award. Pierce yells and pounds his fists and calls the students monkeys and spits on the floor. It was a very proud moment for education. You can't blame the organization who gave it to him. They make decisions based on the recommendation letters they receive and when letters come in from administration they carry weight.

Also, boy was I wrong about Pierce wanting to start fresh. I received a letter from his attorney today. He must have sent the note to me the other day and then immediately went to see his attorney after school.

Dear Ms. Martin:

Please be advised that this office represents A. Pierce. I have reviewed the letter which you sent Mr. Pierce and apparently distributed through the school postal system. Not only does my client take issue with the remarks that you made, but reference to him as a patsy and a dictator are slanderous. Not only do these comments show poor judgment on your part and a lack of respect for my client, it is actionable in a court of law.

Please realize that if my client does not receive an apology, in writing, within ten days, he has instructed me to file suit against you in the Court of Common Pleas for monetary damages. We will wait ten days and there will be no further warning.

Very truly yours,
Mason Nealson
Attorney at Law

MAY 18, 2005

I talked to the union as a courtesy to let them know where the situation is now with Pierce and to give notice of his pending lawsuit. Jim asked me if I would be willing to sit down with Pierce and talk things over. I didn't have a problem with that but I did not feel I owed Pierce an apology and I told Daniels I would not apologize to Pierce EVER.

Jim called me at home and told me that he had spoken with Pierce. Pierce explained that he really did not want to go through with the lawsuit; probably because he had no case as he was the one who used the word patsy and I just said "in my opinion he was not a patsy but a wannabe dictator." He told Daniels he felt I had humiliated him with the election and the letter. Okay, I am going to go all school-girl here and say, hey! He started it first. I couldn't believe I humiliated him; unless he can dish it out but he can't take it. Pierce told Jim that he was willing to drop the matter but he still wanted a written apology. Jim told him that he was not going to ever get an apology from me and Pierce became extremely irate.

Pierce told Jim to inform me of a few things. He said that I was to stay away from anywhere he was. For example if he was walking down the hall and I saw him I was to turn around and walk in the opposite direction. I was not to look at him or to talk to him. Are you kidding me? It is a small building with a teaching staff of thirty. There is no way that we can avoid contact with each other all of the time. He is not going to rule my life. Thank goodness school is almost over for the year.

MAY 20, 2005

The local union felt that I should speak to the regional union about my situation with Pierce. Daniels thought it would be a good thing for Miranda to do as well because she has had almost as many problems with Pierce and Edmonson as I have had. I faxed the letter I got from Pierce's attorney along with some background information to the regional union office about my situation with Pierce. He is a bully at school and yet he wants me to say I'm sorry to him? I didn't say anything wrong. No apology will be coming but he is starting to really worry me. He has always yelled and screamed but he is getting up in my face more often. I don't know how well he can control his rage. Should I be afraid of him? It's been so hard to comfortably do my job when Bart and Edmonson don't care. I have continued to try and talk to both of them about the situation. Edmonson just comments on how Pierce could be in so much trouble with his behavior and that I should pray over the situation. Bart just tells me he doesn't want to hear it; that as far as he is concerned it's a union issue. Is anyone going to try and control Pierce's behavior before he does something serious?

MAY 25, 2005

Edmonson asked me to write a recap about the phone call I had with the parent who called me about his son being bullied. Edmonson told me he is very upset that I dared to have a conversation with a parent. I didn't call this man. He called me because his son gave him my name as someone who might be able to help him. And by the way, isn't that what a good teacher is supposed to do; communicate with parents? The dad told me he has spoken with Edmonson several times and has gotten nothing but the run around. The way his son has been treated makes my heart hurt. The dad asked me what his legal rights were as a parent. It should have been such an easy question to answer but I was afraid with the way I have been treated by Edmonson myself that I would get into trouble if I told him what I actually believed. Edmonson is becoming more vindictive and I don't know what all the legalities are when you know your boss is doing something he shouldn't. So I told the parent very clearly to refer to his copy of the Department of Education procedural safeguards for parents. He didn't know where they were so I told him where to get them and told him what section to look in. EVERY ONE who comes to school should be safe. Teachers need to set an example and not overlook what goes on in the class and administrators should not try to bend the truth or cover anything up. It is a shame to think that the actions of one teacher can give a bad name to the school. We have so many dedicated and hardworking teachers here.

JUNE 13, 2005

Miranda, Daniels and I went to the regional union office in New Canton today to meet with Ryan Matson, the attorney and Kevin Klein, the uniserve rep. We wanted to talk about what to do with Pierce's behavior and talk about mediation. They just absolutely dismissed me— literally with a wave of the hand. Yes! Matson waved his hand in front of my face. They did not want to hear one word I had to say. I was extremely offended but more importantly I still wanted to get some answers as to what to do. When I tried to press them for help or advice, Klein got very flippant with me and told me that they could not do anything to help me because they could not pit one union member against another. By not helping me, aren't they in a sense helping Pierce? I couldn't believe what they were saying. Something needs to be done. Don't they understand that? They also told me if I did anything to have Pierce fired then they would have to defend Pierce to keep his job. So, they can't help me, but they would help Pierce? How does that work? Why is my worth as a PSEA union member less valuable than Pierce? I don't know but it is. Klein may say it isn't, but his actions certainly speak louder than his words. I can't help but wonder if Klein is talking to me as a union rep or as Pierce's friend?

Miranda has been calling everyone she can think of on a higher up state union level to have someone come in for mediation for us but no one will help us. What do we pay union dues for?

JULY 1, 2005

At the June Operating meeting, the math department, one guidance counselor, five paraprofessionals and one shop instructor were laid off. The staff was really upset about this. It came out of left field and there was really no explanation as to why this action was being taken. There was no warning that the massive layoff was coming. I thought there had to be some sort of notice given to the union that they were at least thinking about taking this course of action. Did Pierce get the notice and not tell any of us because he wanted to see these people leave the building? Notice should have been given to the union in April when Pierce was still president. Did Bart and Edmonson tell Pierce that if he kept his mouth shut that they would hold the nomination forms for Educator of the Year and send in letters for him personally?

Things are so shady with administration. There doesn't appear to be much honesty. On the last day of school Holly, the guidance counselor who was laid off, had met with Bart and Edmonson and they told her not to worry about anything. Her job was secure, have a good summer and they would see her in the fall.

There was no reason to do this. We need all of them. A federal grant covered the salaries and benefits of four of the staff members laid off and Elliot had approximately twenty kids coming back to his shop. Why would you lay off these individuals? Why would you close this shop? It makes no sense. Bart and Edmonson have told me that they don't like several of the staff that were let go. I think they're trying to do this massive layoff to cover their tracks. It is nothing short of cowardice.

I knew this was partially coming though. Samantha told me that Kurt, the superintendent from The Mountain District, called her and said that if she got laid off at the vo-tech Monday night she shouldn't worry because they was going to hire her on Thursday. And they did. Samantha didn't fill out an application or interview for the job. She just got laid off and she was hired in the same week at her step with her years in tact. It's close to how it should have been done. They should have followed the rules of the Transfer of Entities, but they didn't. What's going to happen with Andie and Holly and the others that were laid off? I felt horrible the night Andie was laid off. She had gone to Idlewild Park with her husband and daughter for a nice summer outing. She called me after the board meeting to see what happened. She is my friend and I had to be the one to tell her that she just lost her job. It was one of the lowest points of my life. I think it was spineless of Bart and Edmonson to know that these individuals were on the agenda to be laid off and they didn't call any of them ahead of time or even right after the board meeting. I guess they were just planning on letting them read about it in the paper the next day. The situation makes me want to say very bad things about them. Very bad words.

JULY 7, 2005

I stopped by the vo-tech to work on some federal files. What I saw was pretty shocking. Not only did administration not give a head's up to anyone who had been laid off, they did not give them any time to come in to go through their belongings. Their desks and filing cabinets had just been emptied and literally dumped on to the floor. Some of the items were in boxes, some of the items were laying on chairs and tables but most of the items were lying on the floor. Personal items that belonged to Holly were missing. One of the missing items was a geometric design I had done for her and framed. I saw it later that day in the hallway outside of Edmonson's office on a bookshelf. I asked him where he got it. He said that he had picked it up somewhere. Right! I know where he picked it up; he picked it up from the top of Holly's desk before he dumped her stuff on the floor. He is a master liar.

I should have told him that I knew it belonged to Holly because I made it for her, but I don't want any more trouble then I already have; which is a lot. Is that a little cowardice? Yes, I'm ashamed to say that it's more than a little cowardice. Shouldn't I have confronted a petty thief and a liar even though he's my boss? Did I just give him permission to keep telling lies? I hate to admit it but I just contributed to his appalling behavior. I am ashamed of myself.

JULY 18, 2005

Edmonson called a staff meeting this month for the remaining members of what he refers to as the support department. The support department is really any teacher who works with all of the students and doesn't have a specific vocational shop with an assigned state CIP code. He said he was going to pay us for this meeting since he asked us to come in during the summer. That's a first. I don't think I can count the number of times I have gone to meetings after school or in the summer and he never once offered to pay me. I was there along with Charlotte, Amy, Miranda and Hank. This was the first time that Edmonson has ever asked Hank to attend a support department meeting. I thought that paying us had something to do with Hank attending the meeting because he is a man.

Edmonson wanted to talk about his great four step reconstruction plan. Who does he think he is now? Abraham Lincoln. There is nothing honest about him. He talked in circles but basically it amounts to this: we are all to pick up the work of everyone who was laid off in addition to still doing our work. Hank spoke up and said that we cannot possibly do everything and that as our boss he should prioritize what he wants us to do and then we will follow his direction. I don't think Edmonson has a clue what anyone did who is now gone and I don't think he has a clue as to what we do so I don't think he has a clue how to prioritize anything.

Today was one of the few times I believe that I have seen Hank truly angry. He is one of the most admirable, decent men I have ever known and I have seen him upset on occasion but I have never seen him angry until today. Everyone at school knows that Hank served in Viet Nam and that he was awarded bronze and silver stars for valor. He doesn't speak much about the war, but he takes it very seriously; as he should. Edmonson during the course of the meeting said very dramatically, something to the effect that we have lost a lot of our comrades. He said it was just like being in a war and seeing our friends killed, but that we just had to put it aside and go on. It was completely inappropriate and there was absolutely no reason to say what he did. I think Edmonson stays awake at night thinking of things to say that he knows will upset people. He likes to create tension and drama and I think he said this because Hank was there. Charlotte and I were sitting closest to Edmondson and we both reacted by sliding our chairs far back away from the table because by the look on Hank's face we thought he might be coming across the table to get Edmonson. But Hank was true to his nature and kept his cool. I don't know how. If I was in that position I may have jumped across the table to get him. Maybe Edmonson was hoping that Hank would attack him so he could have him arrested and fire him. I wouldn't put anything past that small minded man. I am surprised that Edmonson didn't say anything about his two supposed tours in Viet Nam. I can't believe he actually tells people that. I feel in my heart he is a liar. I don't think he served at all. The truth about his service is bound to come out. Isn't a crime to claim to have served in the military if you haven't? I believe it's called Stolen Valor. I do believe that the only way for Edmonson to have any valor would be for him to steal it.

August 25, 2005
Today began a new school year. It was the first day of in-service for the teachers. There is a sad and empty feeling in the air with so many people laid off. Please oh please oh please let this year be better.

AUGUST 27, 2005

This new school year has gotten off to the worst start yet. I went to the hospital this morning. Things have finally escalated to a physical assault level with Pierce. It was bound to happen. Pierce hit me yesterday at school. I felt like I was in a hockey game. He body checked me and almost put me to the ground. I am in some of the worst pain I have ever experienced and I am no stranger to pain. I was in labor with Alonna for 129 hours. And of course I had the doctor that did not believe in any type of pain medication. I know what pain feels like and this is pain! When I explained what happened at the hospital the woman who was registering me asked me if I really wanted to put it on the report that I was assaulted by a co-worker because once I put it down I couldn't take it back. Seriously? Is that how they advise battered women or other assault victims? I'm just telling the truth about what happened. I felt like they were actually trying to make me feel bad about reporting an assault. Blame the victim. It is what society seems to do. I told them to write it just as I told them in large print so there would be no mistake about what happened. It is what it is and I will not try to cover it up.

I keep going over what happened in my mind. Was there something that I did or that I said that made him want to hit me? No! I didn't do a damn thing. In fact, the first half hour of the in-service yesterday seemed to start out fine. Miranda and I were presenting a segment to the faculty about students with learning disabilities. It was going to be a long session, about two hours but it was really worth it. It's a program called F.A.T. City. It deals with the Frustration, Anxiety and Tension that kids with learning disabilities experience and the program really helps people understand what it feels like to have a learning disability. I think it should be mandatory for all teachers in all districts to watch the video. I was actually very excited about coming to school and presenting the session.

Just before it was to begin, I was standing on the right-hand side of room facing the screening area. There was a faculty sign-in sheet for Act 48 credit on the front table. People signed in and passed by me to be seated. Then Pierce entered the room followed by Rick. He began to pass the front table. I spoke to him in a very civil manner and said, "Pierce, there is a sign-in sheet on the front table for Act 48 hours." At that point he did not speak but he made direct eye contact with me and then slammed into me as to shove me out of his way. He did not stop to apologize, he just continued to the back of the room where he sat down. I swear that I saw him smirk as he hit me.

I was stunned. The hit jerked me back a few feet and I tried to maintain my balance but I was wearing heels and within seconds I was on my way to the ground. I tried to catch myself which was probably a very stupid idea because I could feel my back twist as I struggled not to hit the floor. I landed on my hands and instinctively pushed myself up. My head was spinning. Why did he do that? I was not in his way; he could have easily gone around me like everyone else did. It was unprovoked and it was deliberate. I wasn't sure what I should do. I looked around the room and everyone was talking in small groups. I wondered who had seen what happened. I was filled with mixed emotions. I felt angry and embarrassed at the same time. I don't know why I felt embarrassed though. I was the person who had been hit. It took me a minute to pull myself together and then I immediately went to Miranda and asked if she saw what happened. She said she heard everything but didn't see the actual hit as she was getting papers together. I didn't go to administration right then. I guess I should have but I had a presentation to do and I was just absolutely stunned. Thinking about it right now I should have just gone straight to the office and reported the hit but based on everything that has happened with Pierce I didn't think it would do any good. Edmonson probably would have just told me to pray about it like he tells me to pray about everything else.

I tried to be professional during the presentation but it wasn't easy. Pierce didn't participate in the session at all. He just sat there and glared at me. I kept wondering if he was planning on how he was going to hit me again. He left the room once for about fifteen minutes before the break and then when we took our break he did not return at all. I was actually relieved that I didn't have to look at him anymore.

As the hours went by during the day my shoulder and neck and back began to hurt more and more. I also started having the most God awful muscle spasms in my lower back. At times I thought they were going to put me back to the floor. I was never so glad to see a day end. I cried all the way home.

As I changed clothes I noticed that my shoulder was swollen and bruised. The pain was getting worse. I took a shower, put ice on my shoulder and cried until I went to bed. When I got up this morning the bruising was much worse and I was in agony. My mother drove me to the hospital emergency room for medical care.

In my gut I believe that Pierce followed through on his threat from this past May; that I was not to ever speak to him or look at him again or else. I now know what the or else was; a physical assault. How am I going to go to Penn with him there every day? I'm scared and I don't know what to do. What will Bart and Edmonson do now?

AUGUST 29, 2005
Hurricane Katrina hit New Orleans today; I felt like I might be driving into a hurricane as I drove to Penn. The students started today and I turned in the write up of what happened with Pierce to Edmonson and Bart the minute I walked in the door. I wanted to see them in person to talk about it but they were both conveniently busy. I went into the cafeteria to work with students who have shop registration problems. There were many students for Elliot's shop who showed up and had no idea that the shop had been closed. They were bewildered and had no idea what to do. Why didn't the school call them or send them a letter? They had already been in the program for several years and were working toward a Pennsylvania Skills Certificate for the program. Edmonson finally came in with Peter Griffin. When I asked Edmonson what we should do with the students he hit me on my left shoulder and asked me what I thought we should do. Bastard. I winced. He asked me what was wrong. I asked him if he had read the assault report I just gave him. He said that he had but he didn't realize that I was hurt. What the hell! I told him that I was in severe pain but I didn't want to miss the first student day of school. He asked me if I had a bruise or anything. I was wearing a tank top and a blazer over it. I took off the jacket so he could see the bruise for himself. I think he hit me to see how I would react and if I was really hurt. When I showed him the bruise on my shoulder he asked me how I got it. I was gob smacked. I asked him again if he had read my assault report. He said, "Yes, that's right. I remember." Remember? How could he forget? He had just read the damn report minutes before he came into the cafeteria. He then said we should put the boys from Elliot's shop in Wanda's shop. Seriously? Move from a technology shop to Hospitality?

I was even more astonished when Edmonson just immediately switched gears again and told me I was in a really good position. He said that I should call the police and have Pierce arrested for assault and then he would get fired. He also told me that this wasn't a worker's comp case and I needed to deal with it on my own. He told me he could give me the name of a good attorney who would make sure that Pierce lost his job for good. I'm not sure if he is really that clueless about how to manage the building or if he just wants to appear ignorant so he doesn't have to deal with anything. That is what he is most famous for around the building; just ignoring every situation he does not want to deal with. He just sticks his head in the sand and hopes it will go away and if it doesn't, he keeps his head in the sand until people get tired and the situation does go away.

I told Edmonson that since it happened while I was at work it was a worker's compensation case but more importantly I wanted him to deal with Pierce and provide a safe working environment for me. He did not respond. He just walked away. Off to stick his head in the sand I would imagine.

It hadn't actually occurred to me at first to call the police about what happened, but the more I think about it I don't know if it would be a wise move. It might be what I should do but in the teaching profession if you are arrested then you are automatically suspended without pay. I thought about how angry Pierce is right now and the thought of what he might do if I was the cause of him losing his job. Why can't Edmonson and Bart take care of this? Why can't they discipline Pierce? Am I being as much of a coward as they are? Maybe so, but I didn't step up and ask to be an administrator. Even though Edmonson did not have the credentials for the job, he wanted it and the board manipulated the rules to give him the job so now he should man up and do the job. You cannot pick and choose what issues you want to deal with; unfortunately that is how our administration works. Maybe I should call the district attorney's office just to get some information on what I should do.

AUGUST 31, 2005

There was a meeting today with The Mountain District Special Ed Director, their Transition Coordinator and Edmonson. When Edmonson came into the meeting he hit my shoulder again. He keeps hitting me on the left shoulder since I gave him the injury report. Just a coincidence? I think not. He is one mean man who is taking this opportunity to inflict physical pain as well as emotional pain on me.

The parent who had requested the meeting told the home school reps that his son had worn a shirt to Penn that said *Genuine Imitation*. He said Freeman had crossed out the word *Imitation* and wrote the word *Idiot* with a black sharpie on his son's shirt. Freeman's response was that he didn't cross out the word; he just corrected the spelling after the other boys in the shop had actually done the deed. Well, that certainly makes everything okay! Are you kidding me? Does he realize what kind of trouble he could be in by admitting what he had done? You do not treat students like that. It is cruel and it is harassment. I don't care what your personal feelings are about the student. What is wrong with some of the people in this school?

The father also talked about the number of writing assignments that his son had been issued; writing a paragraph out of the book seventy-five times. What exactly is the point of that? Writing and reading should NEVER be used as punishment. We should encourage students to want to read and write. Reading should be an exciting experience. It is a chance to learn something new or just an opportunity to get lost in an imaginary world. I grew up in a home that made going to the library an adventure and we never left the mall without going to the bookstore. The written word is amazing. It is powerful. Don't use it to punish a child.

Nothing was really resolved while the parent was there. He was told it was more of information gathering session. I have been through too many of those. They are bullshit! After the dad, student, and Freeman left the meeting, Edmonson told the remaining people in no uncertain terms that no more writing assignments would be issued and if they were, disciplinary action would be taken against Freeman. Why didn't he say that when Freeman was there? The Mountain District also wanted Freeman to attend a workshop at the IA on how to deal with special education students. Edmonson said he would make sure that was done. Later in the day Edmonson told me that he had talked to the solicitor and that he now had the green light to go ahead and get rid of Freeman. I'm not sure why he felt the need to tell me and I would wager every penny I have that it is not going to happen. I don't think the school will let him go and I don't think they will make him go to any workshops even though Edmonson gave TMD his word. We all know what Edmonson's word is worth. I had a wonderful English friend who came over to this country as a WWII war bride. She always seemed bigger than life and was such an important part of my life. I lived right around the block from her when Alonna was a toddler. Alonna and I had an evening ritual when it was nice weather. We would go outside for a half hour and blow bubbles and then take a walk around the block and stop to see Rose. She always had some words of wisdom before we left. One of her favorite sayings was, "talk is cheap; it takes money to buy whiskey." Edmonson's talk is cheap and it looks like there isn't going to be any whiskey coming soon.

On Edmonson's way out of the meeting he slapped me twice hard on my left shoulder and thanked me for my work. I literally jumped out of the chair in pain. Brenda, Edmonson's secretary looked at me and just shook her head and walked out behind him. Edmonson never stopped to apologize to me, he just kept on going. The Mountain District staff just looked at me in shock. If you knowingly keep slapping someone on an injured area, is that assault? He would plead ignorance and he would win because he is ignorant.

SEPTEMBER 1, 2005
I could just spit nails!!!! I don't like to have threats, subtle or otherwise thrown my way. Edmonson stopped by my classroom to say he needed to talk to me immediately but I was to come up to his office in ten minutes. He slapped me on my left shoulder yet again and said he would meet me upstairs. The force of his hit felt like a knife was going into my shoulder. Tears were streaming down my face. I almost sent the chair flying across the room backwards and I jumped up and told him to please stop hitting me on my shoulder. My shoulder is still bruised and sore but the main problem is that my sternum clavicle joint has been dislocated. It is popped out and I have to have to see another doctor to figure out what to do about it. It doesn't appear that it is a joint that can easily be manipulated. Edmonson just glared at me, turned around and walked out. When I got to his office he was there with Bart.

During the meeting there was an odd dynamic in the room. Bart came off as a wimp which wasn't a big surprise. He is the director but we had the meeting in Edmonson's office and Edmonson sat behind his desk while Bart sat in a chair by a corner of the desk. He looked like he didn't know what to do with his hands. He tried to put them up on the desk but they slipped off. He looked ridiculous.

Edmonson asked me if I knew why I was there. I said I thought it had something to do with the assault by Pierce. Wrong! Bart jumped in and told me that he was very disappointed in me. He said that the grant summary report was due to Harrisburg at the end of August and I got the report to Harrisburg at the end of August.

I thought I was hearing things. Isn't that what I did? I got the report to Harrisburg when it was due. I had fully completed all parts of the report myself with the exception of adding two numbers to a chart because I did not have access to the needed information. Administration has made a habit of keeping back information you need. I heard Bart tell Edmonson one time to only give people less than what they need and only give them the rest when they ask you at least three times for it. Jerk.

I took the reports to Brenda in the office before 1:00 for Bart's signature and for her to fill in one chart—actually it just needed two numbers. I asked her to fax the copies to Harrisburg and then mail in the originals. It should have taken her no more than twenty to thirty minutes for the entire task. In fact, she called me yesterday and told me that she had a hard time finding the numbers herself but the whole thing was done, faxed and mailed before 3:30. She said she called to assure me that it was done because she knew how important it was that the reports were submitted that day. If she was supposed to have access to the numbers and had a hard time finding them how on earth would I ever had found them? Should I just have made them up?

Typically the grant summary reports aren't done until we get back to school. I write the grant during the summer and the end of the year summary report from the previous year gets done after school starts so all the numbers from the previous year are correct. There is no other way to do it.

I told both Edmonson and Bart that the report was submitted on time and that I had never missed a deadline. EVER! I worked for two different newspapers before and I know the importance of deadlines. If you miss a deadline when you are working in the pre-press department there would be a big hole in the newspaper. Missing a deadline is not an option.

Bart tried to spin it and said he would have liked to have seen the reports submitted around August 1st. I would have come in and done the summary if he had told me that he wanted the report in early this year. He never mentioned it when I gave him a copy of the grant in July and then he was on vacation for almost the whole month of August. He just came back from vacation a couple of days before school started. Maybe I should have just read his mind.

Edmonson kept saying that if it was him instead of Bart in that position he would have been *freaking* on me. For what? Nothing was late. The reports were turned in when they were due. Nobody freaked on Edmonson for not having the proper credentials. In fact, they embraced him and changed all the rules for him.

Dumbasses. They forget they tell me things like when Bart missed the deadline on submitting paperwork on Edmonson's emergency certification and the school was going to have to pay a $500.00 fine. He was hoping that the board didn't find out. He said he would just list the fine in the monthly financial report as a payment to the Department of Education. He must have forgotten that he told me about that. I guess he also forgot that I knew about other reports he was responsible for and didn't get in on time. The school was either fined or they missed out on grant money. Penn even had to return a $20,000 grant for the hospitality program because Wanda and Edmonson didn't get the reports turned in at all. My report wasn't late; it was turned in on the day it was due. There was no fine and we didn't lose a penny of the grant money.

Edmonson told me that Brenda was at the office working until 7:00 p.m. because of me. Did he really expect me to believe that she was there until 7:00 working on finding two numbers, getting a signature and faxing a few papers? His face turned bright red when I told him I had spoken with Brenda from home around 3:30 and she told me the reports had already been faxed and the hard copies were already mailed. I don't know if she was at the office until 7:00, but if she was, it wasn't because she was working on faxing the report until 7:00. It sickens me to watch how Edmonson can sit there and blatantly lie to me like that.

I had to get quiet before I blurted out something I should not have; which I am sure is what they were waiting for me to do. I wanted to ask them what kind of men they were that they would try to drum up some reason to try and scare me just after I had filed an assault report. Just how stupid did they think I was? I just sat there and looked at them both. I only spoke when I absolutely needed to. A former mentor taught me that the person who speaks first in a confrontation loses the power. I wasn't sure what I was going to lose except for my temper. It was pretty evident that I was very aggravated. I think I was giving them Jo eyes. That's what my family calls the look my niece gets on her face when she is upset with someone. She doesn't have to say a word; her eyes just cut right through you. Anyways. I think I had Jo eyes during that meeting because they got all puffed up and told me I needed to act professionally. I needed to act what? All my evaluations have been outstanding. The worst thing that was said during one of my evaluations was when Edmonson actually stopped the lesson I was teaching, called me to the side of the room and asked me what was wrong with me. He said that it just seemed he wasn't getting that warm fuzzy feeling from me. I am sorry, but I didn't know part of a professional evaluation was rating the type of warm fuzzy feeling you were getting from the teacher. He is one sick ticket. There never was, nor ever will be a warm fuzzy feeling thrown his way. I am not interested in a personal relationship with him. Even if he was not my boss I would not be interested in him. I like honest, hardworking, ethical men. Okay, well I was hoodwinked when it came to Mac. I thought he was honest and ethical. I had never been more wrong about anything in my life. But in my defense he was very good at putting on a false front and I was deeply in love. He lied like a champion and I believed every lie he ever told me. Edmonson is not a good liar. He is as transparent as they come. It is very obvious that he is devious and just spends his nights thinking of new ways to cause trouble.

Bart and Edmonson reminded me that there was a thinning out of staff this school year and there could be more staff cut backs at the end of the year and I should watch my behavior and professionalism because I could be one of the ones let go. Watch my professionalism? Watch my behavior? I wasn't the one who was hired without the credentials for the job. I am not the one who lies just to create tension. I am not the one who hides in my office because I am afraid of the students and staff. What kind of example are they setting for the students and parents? What did they think they would accomplish by trying to threaten me? Do they think that I am the type of woman who will cower in the corner? You really should know something about the person before you try to intimidate them. I may be frustrated and I may even be afraid for my physical safety but I am not easily intimidated. If my ancestor George Ross could stand up to the King of England I think I can stand up to a sweaty man who wears his suits too small and a bony, little, thin lipped man. I could feel the strength of my ancestor starting to stir in me.

During the meeting, Edmonson suggested very strongly three times that I should resign as the Federal Funds Coordinator. This is an extra, after school hours, contractual 250 hours position. I said no all three times. Edmonson said if I couldn't handle it than they would have to consider removing me from the position. He said he had someone in mind who could take over the position immediately.

I have done a great job handling the grant. I passed two state audits with flying colors. Do they really think I am stupid? Isn't it convenient how all of this comes up after I report an assault by Pierce? I'm not an idiot. I see how much time Nikki spends in the office with Edmonson with her skirt up to places it shouldn't be and her top unbuttoned far too low. It may be fine for a gentlemen's club, if the gentlemen prefer older, loose skinned women, but certainly not appropriate for a high school. She has been crying poor lately; telling everyone how she is in the process of a divorce and her husband is draining her. I think Nikki is waiting in the wings to swoop in and take the job. I wonder what she is willing to do for the job.

SEPTEMBER 2, 2005

Today was Bart's last day at Penn. At the August 29th board meeting he *retired* and the board gave him a $40,000 bonus toward his retirement. Come on! Let's just all say what really happened. Bart quit. He is fifty years old, although I have to admit that I thought he was a lot older than that, and he only has about eighteen years in education. He doesn't meet any of the criteria for retiring. He started as director on April 1, 2000. People have joked about him being the school's April Fool's joke. Who's the joke on now? Certainly not Bart; he's walking away with some mad cash. Edmonson has told everyone that the Board hates Bart, they were making his life miserable and they were planning on firing him so he made the decision to leave before he got fired. Edmonson said that the board decided to pay him off so he would just go away. I don't know if I believe everything that Edmonson has been saying but Bart certainly has a problem dealing with people. He seems very afraid of them. You can't cower in your office and run a school. Most of the students don't even know who he is. They are probably better off.

I was in a lot of pain this morning so I didn't go to school. I didn't care to say good-bye to Bart anyway. He has never done a thing to help me and now as a parting gift he just threatened me. I guess we're going to have to deal with Edmonson as acting director for a while. Nothing is going to get better; I fear only worse.

SEPTEMBER 5, 2005

Edmonson called me to his office today and kept me there for about an hour. I was very uncomfortable the whole time I was there. He kept talking to me like we are in a relationship. Does he have some delusion that we are already involved or does he think I am going to change my mind about going out with him now that he is acting director? Or does he think that he has some power over me since he threatened my job?

I tried to look as bored as I could, hoping that he would get mad and tell me to leave but it didn't work. He kept rambling. He told me was that Freeman was still giving writing assignments as punishment to the students. Flashback to the August meeting with the Mountain District, "There will be no more writing assignments given or he will face disciplinary action." That was just less than two weeks ago. In Freeman's defense I bet that Edmonson never told him to stop giving writing assignments. Freeman had already left the meeting when Edmonson promised the school district that it would never happen again.

Edmonson also told me that he was sorry he could not help me out with the situation with Pierce. I don't buy it one little bit. I told him that it is not that he can't help me; it is that he won't help me. There is a huge difference. He kept telling me that I was wrong and I didn't know what I was talking about.

He said he did not see how I could have sustained an injury to the degree that I said I had. He's not a doctor and neither am I but anyone can see that my sternum clavicle joint is dislocated. And not only is it sticking out, I am lopsided now. I'm in constant pain and now I've just been called a liar. Is he also calling the medical staff that is treating me liars? What is wrong with this man?

He told me that he was sure that God would take care of it though and that I should just pray about it. What should I pray for? That Edmonson finally has the moral fiber to do something about the safety issue in the building? Wait. I guess to have moral fiber you have to at least have some sense of morality.

For years he has been telling me and Andie to pray about things. I wonder if he tells anyone else that. I must admit that it did kind of upset me when he didn't believe I was injured. The hospital said I was injured. They wouldn't say I was injured if I wasn't. How bad did he want me to get hurt before he believed it? Did he want my bone to be sticking out through my skin? I doubt that he would have done anything about it then either.

SEPTEMBER 14, 2005

Edmonson sent me to Larson Vo-Tech today with Charlotte, Amy, Nikki and Pierce. The purpose was to look over their school and see how they handle their special needs population. I wasn't thrilled about going anywhere with Pierce. I don't know why Pierce always is sent to conferences and workshops by Edmonson. Shouldn't someone else be given a chance? Someone who hasn't called his students monkeys to be trained. We have plenty of teachers who think of their students as young adults who they have the opportunity to help shape their futures. What would be wrong in sending one of them?

Nikki and Pierce drove together. It didn't surprise any of us but I have to admit that it made me feel better having them in a different car. I tried to stay far away from the both of them when we were at Larson. We all had to have lunch together though. Pierce treated Nikki like she was his servant. He ordered her around and she couldn't move fast enough to get him whatever he wanted. It was quite embarrassing. One of the teachers there asked me if there was something going on between Pierce and Nikki. I didn't answer. I just changed the subject. Everyone can see what is going on with them. Especially the students at Penn. Many of them have told me that they are not stupid and that when she comes into the shop Nikki and Pierce whisper and she giggles and he swats her on the behind with a rag. Teenagers are far from stupid. They are very observant as to what's going on. And they talk! Boy do they talk.

SEPTEMBER 16, 2005

I got a flyer from a local agency, the IA, about a bullying workshop. I sent it to Edmonson because I thought it would be good for Pierce to go to. I don't know if a workshop would really help to change his behavior but you have to keep trying, don't you?

I also wanted to go but not with Pierce. I was hoping that maybe it would help me learn how to deal with what happened and how to go on without crying everyday as I drive to work. There have been days when I have had to pull off the side of the road so I could throw up because the thought of being there is making me that sick. I don't have any choice. I have to have insurance and a paycheck for Alonna's sake.

There were a couple of different dates that you could sign up for the workshop but Edmonson has blown me off about it. He won't answer me about going. I don't get it. I thought it would be a very informative workshop. Why would he send us to look at a school like Larson? The only thing in common between our two schools is that we both offer vocational training. Larson operates in a completely different way. They only have juniors and seniors at the school and the students get all of their academic classes there as well. Penn will never operate like that. So why is it ok to send us out to look at something like that but not send us to a session on bullying when that is exactly the problem that we have in our own building with our own staff. More bad words are going through my head.

There was also a mandatory meeting for shop instructors at 8:35 today. Edmonson called me at 8:20, He wanted me to go to from shop to shop to tell all of the instructors about the unscheduled mandatory meeting. He wanted them to send the students to the cafeteria and then go to the computer room. He could have made ONE announcement and everyone would have known at one time. I asked him why he didn't make an announcement. He said he didn't want to disrupt the learning environment. That made no sense. He was stopping the learning process to hold the meeting. He just wanted to make my morning miserable. He is an ass.

I had to stay in the cafeteria with Peter Griffin to watch all of the students while Edmonson met with the shop teachers. Edmonson came over to the cafeteria after the meeting. He told me that he was pretty ticked off with me because not all of the teachers were at the meeting at 8:35. He didn't call me until 8:20 and there were 18 shops for me to go to. It was a tedious task. I'm thinking very bad names to call him even as I think about it now. I will say it again, he is an ass.

September 19, 2005
A few weeks ago Edmonson asked me who I told about what happened with Pierce on the day that he supposedly ran into me. He didn't run into

me; he assaulted me. There is a difference. He then set up taped interview sessions with the people I told. He didn't bother to talk to anyone else in the room though to find out if they saw anything. I also heard that he interviewed Pierce and Rick. Edmonson told me that I could have copies of the tapes and the notes but I haven't received them yet. I have asked him about it several times but he just asks like he doesn't hear me talking. He must have heard me though because today out of the blue he told me that he couldn't release anything to me because I haven't put a formal request in writing. I jumped right on that. I emailed him a formal request and I also asked him to outline the reasons why no disciplinary action was able to be taken against Pierce. I don't think I should hold my breath waiting for an answer from him. I don't understand how I could have been hit on the second day of school and still nothing has been done. If this had happened to someone else would something have been done?

SEPTEMBER 26, 2005

Man! I was hoping to get my extra check this Friday for the work I had done on the grant. I submitted my time sheet on time to get paid but instead of a check I got an email from Karen. She said Edmonson had the timesheet on his desk and he didn't give it to her until after she ran the payroll. She said she asked him for it several times but he never gave it to her. He had to approve the timesheet before I could get paid.

How would he like it if someone kept money from him? I know he was just trying to show me how he can mess with me financially if he wants to. What a jerk. I am a single parent supporting my child and he has intentionally kept money out of my hands that I needed this weekend. Why should he care about my child though when he doesn't even care about his own children? Karen told me he has two children on his health insurance but in five years time he has never spoken one word about them to me or anyone else that I know of. I would wager that the only thing he does for them is what he is forced to do. How does a man get to be in a position of making decisions that affect the lives of so many children when he doesn't even have the decency of caring for his own children? It just boggles my mind. Try to keep all the money out of my hands that you can bucco. My relationship with my daughter is rooted in love, not a financial obligation. What a jackass!

OCTOBER 3, 2005

I am getting more afraid every day. Pierce is becoming more aggressive and unexpectedly volatile. He has been strutting around with his chest all pumped up like he has gotten away with something; and if truth be told, he has. I just don't feel safe being around him. He walks toward me down the hall and then will lunge in toward me and laugh. I can feel my whole body tense up preparing to be hit again. It just adds to the pain. The pain is getting worse and this stress is not helping my pain at all. It has been five weeks and Edmonson hasn't done anything about the assault. I told him I am afraid that something really bad is going to happen. I don't feel safe working in the same building with Pierce. He actually snickered and told me that I was just being an over reactionary woman. He told me not to be a drama queen.

OCTOBER 6, 2005

I have so much work to do and Edmonson keeps calling me to the office to tell me things that are none of my business. He wanted to tell me that he had walked into Freeman's shop and saw that a student had been issued a writing assignment. Freeman told the boy to write out the entire student handbook by hand three times. Edmonson told me he did not understand why Freeman was still issuing writing assignments. I said, "I have a clue for you. Could it be because you have never done anything about Freeman's antics and he knows that you won't do anything?" Oh God. I probably shouldn't have said that but I am in a great deal of pain and I get really cranky when I am in pain.

I decided I might as well just go for broke so I asked him what he planned on doing about my situation with Pierce. He told me that the investigation was still on-going. I told him how frustrated I was. I didn't understand what there is to investigate? I asked him if there was someone else higher up I should be talking to. He got very snippy with me and said that he was at the top of the food chain. Who the hell talks like that? Top of the food chain! He said he would let me know when his investigation was concluded. I wonder if that will be before Pierce hits me again. Probably not.

OCTOBER 7, 2005

I was leaving for a meeting at The Mountain District and was approaching my car when I noticed that my car had been badly keyed. It isn't a new car but I take good care of it and it wasn't just a little scratch. It had been deeply keyed down the whole passenger side and all over the trunk. I felt so violated. Instead of driving to the meeting, I drove my car around the back of the school to my classroom door and went back into the school and reported the incident to Peter Griffin. I didn't want to leave the school property so they could tell me it had happened somewhere else. I broke down and cried. I hate when I cry at school.

I had tried to call Edmonson but I was told he was unavailable. Peter told me that he knew that it was Pierce who did it, or got someone to do it. He said he thought they should have gotten rid of Pierce before when they had all that stuff on him. All what stuff? Kathy? Peter said that the rumors of drugs at school in his vehicle weren't rumors but fact. I don't know anything about that. It's just all very fishy. I hate this kind of stuff. All I wanted to do was teach. I didn't come here to be asked out by Pierce or Edmonson. I didn't ask to be assaulted. I'm upset, hurt, and NO ONE WILL HELP ME! I told Peter that I wanted to call the police but he said that based on school law he is the police at school and he is the person who would handle the situation. That didn't sound right to me so I again reiterated my desire to call the States. He again refused. He told me he was the one with the authority to handle this situation. So I told him that I wanted an official report written up. He asked me if I was sure I wanted to have a police report written up. Of course I was sure. Why would anyone think that I would just want to let this vandalism go unreported? Why do people keep asking me if I want to report things? This harassment has got to stop. How many things that happen to women go unreported because people like Edmonson and Griffin pressure them not to file a report?

Edmonson came down to the back of the school about ten or fifteen minutes later in the security golf cart with Peter. They looked at the car, Peter pointed out the keyed areas to Edmonson and they drove off. I thought they were going to come inside to talk to me but they didn't. I emailed Edmonson and asked for a copy of the parking lot surveillance video and a copy of the incident report.

Let me be clear about this; I never accused Pierce of vandalizing my car. I know that I arrived at school this morning and Pierce pulled in beside me to the left side of my vehicle. He followed me into the school close enough that I could hear him keep clearing his throat and at one point I actually felt his breath on the back of my neck. He did that all the way into the school. I think he wanted me to turn around and say something to him but I never looked back. I was nervous and shaky but I never turned around. I was hoping that he didn't notice how much he was getting to me. I went straight into the office to sign in. Pierce walked into the teacher's lounge. Jeff and Stan were in the hall when we both walked in. I didn't say anything to them because what do you say? Help me. Pierce is trying to scare me? I really think he was. He has bragged to people that he has a master's degree in psychology and he knows how to manipulate people and situations.

I had a doctor's appointment after school today. My blood pressure was sky high and my pulse was still racing. My blood pressure is normally on the low side. The doctor said that with the work I am doing at school and the toll it is taking on my shoulder and my pain level, not to mention the level of stress there, my shoulder is never going to get better and I need to take some time off from work and get it taken care of instead of trying to keep going to therapy after school. She wrote an off-work slip for worker's compensation effective immediately. I'll call Edmonson and send a copy into the office. Maybe I have been crazy to try to keep working through all of this, but that is how I was raised; people in my family work hard. Also, I'm struggling to make ends meet as it is. Going on worker's comp means that there will be less money coming in.

OCTOBER 10, 2005
Charlotte called me. Edmonson had a meeting with her today. I guess since I am not going to be there for a while he is going to start having meetings with Charlotte. He seems to have a need for an audience. Maybe it makes him feel important. He told her that "Mr. Pierce" had not moved his truck, that a student had moved it so he could not have possibly keyed my car. He also said that I should have not parked next to Pierce. I did not park next to Pierce! Amy had pulled into the parking lot behind us. She saw that I was the first one to park. Pierce parked a space over from me. Why would it have mattered where I would have parked? It didn't change the fact that my car was keyed. And why would he believe Pierce over me? More importantly why would he talk to Pierce about the incident but not talk to me? Why would he tell Pierce that I accused him of vandalizing my car? I never said that. Peter said that he knew Pierce was responsible for the vandalism. Edmonson was trying to inflame the situation between us. Is he that upset with me for not going out with him that he is trying to make Pierce really want to hurt me? I wouldn't put it past him.

Edmonson told Charlotte that there was nothing he could do for me. He said there was nothing the police could even do for me. How does he know that? He said that Pierce was "*good.*" Edmonson told Charlotte he knew Pierce would hit me again when he knew there were no witnesses around. Very comforting. He asked Charlotte if she knew what I planned to do. He said he thought I sounded stressed; that I did not sound good and he thought I should probably take some time off. Maybe I would be less stressed if someone would just help me. I don't know how I'm going to handle this pain. The pain is there everyday. I can't get comfortable. I can't sleep. I can't use my arm. It hurts and it was all so unnecessary. This could have all been avoided if Edmonson, Bart or the board would have just talked to Pierce a long time ago and told him that bullying behavior would not be tolerated in the work place. I think that as a military man, if Pierce was given a direct order to leave me alone or be held accountable, he would have stepped back. More than one person in the school has said that it has been a back scratching pact between Edmonson and Pierce since Edmonson came to the school. Pierce knows how Edmonson lied about his credentials and Edmonson knows about all the things Pierce has done at school. They are watching each other's backs but they occasionally have to make it seem like they are taking a firm stand against each other. They really aren't fooling anyone but themselves.

Miranda also called me today. Edmonson told her that she needed to attend an Integrated Learning Conference in November at University Park. He said she would be attending with Nikki and Pierce. I have lost count of the number of conferences that Edmonson has sent Nikki and Pierce on together. He told Miranda that no one else would be going with them. Miranda did not seem very happy about having to attend alone with the two of them. She said she talked to them about driving up together and sharing a room with Nikki but they told her no. I guess they don't want her to interrupt their school paid vacation. How rude. I wonder what Pierce's wife would have to say about all of this.

OCTOBER 13, 2005

I am feeling guilty about not being at work and worried about things that need to be done because it feels like I just left school so abruptly. After physical therapy this evening I stopped by Penn to check on loose ends. I had Alonna and a friend of hers with me. Wanda had emailed me a paper from her college English class and asked me to proof it. Actually she more or less just told me to do it for her and told me that she needed it back the next day to turn in. People constantly ask me to proof things for them. I like to write but I don't care for proofing things. Proofing is a necessary evil. You have to ask someone else to do it for you because when you read your own work you see what you think should be there. I had a college professor who said good grammar and correct spelling in formal writing were a courtesy to the reader. I try to pass that along to the students at school. It is important, but not always fun. The best part about writing in a diary is that you don't have to worry about grammar and formality. You can say things however you want, and occasionally overlook the rules of capitalization.

I was really amazed at Wanda's nerve. The woman doesn't even like me. She is one of Edmonson's pets. He can do no wrong in her eyes. Personally I have never thought Wanda was that bright but when I looked at her paper I was absolutely bewildered. I have seen some bad writing in my time but I had no idea what to do with this paper. To make any sense out of the topic I would have to rewrite the whole paper for her and I was not about to do that. I made some grammatical corrections and sent it back. I shouldn't have even done that. She probably thought I would rewrite it for her. Divas like her usually expect to have things taken care of them for her; just another short skirted, blonde who really could use a make under and can't write a coherent sentence. And the damn paper was in a script type face. Why is everything she writes in a script type face? Script is fine for poetry and invitations but not for English papers.

Amy had also sent me an email. She found a Bullying and Social Aggression Teleconference she thought would be good for the staff to listen in on so she sent the info to Edmonson. He emailed her back and said it was a great idea, but the timing was out of whack. We needed to be focused on the program re-approval because we were a year late in getting the process completed.

My, oh my! Let me try and process this. I actually got a report into the state on the day that it was due but now his team is an entire year late on the paperwork for program re-approval. Is anyone *freaking* on him for this? I would venture to say not. Probably because the board doesn't know what really goes on at Penn. They meet once a month and swallow whatever is fed to them by Edmonson. Slick Willy in action with his false flattery can put on a good show. Why can't we take an hour and a half to prevent further bullying at school? After what happened wouldn't it be a valuable learning tool?

I have an even bigger problem right now though and I have no choice but to talk to Edmonson. All of the federal grant files from the past five years are missing from my room. Edmonson had to have come in and taken them. Who else would want them? I don't think he should come in and take things without talking to me about it beforehand but he's done things like it in the past. When Andie got laid off we moved her computer into my room so she could retrieve any info she needed from it and so the kids would have a computer they could use in my room. Peter and Edmonson took it within hours after Andie and I left that day and she never got to retrieve her information. They knew we were moving it when she was there. Peter had told Andie it was okay. Why didn't Edmonson say something then? Just like him to be sneaky and wait until we leave to run and grab it.

Karen also told me that when she went on vacation during the summer for a week she found her office had been rearranged and things were missing. Edmonson told her that her room was messy and he was cleaning it up. That is just wrong. He should stay out of other people's offices. She was afraid to say anything though because of all of the lay-offs.

OCTOBER 14, 2005

I talked to Edmonson; he said he doesn't know anything about the missing files. It was very strange. He didn't sound the least bit concerned or upset that federal grant files are missing. He never said anything about a plan to try and find them. I'll just come right out and say it. I think he knows exactly what happened to them. If he was going to *freak* on me for a report getting into Harrisburg on the day it was due, wouldn't you think that he would sound just a little bit concerned about five years worth of missing federal files? I believe he knows where they are.

There are two possible reasons for him taking the files. Either he is hoping that I will be held responsible for the missing files or it has something to do with his other personality malfunctions. There are two big ones. He is a compulsive clean freak and can't stand it when he sees things that are out of place in his eyes. He also has an obsessive need to be in total control of everything. I have seen him take things that he will never use and hide them away just so he will be in control of them. It doesn't matter that someone else could put the items to good use. Even things like notebooks and pencils. He needs to be the one who is in control. Now that's freaky.

I would have to say that he took the files to try and get me in trouble because they weren't sitting out. They were in a filing cabinet. Two drawers filled with federal files were taken but the other two drawers were left alone. I wonder how he planned on using them to get me in trouble. I bet he didn't plan on me discovering them gone so soon.

OCTOBER 15, 2005

I called Harrisburg to report the missing files myself because I don't know what my liability is. Harrisburg said I should be okay because I didn't have any of the financial documentation. The financial records have always been kept with the bookkeeper. The whole thing just bothers me though. I don't feel very comfortable when someone says I *should be* okay.

Dorrine Pryce, who is employed as a paraprofessional with the IA, was working in the Life Skills classroom at Penn. Apparently a student broke away from her and she was somehow injured. The IA immediately pulled her out of the building and gave her another placement as she said she did not feel safe in that environment. When I was told about this incident, I was really aggravated with Penn. Dorrine's safety was addressed right away by the IA, as it should have been, but my safety issue still has never been addressed by our administration or the board. I try not to think about it very often, but I don't know when Pierce could just go off on me again and this time really hurt me. From everything I've seen of him, I would say that Pierce is a man who really holds a grudge.

OCTOBER 18, 2005

Miranda called to check on me. She hasn't been physically assaulted at school but she has dealt with her own issues of harassment. She was scheduled to go to Valley High School to talk to the 9th graders about our upcoming Open House. Usually the support staff goes with Miranda to school presentations because we work with all the shops and can answer questions about the programs as well as how the support department works. Amy was supposed to go with Miranda but Edmonson wanted Wanda to go. Wanda told both Miranda and Edmonson that she wouldn't be able to go because she had a visitation with her class set up on that day at River View in Morgantown, West Virginia. Edmonson called River View and cancelled her visitation. Miranda said Wanda cried like a baby over the way Edmonson had treated her. I guess she was shocked that she didn't get want she wanted from him this time. I have no sympathy for her.

I remember last year when Miranda was scheduling presentations at the high schools; Wanda wanted to go with Miranda. She said she needed to focus on getting her numbers up. Edmonson told Miranda that Charlotte and Wanda would accompany her instead of me. He had said that Charlotte and Wanda were both eye candy and that the boys would want to sign up to come to Penn just because of them and that the girls would be able to relate better to them because they were both in their twenties.

Okay, I get it. Charlotte is extremely pretty and Wanda is a Monet; pretty from a distance but loses something when you get up close to her and you see how much make up she has packed on. Plus, I'm old enough to be both of their mothers. But what difference does the way I look matter? His thinking is twisted and insulting. What am I to believe? I'm attractive enough for him to want to have sex with, but he doesn't look at me as someone a fifteen year old boy would be into. Well, thank goodness for that part. Women who are into boys or would like to think that teenage boys are into them are pretty twisted themselves.

OCTOBER 19, 2005

Hank and I both serve on the Education Council for the County Chamber of Commerce. We represent Penn. Hank has been on the Council for a number of years and Bart asked me to take over for Holly a year or two before she was laid off. She had taken some time off from work to adopt a beautiful little girl from China. It was such an exciting time because she and her husband and sons had been waiting for so long. The trip had been postponed because of the SARs epidemic. It was a glorious day when they got word to book their flight to China. Anyways. I love serving on the Education Council so I talked to Holly after she came back from her sabbatical and she was gracious enough to let me continue to serve. I asked the teachers to have the names of the students they wanted to nominate emailed to me or Hank by the end of the day on the 18th. I can check my school email from home so I would have made sure that Hank had all the information that he needed to get to the Chamber. The information was due on the 20th. In his great wisdom, Edmonson sent out his own email instructing the teachers to submit the names of any student who has an outstanding theory grade *to him* by the 21st so he could select a student of the month for the Chamber. He said he would be handling the Education Council from now on.

Technically he has the right to take over the council but he should have talked to me and Hank about it. It's just another example of him acting like a selfish little boy who doesn't want anyone else to have any toys. How old is he? Will he ever grow up? I think it may be too late for him to learn how to properly behave. If he really wanted to handle the students of the month that would be fine but he doesn't know what he is talking about. He should know that *two* students should be selected, that they have to be juniors; that bio sheets need to be filled out and the students need to submit photos for publication in the newspaper. If he knew what he was doing he wouldn't ask for the wrong information the day after it is due to the Chamber. He is just hurting the students.

OCTOBER 20, 2005

I have questions about worker's comp and my union dues. Daniels said he wasn't sure how to handle it so I emailed Kevin Klein. He did answer my email but I have no idea what he is talking about? He told me to take Family Medical Leave. I don't need FMLA. I need therapy for my shoulder, which is a comp issue and I need to know how much my union dues will be while I'm off. I would like to stay a member of the union. What I would really like would be someone in the regional or state union to help me with Pierce.

Klein said Pierce was supposed to talk to Ryan Matson, the regional attorney, but cancelled at the last minute and didn't want to reschedule. Klein said that Matson can't push the issue if Pierce doesn't want to talk. It looks like they're just going to drop it. Why doesn't he understand how dire this situation really is? Why won't he help me; especially when I told him that I have not received any help from anyone at Penn? I deeply believe it is because Pierce has always bragged about how close he is with Matson and Matson is choosing friendship over doing the right thing.

OCTOBER 30, 2005

It is sad that I feel a weight has been lifted off of me since I have been off work. I am going to therapy and doing what I am supposed to do so I can physically heal but I still feel I need to honor certain obligations I made to the school. I had designed and printed a flyer for the November Open House which was to be given to the Chamber for distribution. Charlotte stopped by the house to pick it up and take it to Wanda who is the chair of the Open House committee. Miranda called and told me that Nikki and Edmonson changed the flyer and included door prizes for potential students. She emailed me a copy of the new flyer. I taught design on a college level and I've got to say that I hope no one thinks I did the flyer because it is absolutely horrible. I would not have given it a good grade. I think they just felt the need to change it because I had done the original. Petty, petty people.

I also got a call at home from a student asking about how student council money can be used. I'm used to students calling me at home and even stopping by my house but I was a bit thrown when they called asking me about club money. I am not the student council advisor but it works the same for all clubs. The money belongs to the students and they have to vote to authorize money to be spent. The student told me that Edmonson authorized student council funds for the open house; however, there was never a student council meeting or a vote on spending the money. This is a blatant violation of Pennsylvania school law. This seems to have gone on a good bit at Penn. It is the students' money. You cannot just go around spending it without following the law; but Edmonson does; and gets away with it. Someone should probably report him to the state. Should I do it? I probably should but with everything else that is going on I am leery. What if I report it and then the State doesn't do anything and it causes even more trouble for me. Am I being cautious or a coward?

NOVEMBER 2, 2005

I don't know how long I'm going to be off work. I realize that there is pain involved in going through physical therapy but this is ridiculous. Should I be in this much pain? It is constant. Oh how I wish I could sleep through the night without the pain waking me up. And if it isn't the pain waking me up, it's worry about the federal grant. To be able to oversee the grant I have to be there to get the daily information that needs to be recorded and I'm not there so I have no way of doing my job. I don't have any choice; I don't see any option other than to resign as coordinator because I can't be there to handle the day to day operations while I'm off work. It looks like Edmonson is going to get his wish and I'm going to lose another $5,000.00 a year. That part really makes me sick. The grant was a lot of work but it helped me buy things for Alonna that I couldn't otherwise afford. I don't know how I'm going to scale back but I'm going to have to. I hope I can explain this to Alonna so she'll understand. I know she will try to comfort me. She is the sweetest girl I have ever known. I couldn't ask for a more loving daughter. I wrote the resignation letter, emailed a copy to Edmonson and mailed a copy to the president of our board.

NOVEMBER 10, 2005

No one has been able to answer my questions about how much I need to pay to keep my union status current. Klein says he'll check into it. I've heard those words so many times before. They don't mean anything. I can't be the first person who has ever run into this situation. Why wouldn't he know? How hard could it be to find out? I guess he doesn't think I'm worth the extra effort.

NOVEMBER 11, 2005

It's bad enough that Edmonson won't lift a finger to help me with the problems I have had with Pierce but now he is telling lies about me in staff meetings. Yesterday he told the entire staff I wasn't returning any of his phone calls and it was my fault that the shops weren't getting their purchase order requests. What a lie! Since I'm not at school to defend myself I'm an easy target to blame for things not getting done, even the things that are not part of my job. I wonder what he has been telling the board about me. I sent Edmonson a fax and asked him for a written apology/retraction with copies going to the faculty because his lies were damaging to my professional reputation. It is time for this man to be held accountable for his lies.

I will have to thank Sam the next time I see him. He spoke up during the meeting and said the items he was asking about for his shop weren't grant related so they wouldn't have anything to do with me. Edmonson just ignored him and kept rambling about how hurt he was that I wasn't taking his calls because we had been so close. What a liar! Or does he really believe what he said? The thought of that is really scary. That would make him even more delusional than I thought he was. Edmonson did not call me except for the message he left me at the end of October. Of course I would talk to him; if the conversation was related to school business. I don't think he wants to talk to me though. I faxed him all the information he needed when I resigned. There were no loose ends. But if he needed to call me to clarify something he could. The school has both my home number and my cell number. He hasn't called.

Hank also told me that at the meeting Edmonson asked if anyone wanted to take over the federal grant and in a heartbeat Nikki's hand flew up and

Edmonson said, "Done." Edmonson didn't give anyone else a chance to respond or run it through the board; he just approved it on the spot. It kind of sounded like a fixed auction. I don't even want to think what she gave Edmonson in return for the job.

NOVEMBER 14, 2005

See, my phone works. I got a message from Brenda. Edmonson had her call me. He wants me to come in to train Nikki on how to take care of and write the grant. He said that it was very complicated and I would have to go over things so the school wouldn't be in jeopardy of losing any money. No way. I wouldn't teach that bitch how to spit. If I could go in I would be working. She has been trying to take over for months. She can learn on her own. When Kathy left and I took over the grant there was no one to teach me and I had an audit to deal with in just sixty days after taking over. Nikki can read. She can figure things out the same way I had to.

I actually just wanted to return the call and tell him to bite me. I know I'm just being cranky but pain has a way of making a person very cranky. Bite me. That's another statement that is very unlike me but ever since Alonna watched the remake movie of the Little Rascals it keeps popping in my head. Alfalfa said it I think. "Oh, bite me." Not a great line for young children to learn but it is very catchy. It has a little bit of a bite to it. Pun intended.

It is hard to believe that my problems at Penn have been going on for years now. Everyone who seems like they would be in a position to do something to help me just brushes me off. This whole situation is now not only affecting me but Alonna as well. She went back on a homebound status mid-October. She is so worried about me and her stomach pain is back. I don't know if the pain is just getting worse again or if the stress in the household is contributing to her pain. I try to put on a brave face but she knows me so well. I'm all she has and she worries.

I had to meet with Bryson Mancini, the superintendent of Unity Area School District, to talk about Alonna. The guidance counselor and principal were also there. They seemed sympathetic and I did feel a little ashamed that I broke down and cried in front of them. I'm Alonna's mother. I'm supposed to protect her but I need help to protect myself so I can assure her that I'm safe. After the meeting I spent about another half hour or so talking to Mancini about the situation at Penn. As one of our sending school superintendents he certainly should have some input into what goes on at Penn. I told him about the attempts by Pierce and Edmonson to date me and I said I felt what was going on was payback for rejecting them. We talked about the assault and I was stunned to learn that he claimed he didn't know anything about what was going on. I told him that Edmonson had told me that there was no one higher up that I could talk to about the situation. Mancini said not to worry. What does that mean? Is he going to help me? I need answers and I'm not getting any from anyone.

NOVEMBER 15, 2005

Miranda ended up driving to the Integrated Learning Conference alone. Pierce and Nikki went to dinner together every night and acted like they didn't even know who she was at the conference. I felt bad that she had to go with the two of them alone. Edmonson knew what it would be like for her and he deliberately put her in that situation. I can't believe he didn't allow anyone else to go. Someone else would have gone. The school has sent five or six people before. Of course he certainly never asked me to go to any of the conferences. He and Bart would not even approve a request for me to go to the Special Needs Conferences in Harrisburg when every other special pops coordinator in the state went. Instead every year Bart would go alone with his wife. Sort of another school funded vacation. He is another one that never shared any information with me when he came back from any of these conferences. As federal funds/special pops coordinator I should have at least been told what was discussed. I always have to find out through the grapevine from people who went from other schools.

DECEMBER 15, 2005

Today was the first time I have been at Penn since October. That feeling of anxiety swept over me as soon as I turned onto the road leading to the school. Some of the union officers wanted to talk to me about the grievance I filed against Edmonson. I wanted an apology for the lies he told about me in the November staff meeting. They said they don't think I will ever get an apology from Edmonson and the whole thing is fruitless. They are right. But should I fight the battle for this apology or should I choose my battles? I would typically feel that an apology should be fought for. I feel I am owed an apology from Edmonson but the officers are right in this case. I have a feeling I need to choose my battles wisely with him. I will just have to suck it up and let Edmonson think that he has won this time.

Oh, oh! I did see Edmonson when I came in to the school. He was about fifteen feet away and he looked right at me but he turned very quickly and literally ran down the hall and ducked into one of the rooms. Way to be conspicuous. What did he think I was going to do to him?

DECEMBER 19, 2005
After watching Edmonson run down the hall the other day, the letter I got in the mail today made me laugh. It was from Edmonson. He said that he heard I was in the building the other day and he was so sorry that I had not stopped in to see him; that it would have been good to see me again. Seriously? I don't think he could have run down the hall any faster when he saw me. Those little feet can fly! Why am I still amazed by him? He talks about me in staff meetings and then when I file a grievance he twists everything around and talks in circles so it comes out like he is the injured party. Did he take a class on double speak or does it just come to him naturally?

He said that he finds it unfortunate that someone would take a positive comment and turn it into something of a derogatory nature. He said to please take care, wished me a wonderful holiday season and said he hoped to see me soon.

The thought of going back to Penn leaves me with a bad headache. There are so many emotions running through my head. I miss many of the people that I work with and I miss the students. And I miss the work. I have always worked. It has been necessary to be off all this time and I am slowly healing. I have had to rearrange my life though. I can't use my left arm for any length of time. I can't pick up things with any kind of weight to them and I can't reach up which makes the simplest thing like dressing very hard to do. Alonna has to help me pull tops over my head or zip up things if the zipper is in back. I am hopeful that one day I will be able to get back to what I am supposed to be doing. But I am still very afraid. Nothing I have heard about Pierce or Edmonson makes me think that anything has changed for the better.

DECEMBER 24, 2005
It's Christmas Eve and I should be happy but I am feeling sick over a letter I got the other day from the school's insurance company. Their doctor said I'm pre-injury status and I have to go back to work. If I don't go back I will lose my job.

I had to drive to Greensburg to see their doctor in a wicked snow storm two weeks ago. It's over an hour drive on a good day from my house. My mother went with me and that was great. She helps keep my head on straight. When I was a teenager I always liked my mother but I don't think I could really appreciate her until I became an adult. She is my role model and my sounding board. I know that she will always tell me the truth about a situation whether I want to hear it or not.

I know she felt bad about not driving but it was snowing so hard and she has to have cataract surgery and she shouldn't have to be driving me around. She's an amazing woman and is in much better shape then me. She can do an easy five or six mile a day walk when the weather permits. Gracious do I wish I had her strength and stamina.

I had tears streaming down my face from the pain when I got to Greensburg. Keeping my arm up and being tense from driving for two hours in a snow storm was almost unbearable. I dreaded the thought of how much I would hurt by the time I got home. Their doctor only looked at me for seven minutes. He had me move my arm around, and when I couldn't move it he pushed on it and the tears were just pouring down my cheeks. I hate to cry in front of people but when you are in pain and your arm won't go up and there is someone pushing on it I think tears are inevitable.

I called the insurance carrier and asked for a copy of the report. They said I couldn't have a copy of it; they said it is their report and I have no right to see it. How can that be true? I think it is another lie. It's my medical condition. It makes me believe that the insurance carrier has paid the doctor to write what they want to hear.

I called Edmonson to talk about my return to work and to tell him that I was going to file whatever paperwork was necessary to make sure that my medical coverage would still be taken care of. I am by no means pre-injury status. I tried to stay on topic but he started talking about Charlotte. He asked if I had talked to her because he was worried—no—he needed to clarify—he was extremely worried about her. He said that there was a student at school who had chicken pox and she was freaking out because she never had chicken pox. I don't believe that. I mean, I don't know whether Charlotte has ever had chicken pox, but she is very professional and she doesn't *freak out* about things; especially something like that.

The conversation then took a very strange turn. He told me a story about being attacked. He had gone to his parents' home, where he has been living for the past four years, and went into the sun porch. He noticed that the screen door was slightly ajar. It was dark but he felt that someone or something was watching him. Then out of nowhere a huge hawk, with a ten foot wing span came swooping down on him. Yes; a ten foot wing span! He desperately tried to fight it off; trying to push it back but the hawk was strong and his talons were clawing deep into his head. He fought hard and pushed the hawk out the door. "True Story." He always says True Story when he tells a story that you know is an absolute lie. I wonder if he knows he does that. I am not an animal expert but I know enough about animals to know that if a hawk with a ten foot wing span had his talons deep in my head I probably wouldn't be alive to talk about it. At the very least I would have some major gashes in my head and probably scratches on my face and body. There would also be a lot of blood. Head wounds pump out a lot of blood. Maybe he still had a lack of blood flow to his head because he seemed to zone out when I tried to talk about safety issues for my return to work. Because I couldn't really get a word in edge wise I sent another letter to Edmonson asking for assurance for my safety while at work.

JANUARY 9, 2006

First day back at school. I shook all the way there. It only took five minutes in the building before Edmonson called me to his office. He had such a smug look on his face I knew he was up to something. He broke out into a big smile and he told me I couldn't stay. I swear to God that he even snickered right before he told me I had to leave because my doctor had restrictions on my shoulder and they didn't have a light duty job for me.

I have to admit that it felt a little bit satisfying to see that smug expression slide off his face when I said I wasn't leaving because my restrictions didn't interfere with my job description. Although in the past I had done whatever was needed to be done at school I assured him that from now on I would just work within the confines of my job description. Edmonson now looked angry. He wanted to know how I had a copy of my job description. Is he a loon? Why wouldn't I have a copy of my job description? I had to sign it. Did he honestly think I would just sign a document and then not keep a copy of it for my records? Edmonson was really thrown off balance. He started to shake and said he had to call the school solicitor right away. He called while I was there and put the solicitor on speaker phone. The solicitor also told me I had to leave. I told him the same thing I had just told Edmonson. I was not going anywhere.

I didn't tell them that last week I had called the worker's compensation office in Harrisburg to find out what I should do. They told me that if I did not go to work it would be considered employment abandonment and I would lose my job and not be eligible for unemployment or any type of benefits. We talked about my job and they told me to read over my job description. They said I did not have to do anything that was not in my job description. I want to work. I have to provide for my daughter. I just want to get my shoulder fixed, be pain free and work in a safe environment.

I thought it would be best to let those two great minds figure out why I was right. Edmonson and the solicitor told me they would have to check into whether I could stay and get back to me to let me know what they found out. I can tell that they're just so thrilled that I'm back. I think Edmonson actually believed I would walk into his office and he could send me away and then they would be able to fire me. He doesn't know me very well. I will do what I have to do to provide for my daughter. One of the most important things I have to do is to know the law and my rights so they can't get away with something shady like they just tried to do.

Right after that meeting Edmonson sent Stan down to my room to tell me that they were taking my office away from me as they needed storage space. I had only been in the building for about a half hour and it was starting out on a very, very rocky path. Actually Stan had come down to measure my office; he had no idea that Edmonson hadn't told me about the plan. He had seen me leaving Edmonson's office and he thought I knew what was happening.

I felt sorry Stan had been put in that position. Edmonson wasn't man enough to tell me himself. There are at least eight rooms I can think of off the top of my head that aren't being used and would make better a better storage area than my office. You have to go through my classroom to get to the office area. It will be a constant intrusion. I think Edmonson is just doing this to try to get back at me for returning to work. By the way, no one seems to know anything about Edmonson being attacked by a hawk. I guess I'm the only one that he shared that story with. His head seems to have healed amazingly well; I didn't notice any scars from the attack.

JANUARY 10, 2006

Someone really doesn't want me back at Penn. I came to work today and there was a note left under my door telling me not to get too comfortable because I wouldn't be there that long. At first I hoped that Amy or Charlotte was playing a joke but in my heart I knew they weren't. They aren't like that. I checked with them anyway and I could tell by the looks on their faces that they hadn't done it. I took the note to Edmonson. He told me I'd have to call the police if I wanted to do anything about it. How typical. Wasn't this something that he should handle? I will handle it if he doesn't want to.

I called the Pennsylvania State Police and talked to Officer Weiss around 9:15 a.m. He said since I didn't know who left the note and because I wasn't willing to point the finger at anyone there wasn't anything they could do. My boss should deal with it internally. Looks like nothing will be done. Isn't it funny how when I wanted to call the police in October Peter told me that he was the police at school and he had equal authority, but now they suddenly don't have the authority and they aren't going to touch this. I realize that this is more serious than vandalism of my car but how can you claim to have authority one minute but then say you don't have any authority the next?

I told Edmonson that I called the police. He told me that I shouldn't have done that. I think the man is losing his mind. That is exactly what he told me to do. He said that he had just talked to Bryson Mancini and they agreed there really wasn't anything they could do. I wonder what Edmonson told him. Boy, that Bryson Mancini is some guy. He told me back in the fall not to worry. I guess he is no better than any of the others I have dealt with.

JANUARY 11, 2006

Peter called me in my room this morning to tell me they had called the Pennsylvania State Police for me. I told him I had done what Edmonson told me to do yesterday and I had taken care of it already. He said they were on their way and I needed to talk to them when they got there. That was cool. I wanted this properly reported anyway. I asked him to call me when they arrived.

When the trooper got there Peter called me to come to the office. I asked if he would send him to my room. Peter called me back and said that

Edmonson didn't want to "alarm" any of the students by having a state trooper walking through the building. Are you kidding me? That's so unbelievable. We have had drug dogs and troopers and probation officers walk throughout the building dozens and dozens and dozens of times. Students have been arrested on occasion and taken away in handcuffs. How would a trooper walking to my room alarm anyone? I believe Edmonson wanted me up in the office area because the walls are thin and he wanted to be able to hear everything I was saying so he could spin the situation.

I talked to the trooper for a good while. He thinks someone is trying to frighten me. He said no matter how scared I am I should hold my head up high and put a smile on my face. He told me if anything else happens that I should contact him immediately—even before I contacted the office. He also told Peter to watch the security tapes to see if there was any indication of who might have done this. Peter said that it would take eight hours per tape to watch and there were several tapes to watch. He said they had to be watched on a special machine at school and he would watch them as he was able. Peter also said that if one of the custodians had placed the note in my room it wouldn't show up on the tape. I said I didn't believe any of them would do it. I get along well with the custodians. Peter said that maybe someone gave them the note to place in my room without telling them what it was. Sounds a little contrived. I didn't want to come back to work like this. Am I going to get hurt again? Does anyone care?

JANUARY 12, 2006
I tried to log onto my computer this afternoon and it said that I was already logged in at another location. Is someone else using my password? I don't want to start feeling paranoid but first the grant files come up missing and now someone is logging onto the school computer system using my password. What would they be doing logged on the system as me? I had a bad feeling about it. I reported it to Edmonson but I don't think anything is going to be done. I asked Peter to change my password. The school gives us our passwords. We can't make up our own.

JANUARY 29, 2006
Alonna's birthday; always a bright spot in my life, it is my "birth" day. It was this day fifteen years ago that the most important person I have ever known came into my life. I have been on my own with her since I was five months pregnant and I almost lost her at birth. Actually we both almost died that day. I went into labor six weeks early and the doctors could

not stop it. After five days in hard labor and with no pain medication I came close to having a stroke. The doctor told me that they had to do an emergency c-section right at that moment and they would have to put me under. I knew it was serious but when the team was running with my bed to the operating room I realized that it was very serious. I didn't want to die. I wanted to live and hold my baby. I pulled through but I didn't get to hold Alonna for several days because she spent the first two days of her life in the neonatal intensive care unit at a different hospital. Those were the longest two days of my life. I don't know if there has ever been a child more wanted than she was. I lay in that hospital bed for two days without her and it helped to put life into perspective for me. I had faith that she would pull through and I knew I would devote my life to her. Since that time I have made every decision based on how she would be affected.

I found myself thinking more and more about how the situation at Penn is affecting Alonna. I knew I couldn't continue with work the way things have been so I had a long talk with my mother. She is the wisest woman I have ever known. She and my father taught me that life isn't always fair and there are many things that we can't control and just have to deal with but sometimes we have an opportunity to stand up for ourselves and force people to do what should be done.

There are laws made to protect people and it was time to investigate the legal side of this issue. She told me that it was time to see an attorney. She had the perfect attorney in mind and she took me to see him. He was a brilliant attorney who I vibed with right away; spiritual and very reminiscent of Jerry Garcia from The Grateful Dead in his later years. Long gray ponytail, bushy beard, rumpled suit and tattered, leather backpack. The legal process is extremely complicated and speaks a language that is foreign to most of us. He was very truthful about the process I needed to go through to try and resolve the situation. My Garcia laid it on the line. He told me we could file a lawsuit on a state level quickly and see what would happen or we could take the long road and do it right. My father always did things the right way. I knew that I needed to do this the right way. The right road would take years. There would be lots of subtle pressure on me to drop the issue. There would also be a lot of attacks on my character even though I was the victim. He needed to make sure I was committed and up to the challenge. I was. This case was about a teacher giving a lesson in accountability and justice. I knew I would see it though no matter how long it took.

My Garcia assured me that he would work hard on the case but he also made it clear that the hardest working person on the case would be me. No one knew what happened to me better than myself. I would be the one who had to gather documentation and organize it so it was clear and would accurately tell my story. I needed to pass things along to him in as much detail as possible so he would be able to translate it into that foreign language of the law for the courts.

I must first exhaust every administrative remedy. He kept saying that over and over; the law demands that I must first exhaust every administrative remedy. I had done all of the reporting to administration with no help forthcoming, tried to get the regional union to intervene with no help forthcoming and now it was time to file a report with the Pennsylvania Human Relations Commission and the Federal Equal Employment Opportunity Commission. I never knew they existed. They handle complaints of housing and employment discrimination. They are short staffed and overloaded. He walked me through the steps I would need to take. The complaint would have to come through me. I was not afraid when I put my signature on my declaration to the PHRC and EEOC. I got my strength as I thought about my ancestor, George Ross the Signer. I wondered how he felt as he himself signed his name to The Declaration of Independence in 1776. Hopefully my PHRC/EEOC filing will be the start of a new way of handling things at Penn.

A week went by and then I received a phone call from a woman at the PHRC. She was an initial screener. She was very helpful and told me that I needed to change or clarify a few points. It seems that not only had I included the ways in which I was harassed and ignored by my employer, I had included information about how he had treated other individuals at the school. I was told that information needed to be taken out. Why? The screener told me that I had reached the point in the process where I needed to be concerned for and solely focus on myself and my situation. I could encourage others to follow their own legal path but other than that, there was nothing I could do for them and she said I needed to stop thinking about others. Wow. That seemed so harsh. I grew up in a home where worrying about people's feelings and taking care of others was a part of everyday life. My mother became a social worker to help others. I became a teacher to help others. My whole family volunteered with various organizations to help others. How does one just get over something like that?

The intake workers from the PHRC helped me understand that filing a complaint is an individual thing. You must stand alone. You can still care about other people and by filing the complaint I may encourage others to find the strength to stand up for themselves. She was kind, made sense and she was right. I would make the necessary changes.

I received the official complaint from the PHC in the mail. I just needed to review it, sign it, and mail it back to them. This was the real moment of truth. I signed it and a wave a peace came over it. I put the complaint in the mail.

The legal process was about to begin. I would be one of about 12,000 individuals who file federal sexual harassment discrimination charges with the PHRC/EEOC. I was told that about two thirds of cases go unreported. Sexual harassment discrimination is illegal but it is not criminal and it obviously is not taken seriously; not even in a school system where we are stewards of our youth.

FEBRUARY 1, 2006

Finally, after asking for four months Edmonson has said I can have the transcripts from the assault interviews. I find it hard to believe though that Edmonson would only talk to the people I said I told about the incident. He told the W/C carrier that he talked to everyone in the building. I asked a few people if he had talked to them. He did not. Big, big fib. I wonder what possesses him to lie about things he knows can be so easily found out. I don't think he can stop himself. I think he lies more than he has ever told the truth.

Before I could have the transcripts though Edmonson said I had to get releases from people to get the transcripts; actually I had to do it twice. I got releases from Hank, Charlotte, and Miranda but then Brenda called and said that the release said I could have the tapes but it didn't say anything about the *transcripts* of the tapes so I had to get another one; a total of two releases, one for the tapes and once for the transcripts. I didn't get one from Pierce or Rick though. Wonder what they said. Shouldn't I get to hear what Pierce said? After all, Edmonson showed him my incident letter. I guess somewhere down the road through the legal process I will get to hear what Pierce has to say about the assault.

February 6, 2006

I finally got the transcripts from the conversations Edmonson had with Charlotte, Hank, Miranda and me. Most of mine was pretty standard, but there was one key section. Edmonson asked me if there was anything else that would shed light on what happened. I wanted to clarify and I asked, "Why has it escalated to this point." Edmonson said, "I think it is pretty evident based on history…" He said it was evident and yet he has done nothing. What kind of leadership is that?

Then I ready Miranda's statements. She said everything occurred exactly as I had stated in my letter. Obviously he let everyone including Pierce read my complaint letter. She stated that she would not feel safe putting herself in a position where she would be alone with Pierce in a room. She said she would not put herself in a position where she would have to be fearful. Then Edmonson abruptly ended her interview.

Next was Charlotte's interview. Edmonson let things slip that clearly showed he knew about Pierce's bullying. He was questioning Charlotte about a time when she thought Pierce was attacking Miranda and she went to save her. He said he was told that Pierce was pounding his hands on his chest. Charlotte said yes that he was doing that and she was afraid that Pierce was going to hurt Miranda because he was angry and yelling. Then Edmonson jumped topic and said, "Is there something going on; is there a problem that administration doesn't know about?" Charlotte said that she thought administration was well aware of the problems. Edmonson said that unless everyone puts it in writing he can't do anything about it. That is just crazy. People are afraid to put things in writing because they know Edmonson has shown what I wrote about the assault to Pierce. It's true. Edmonson just wants to fuel the fires and create more drama.

Edmonson then asked Charlotte if she was afraid Pierce would physically harm her because he said, "there is an expression that Maria uses; she says that he gets in your face." Charlotte said that she couldn't be sure if he would ever hurt her or not because he really seems to have a temper. Then boom, Edmonson suddenly ended her interview.

Hank's interview came next. Edmonson tried to blow him off which is no wonder because of his ill feelings toward Hank but Hank made sure that Edmonson heard that we have all witnessed inappropriate things going on and nothing was being done about it. This interview lasted just minutes.

After reading what everyone had to say, how on earth could Edmonson just have blatantly dismissed what happened? He just did not want to deal with it, he didn't think that I was worth the effort of looking into what happened and he was seriously afraid that he was going to get an ass whooping from Pierce if he actually did push the issue. He most surely is afraid of Pierce.

FEBRUARY 8, 2006

I received another summoning from Edmonson to his office today. He said I was not to initiate any type of conversation with Pierce again—EVER. I told him I had just sent Pierce an email about a student. Edmonson said Pierce complained to him that I was bothering him. How is asking for needed information on a student bother him exactly?

Edmonson said he could not guarantee when Pierce would become volatile with me again. Not if; when. See! He knows. I knew he knew! But his solution is to shut me up? This is going to make working more difficult. I have to ask Charlotte to ask Pierce things for me. We need some kind of professional help around here. I'm being bullied and harassed and even Edmonson thinks that Pierce might hit me again. I don't know if he will but it is very frightening coming to a place every day when you don't know if it is the day that you are going to get hurt again. What did Pierce say to Edmonson today? It's obvious that he said something strong enough for Edmonson to believe I am not safe at work but he's not doing anything about it. Why won't anyone help me?

FEBRUARY 10, 2006

Edmonson wants me to chair the spring open house. I told him I'm just coming back to work and have a lot to catch up on and don't really physically feel up to doing it. He kicked me in the shin. He didn't swing at the air beside me; he actually kicked me in the shin. It wasn't real hard, but it startled me and I jumped. I almost fell and Edmonson just snickered. He said something like Oh come on, this is the easy part all you have to do is delegate. I don't think I really have a choice whether or not I do this.

...

And I am now more concerned than ever about my safety. Hit by Pierce, kicked by Edmonson; what's next?

FEBRUARY 14, 2006

Today was the first time Edmonson has been in my room since I came back to work in January. He came to see me to see what I knew about a feud brewing between two shop teachers. I wouldn't tell him even if I did know anything. He really should sit down and talk to them but he just lets conflicts brew. I don't want to be dragged into the middle of something that's none of my business. Edmonson said he wanted me to intervene and try to bring them together. There is absolutely no way I am stepping into this situation. I'm sure he just wants to throw me in the middle of more trouble. I don't need any more trouble.

Almost everything was moved out of my office except for the computer and phone so they could start construction on the storage area. Edmonson looked around my office area and said he didn't think the room was big enough for all of the storage files to fit in there. Is he messing with me again? He even mentioned that you have to go through my room to get to the new storage room. I guess it's just one more little dig. I just want to scream. What does this mean? Am I supposed to put everything back? I don't know. Trying to follow his thought process is like trying to follow a swarm of mosquitoes attacking your head.

He jumped topic again and told me that the school was cited because I didn't submit financial reports to the state. What the heck is he talking about? What financials? It's not my job to submit any financial reports to the state. I think they have someone who does that who is called the Bookeeper!!!!! Why would I ignore state reports if I were supposed to do that? And where would I have gotten the information for the financial reports? I don't have any financial records. I don't even know what happened to the missing federal files. Edmonson has ignored me every time I have asked about the files. Charlotte did tell me that in October of last year it appeared that someone had come into my room and really cleaned it and organized things. She and Miranda wondered if I had been in. It wasn't me; I am more of a disorganized, organized person. I wonder who was moving things in my room. She also told me that Private Eye Peter came down to my room about a week after I reported the files missing. He went into Charlotte's room and said that he didn't understand; that the file drawers were still there. I did not say that the physical file drawers were missing. I said that two file drawers worth of files were gone. Top notch detective work.

FEBRUARY 16, 2006

Edmonson called me and asked me why I was in such a hurry to move my office. I said I didn't understand what he meant. He told me that I needed to be moved and the room converted by the end of January. He said, No, no, by the end of the school year. He said I could move my office back if I wanted. I can't move anything! A couple of boys from school moved the furniture out of my office and it just all got pushed together and nothing is organized. It's not my usual disorganized, organized state. It's just a mess. It's so hard because the students did what they could for me but they can't work with me for days just making room for everything and arranging things.

Since my office was pretty well moved out and Edmonson said he didn't need the office until next year I began to draw up a plan to convert my old office space into a reading room for the students. I think it will be cool. I can get lots of trade magazines and DVDs on the trades. It can be very inspiring and get students more interested in reading for pleasure and to enhance the knowledge of their trade area in a fun way.

FEBRUARY 17, 2006

I told Edmonson about my plan for a reading room since he didn't need the space until summer. Within thirty seconds after I told him, he decided he needed the space right away. What a surprise. Is he trying to play mind games with me or does his mind work like a yo-yo? Or maybe he just gets some kind of sick treat by making my head spin.

He had Stan bring some things right away. He put some boxes of old files, which were really garbage, in my room. The stuff in those boxes should have been destroyed ten years ago. They were copies of old student IEPs. The home schools have the originals and we get copies. The copies should have been destroyed after the student graduated. He is a pig! I still need to get my computer and phone moved out of that space. I've been waiting for over a month for that to be done. It's very inconvenient to not have the phone or computer by my desk.

FEBRUARY 19, 2006

Someone fired a gun outside my kitchen window late last night. It scared Alonna; me too. Is someone from school trying to scare me? I have lived here for over twelve years and nothing like this has happened before. Is it somehow connected to what's going on with the school? Is it safe to go outside of my own house? I called the state police but just got the same old run around. They don't have the man power to come out and investigate. I should call them back if someone actually tries to break in or if a bullet comes thru the window. That is just so freakin' comforting!

FEBRUARY 22, 2006

Last night was even scarier than the gunfire outside of the house. I walked down to the mailbox to get the newspaper this morning and I fell to my knees in shock. Someone set my front yard on fire in the middle of the night. It has to be connected with what is happening at the school. There were board and logs spread out and charred. It was not a random act. This took some time. I am feeling truly blessed though because there was an unexpected snowfall last night and it put out the fire. I think someone in Heaven was looking out for me and my family last night. I just wasn't sure how I was going to go into the house and tell my mother and Alonna. They would both be so frightened. How are we going to feel safe going to sleep at night? I called the state police again. Same old story. They could come out but it would be fruitless. There are no witnesses, no real suspects. They don't have the time or resources to do anything with this situation. If my home would have burned down I guess they would have come out. Thank God for my heavenly intercessor.

FEBRUARY 27, 2006

Edmonson sent Tyler Smith down to measure again for the room. Tyler told me that Edmonson wanted the project done now. He asked me when would be a good day for me. I told him that Thursday would be okay. Tyler left and not long afterwards Edmonson came in. He said that he needed Tyler's class to do the project the next day, Tuesday. Wow. I have this vision of Edmonson just sitting in his office thinking of everything little thing that he can do to make my work life difficult for me. There was no reason why Tyler's class had to do it the next day.

FEBRUARY 28, 2006

Miranda is really upset. Pierce was waving a dead rat in the face of a female intern and then he laid it on the computer keyboard of the male intern.

Edmonson is covering up for Pierce again. He told Miranda it was a stuffed animal rat but he wouldn't show it to her because he said he had it in the office safe; for safety reasons. That doesn't make any kind of sense at all.

Miranda wasn't looking for trouble. The interns went to her for help and they said it was real. Bob was very upset; he was afraid of germs on the keyboard. His young son uses the computer and he didn't want germs from a dead rat passed on to him. Edmonson told Miranda that she should stop trying to find things out about Pierce. Again, she didn't do that. The interns went to her for help. What should she have done; just looked the other way like Edmonson does? There is something shady here with Edmonson. If it was simply a bad joke and was indeed a stuffed animal rat then why wouldn't you just want to clear it up and show it to Miranda instead of having it locked up in the school safe? Locking up a stuffed animal rat in the school safe? Come on, that just sounds stupid.

MARCH 7, 2006
Edmonson told Amy that she wouldn't be able to get some of the supplies she needed because the school was cited because I had not submitted a financial report to the state. She knew that didn't sound right so she came to tell me about it. I went looking for Edmonson but he has been dodging me all day. I need to get this cleared up. If there was something that was not turned into the state from when I did the grant I would like to know about it. If it was a financial report the bookkeeper would have a copy of it. If it was another grant report then I am not quite sure what to do since the grant files are still missing. Did Edmonson take the files back in October and wait all of this time to make up a story like this? He definitely is that devious. And a jerk!

There was another eighth grade tour today. Edmonson told Miranda I had to be a tour guide. I have been doing it for six years and now there are other people in the building who could do it. He's pulling me away from my job as a teacher to do this. He's the boss though. He makes such intelligent decisions.

MARCH 8, 2006
There is no doubt. Edmonson is out to ruin my professional reputation! Karen told me she was in the office when Edmonson took a call from the worker's comp rep, Sharon Knight. Karen said Edmonson told her that I was a pretty nice lady but I had a lot of personal problems. I have never

discussed my life with him. How dare he presume to know anything about my personal life? Of course there is the issue of Pierce, but he could do something about that. I wish he would just stick to the facts. I wonder if he would he even know the truth if it bit him in the armpit? I sent him an email to ask him about his conversation with Sharon. I wonder if he'll deny it or just be man enough to admit what he said. I would bet money that he just ignores me again.

I wrote a letter to the trooper I spoke with in January. I wanted to go on record as reporting the gun shot blasts, the car vandalism and my front yard being set on fire. I also wanted to let them know that I never received a follow up from Edmonson about the video tape that they were supposed to watch to see if anyone was around my mailbox or classroom. I have a feeling that I better make sure I document as much as I can.

MARCH 9, 2006
I was leaving the school and I noticed that my car had once again been keyed, the gas cover was open and the gas cap was partially off. My car was sputtering very much as I tried to drive it. I phoned my brother who is a mechanic. He said it sounded like someone may have poured water or something into the tank. He told me to fill the car with premium gas and put in two bottles of dry gas. I reported the problem to Peter. Peter said that he was going to contact the police again. I told him I would stay to talk to them and he told me no that I should leave and he would handle everything. Shouldn't I be there to talk to them since it was my property that was vandalized? I will follow up to get copies of the police reports but I doubt any will exist since I won't be there as the property owner and the vehicle won't be there.

MARCH 10, 2006
I went to River High School with Miranda. I think Edmonson let me go because he just wanted to get me out of the building. On my way out of the school Edmonson stopped me and asked me what I thought he should do about the problems at school. Is this a trick? Is he trying to get me to criticize him so he can write me up? Can he write me up if he asked me the question? I have to watch what I say to him and how I say it to him. I told him I really think he needs to handle things head on instead of letting things build up and fester. I wanted to tell him that he could start acting like a man and stop contributing to the problem with all of his drama needs but I kept my tongue. It's going to be a long year.

MARCH 13, 2006

My front tire was scraped at work. There was no way it was done accidentally. I started to drive away and the tire blew out. Thank goodness I was only going about 10 mph. The way the tire blew you could still see where something had been used to wear it down. It was like the equivalent of running a nail file across your bare finger nail. Someone was trying to make it look like an accident and probably hope that I wrecked along the way. Finally today Edmonson told me park I can park in view of the cameras.

I'm beginning to feel like a zombie. I haven't been able to sleep and during the day I'm always looking over my shoulder. I wonder if my car is going to explode while I'm driving it or if I'm going to get shot at home or if the house is going to burn down. Mostly I worry what this is doing to Alonna and my mother. I can tell that they are both very worried for me. I keep wondering what I could have done to prevent all of this from happening? I don't know; short of sleeping with Pierce and Edmonson I don't see how there was anything I could have done to stop this runaway train. Please oh please just let me not get killed. I am the only parent Alonna has. She needs me. I need her.

MARCH 14, 2006

Edmonson said Pierce is ticked off at me once again because I complained about literature he has in his class with scantily clad women on it. I only gave a copy of it to Edmonson because a student's mother gave it to me. She was upset about it but she didn't want her son to know that she said anything about it to the school because she was afraid it would make things hard for him in the shop.

Of course Edmonson would have had to tell Pierce that I talked to him about it. Maybe Edmonson really does want to see me killed. I am a pretty liberal person but I agree with the mother; there are things that are just not appropriate for school. Distributing company literature with scantily clad women on it may be an accepted practice in the business world but it should not be accepted in a school.

MARCH 16, 2006

Will this ever end? At this moment I should be thankful that I don't have a new car. Yesterday was vandalism act number four. My car was keyed again. It was supposed to be safe under the security camera. I felt numb as

I walked back into the school and asked Peter if I could review the security tapes from the parking lot. He said he'd get back to me. Now I know I am not the smartest techno girl in the world but even I can figure out how to hit stop, rewind, and play. What are they hiding? Why don't they want the truth to come out?

Is Edmonson protecting Pierce, someone else or is this part of his own sick game? Why won't Peter give me the name of the trooper who he allegedly spoke with about my car the last time it was vandalized and why won't he give me copies of any of the vandalism reports? There is only one answer; there aren't any written reports and they never called the police.

MARCH 17, 2006
Miranda feels like she is between a rock and a hard place. To put it mildly, Pierce and Nikki seem to make a point of acting inappropriately at school when they are around Miranda. The surprising thing is that they don't care if students are around when she is there and they are putting on a show to make her uncomfortable. I would like to think that they wouldn't stoop that low but I have heard it from students too. As a matter of fact, Pierce and Nikki have been getting touchier in front of the students when Miranda isn't even around. Are they like two year olds who cover their eyes and think you can't see them, or do they not care who sees them flaunt their affair? As far as I'm concerned Nikki can rub her boobs over every man she comes in contact with; just don't do it in front of the students. Miranda has been hoping that Edmonson would put on his big boy pants for once and finally sit them down and have a talk about how to behave at school. I don't think we are going to hold our breath.

MARCH 25, 2006
Pierce has been expanding his bullying zone. Lately he has been off the hook rude to Shannon our guidance intern. He even threw her out of his shop. Miranda had to speak up about this issue; she is responsible for Shannon. I thought it was great that Shannon actually went to talk to Edmonson herself. I know she was nervous because she is young; just a senior in college and Pierce can be so intimidating but she stood up for herself. What she got in return was bullshit! Edmonson said that he doesn't excuse Pierce's behavior but *Pierce was having a bad day.* Poor Pierce. I have had over a thousand bad days since I have worked here. Having a bad day does not give you the right to scream at a co-worker in front of students. There is no excuse for his bullying. How long is Edmonson

going to let Pierce treat people like dirt? Shannon is such a nice woman. I hope she doesn't get the impression that all schools are like this. I hear tell that there are actually some administrators out there who do the right thing—I wonder where they are. Seriously, there are a lot of good people in education; unfortunately there are a lot of not so good people too. It's like that in any profession, but the field of education should be different because we are modeling behavior for our future leaders. Students learn mostly by example. What example is our school setting? How much damage is Pierce doing to our school's reputation?

Out of the blue Edmonson told Miranda that everyone knows about Nikki and Pierce's affair. He told Miranda that Pierce's wife would cause a lot of trouble for him if she knew what was going on. He went on and on trying to goad her into calling Pierce's wife. But he is the one that needs to step up and take care of school business. Miranda is not the type to call and cause trouble for someone at home. Her only concern is what is going on in front of the students.

MARCH 26, 2006

Sleep has not been coming at all these past few days. I keep wondering what life would be like if I had never come to Penn. Would I be happy? Would Alonna be able to enjoy a carefree childhood instead of always worrying about me? I cry so much. I feel so guilty. Am I in some way responsible for the pain Alonna tries to hide from me? I wish I knew what the right thing to do was. I keep writing to Edmonson and the board about all the harassment I have been experiencing and they just continue to ignore me. I have a folder full of letters and emails to all of the board members explaining the harassment and bullying and giving them my phone number, address and email; none of them have given me the courtesy of contacting me. Isn't the school board supposed to be the guardians of the school? Aren't I part of the school? Shouldn't they be my guardian in a sense then too? If the board really cared to do what the voters have entrusted them to do they could very easily have done something about both Edmonson and Pierce. Their behavior is not only reprehensible it is a violation of the Pennsylvania School Code. It's laid out very clearly in black and white. If I was a suspicious person I would say that Pierce really does have some dirt on Edmonson and the board members. It's either that or that think I am a trouble maker and don't want to deal with these problems. It is so much easier just to blame the victim and hope she will just go away.

MARCH 29, 2006

I am not sure how much more I can take of this emotional rollercoaster these men have been sending me on. There was a fleeting moment of hope when Bryson called and said that they would like to sit down and talk with me. They called it a "Meet and Discuss" session; I called it bullshit. A charade so they could say they had done something. Bryson, the solicitor, and Edmonson just sat there and looked at me like I was an alien when I said I expected them to create a safe, hostile free working environment. They said they needed a clearer understanding of what the problems were. I'm the alien? What planet have they been living on for the past few years? How could they not have a clue what the problems were? I bit my tongue, explained yet once again and then suggested that they go back and review the dozens of letters and emails I had written to them. They said they would check into things and get back to me. Haven't I heard those words before? I think maybe they meant to say, *Give us a chance to meet privately, get our stories straight and then we'll get back to you.*

MARCH 30, 2006

I was very excited for our after school workshop today. A friend of Edmonson's came to Penn for a session on unlawful harassment and staff conflicts. I was willing to give James Kanya the benefit of the doubt even though he is Edmonson's friend. Friends are special people; they are as important as family. You don't choose your family but friends are the people that you actually let into your life. I wondered why this intelligent looking man chose to let Edmonson into his life. Maybe Edmonson was just lying about their friendship. Just because you know someone doesn't make them your friend; and Kanya was getting paid a very pretty penny to do the session. Anyways. Pierce came in late, sat down, put his feet up on the chair next to him and leaned back. Edmonson came in behind him, went to the front of the room, and said that we should get started so we could *get the hell out of here early.* He then began to ramble on about his vision for a new Penn. He talked about the layout and the colors and the atmosphere; funny how his vision didn't seem to include anything about the students or actual learning. Twenty-five minutes later Edmonson let Dr. Kanya speak. His presentation was very enlightening and just confirmed a lot of things I felt were true.

*Too many times people are saved from consequences,

*When you see harassment and no one does anything, you're setting someone up to do something more serious,

*Consequences help change negative behavior,

*Harassment is about gaining power; people look for it.

*Putting someone in a situation where they are uncomfortable all the time is harassment. It's not just hitting and physical abuse.

*Harassers harass because it makes them feel important. Typically it's a way of life—how they've been brought up—a family history—sometimes they feel life has screwed them over; they're angry at their family and exhibit maladaptive behavior. They have a screwed up logic.

*They try to push others down to push themselves up.

Pierce just sat there during this talk with his whole body hung over the back side of the chair beside him. We are a small group of teachers. There are less than thirty of us. Everyone could see what he was doing. He sometimes laughed and sometimes smirked. He thinks this is a joke. It's no joke to me. All of the things that Dr. Kanya talked about are things that are happening here. I felt worse as each moment passed and Edmonson just sat there. I don't know if he didn't care or if he was afraid to confront Pierce. If he can't control him during a meeting with a guest there how can he control him at all?

Kanya had only been speaking for twenty minutes when Edmonson got up and cut him off. He said instead of making us stay until 4:00 he was going to let us go now as long as we promised to take and read the handout that he was laying on the table at the front of the room. Pierce actually laughed out loud, just got up and walked out without bothering to stop and take one of the handouts. I felt so angry that Edmonson continues to promote Pierce's behavior because he permits his very rude, aggressive, hostile behavior.

I spoke to Dr. Kanya for a few minutes after the session to see if he was coming back. He said he felt there were a lot of problems at the school and we needed more sessions but he had not been asked to come back. Big surprise!

MARCH 31, 2006

I looked at the handout Edmonson gave us yesterday. It is Policy Number 448: Unlawful Harassment. I think Edmonson needs a dictionary to understand the word confidentiality. The policy clearly states that confidentially must be maintained for concerns that are reported either in a verbal or written form. This has never happened in my case. Edmonson has always told me that I have to put things in writing or he can't do anything but when I put things in writing, like when I was injured by Pierce, Edmonson showed my write up to Pierce, Nikki, Rick, Miranda, Charlotte, and Hank. I'm not sure whom else he showed the report to. After he showed them the report I was told by different teachers that Nikki and Pierce were repeatedly making fun of me. I don't see anything funny about being assaulted and harassed by a man that is a foot taller than I am.

Brian O'Reily told me he hit his elbow and his reaction was to hold his elbow and wince. Nikki was there and she started laughing and asked Brian if he was going to file a worker's compensation claim. She of all people should know that a physical injury is nothing to laugh about. What kind of a person makes fun of someone's injury? I guess a very small minded person who has a shady relationship with a bully.

APRIL 5, 2006

I went to see Bryson Mancini today. Technically he is Edmonson's boss. I think. In any event he is in a position to be a voice to the board as he is our Chief School Administrator right now. The home school superintendents rotate every two years being the CSA. I bet he can't wait for his turn to be up. They get paid for it though; five thousand on top of their salary. I thought I could plead to his sense of decency and talk one on one without Edmonson being in the room about how things really are at Penn. We talked about Pierce's behavior and the assault. We talked about Edmonson hitting my shoulder and kicking me in the leg. I told him about all of the times Edmonson asked me asked, Pierce asking me out, my car being vandalized, my office being taken and how Edmonson handled the threatening note I received. We talked for about an hour or so. We also talked about the fact that I just received a teaching award for my work with special needs students. He took my hand, looked me in the eye and said that he would do everything in his power to help me. He promised me. I left the meeting finally feeling that maybe something was going to be done about the situation at school. A promise is a man's word and a man is only as good as his word, right?

APRIL 4, 2006
Kevin Klein emailed me. He said that the solicitor wanted him to meet with two teachers about a complaint that had been filed with the PHRC and EEOC. He wanted to know if I knew anything about this. Of course I knew about the complaint. This has so much more to do than just an issue between two teachers. Why don't they understand? Obviously Kevin knew that this involved me because he emailed me about it. People keep talking about talking, but nobody is talking. It is so bizarre.

APRIL 11, 2006
Edmonson told the board that he didn't need an Assistant Director; he could handle everything on his own. Either he doesn't want to feel threatened by anyone who may actually be better than him at the job or he thinks he can get away with a lot more if no one is looking over his shoulder.

Edmonson also scheduled me to do a special education presentation for the faculty today. He just told me yesterday. Having to do the presentation brought back vivid flashbacks of the day Pierce hit me. I was so nervous. Pierce sat there glaring at me the whole time. Every time he moved I jumped. I was petrified that he felt bold enough to hit me again in front of everyone just because he feels he can and no one would do anything about it. It's so hard to be in the same room with him. I instantly start shaking and get sick to my stomach.

APRIL 15, 2006
It is Easter Saturday. I got a flower delivery today at home. A dozen long stemmed red roses. I don't have a special man in my life so I was excited to see who they were from. My excitement quickly turned to frustration and a sense of dread. They were from Bryson Mancini. There was a typewritten note in an envelope. The note was only a few lines long. He congratulated me on the teaching award I was going to receive and said he would do everything he possibly could to help me with the situation at Penn. And then there it was. He asked me if we could get together for dinner. My mind was just reeling. What in the world was going on? Honestly, I just

don't understand it. I have a tendency to dress on the more trendy yet professional side and I am not unattractive, but I am not someone who men would be beating down their doors to get to. So exactly what is going on? Is it because I am a single parent? Do they think I am an easy mark? I don't know. I don't understand it and it is really bothering me. Is there some unwritten rule that if you want help at work with harassment then you have to be willing to prostitute yourself? Doesn't that negate the whole cry for help? There is no way that I am having dinner with him. He's my boss's boss and he is married. Double trouble. Surely there has to be someone who will help me just because it's the right thing to do. I am really beginning to lose hope.

APRIL 20, 2006

Edmonson does not want me, Charlotte or Amy to go with Miranda to the sending schools to talk to the students who have filled out an application to attend next year. He furloughed the math department and now six weeks before school is over he decides to start a new project called The Math Academy. It is a computerized game. He wants us to spend the rest of the year in the computer lab watching the kids play this game instead of helping students with their shop theory work or studying for finals. I heard he has a stake in the program. Can we all say kick back?

Going to the home schools was always a good opportunity for us to meet potential students. We could answer questions, clear up misunderstandings about their program selections and try to help make an appropriate placement. I'm very disappointed about not going. I can see this one decision causing big problems for next year. Edmonson thinks that our being out of the building for a day or two is a play day. It is not. Those few days spent at the home schools helps head off a lot of problems for the next school year. Poor Miranda. He is putting double the workload on her shoulders. He is an ass!

APRIL 25, 2006

A woman from the Children Security Service came to Penn to talk to us about mandated reporting for suspected abuse. There was a disagreement between Edmonson and the CSS representative about what to do in that situation. I'm more confused than ever. According to Edmonson, because he's the F'n boss, we are supposed to call the office to report any suspected abuse and he will handle it because he has a doctorate. The CSS rep said we should call the confidential hotline. But if we don't do what he says then are we being insubordinate? I know enough about him to know that if I do report something to him I better not hold my breath waiting for any action from him. I'm sure Edmonson will help the student just like he has helped me.

The big problem with Edmonson, as I see it, is that he wants to be in charge of everything. And the fact that a woman told him what should be done just seemed to push him over the edge. He wants to control every situation because he wants to look so important. But it backfires on him continuously because so many things fall through the cracks. He doesn't care though. He just blames the screw up on someone else. He doesn't care how many reputations he has ruined.

April 29, 2006

I was raised with a strong work ethic. No matter what the job was it was worthy of doing your best. I was also raised not to ever strut or boast about what you had done. I think that's why I was a little nervous about being recognized at the Educator Awards presentation on Thursday. I am not like Edmonson who is constantly seeking the spotlight. I am more of a behind the scenes kind of woman. But as it turned out, last Thursday evening was such a nice event. My mom, sister and nine co-workers came to the dinner. It was so touching. The timing for the dinner was not the greatest however. Miranda and I were at the Student Leadership Conference in Pittsburgh with six students but we cleared going to the dinner with Edmonson and the Leadership administration. We didn't think we would be gone more than five hours. Shannon stayed in Pittsburgh to chaperone the kids at the dinner and dance. There were also at least 20 other chaperones from other schools there who all said they would watch over our kids. Edmonson said he was coming to the dinner but he didn't show. I took it as a slap in the face. It doesn't look real nice when your boss won't come to a dinner where you are an honoree. Edmonson was the only director not there. It was very obvious by the empty seat and the only place card left sitting on the registration table. Everyone noticed and commented on it, wondering where he was. Oh well. The truth is that it made it a nicer evening for me without him there. It would have been weird to have him there offering any kind of false praise.

May 1, 2006

School has been a joke for the past couple of weeks. I don't have time to help any students because Edmonson wants a daily count of students who have used The Math Academy program. Edmonson said he is pushing the program so hard because the school gets money for every time the program is used. I don't believe it will be the school getting money for the student count! Amy, Charlotte and I filed a grievance so we can do our real jobs. I don't know how long this procedure will take. Edmonson thinks I put everyone up to doing this. I didn't. We can't do our jobs and watch the students do the computer game. Plus, yes, I will admit this. I hate math. I just don't have a math brain. I am more right brained. I focus more on the creative way of doing things. I hate it when a standardized test insists that you show your work. Sometimes you can just figure out things in your head and take short cuts in your head and still arrive at the right answer. It's not like baking, where everything has to be done in exact, precise measurements. I can't bake either. I think it's the exact measurement thing I'm not fond of. I like to cook more. Just throw in some of this and some of that and make it up as you go along. It still comes out delicious. These students need a math teacher to help them understand math not a babysitter so someone can get paid a little extra money on the side.

MAY 4, 2006

I knew taking my office for storage was going to cause problems. People come into my room to go to the storage room even when I am not there. There's nothing I can do about that but when I got back from a meeting today my room was standing wide open. There is confidential information in my room. It shouldn't just be standing open when I'm not around. Who knows what is missing from my room. It would take hours to go through everything to see if anything is missing. Is there another important file or files missing? How hard is it to open a locked door and then make sure you lock it when you leave? Just confirmation that I am working with some educated people who think they are superior but have absolutely no common sense. Or am I being set up again? I used to be such a trusting person. I don't like this feeling of always questioning if someone is trying to set me up or hurt me in some way. My level of distrust escalated tenfold today after I reviewed my personnel file. I remembered Hank mentioning that it would be a good idea to review it every year. I took his advice and scheduled a time to review my file. I was very glad that I did. You would think that it would be in chronological order but it was a total mess. It was as if someone had dropped it and just thrown all the papers back into the folder. Papers were upside down and backwards and nothing made sense. None of the letters or emails that I had written about the harassment or vandalism was in there. Neither was any of the paperwork for my worker's comp claim. There was no mention of any State Police report for the letter threatening me. There was, however, a letter of reprimand in the file from Bart for the State Performance Report being faxed to the state on the day it was due. Again, I can't quite get my head wrapped around this. Doesn't turning in something on THE DAY it is due; mean that it is not late? It's not like they would review it and send it back for corrections. It's a performance report. It is what it is. I used to work for a newspaper. I am very aware of the importance of deadlines. I did not miss a deadline! You don't miss a deadline when you work for a newspaper. You can't have a big hole in the page. It is also against the contract to put anything like that in your file without seeing it and signing off on it. Typical of them just try to slip something in. Or was it Edmonson? I never saw a letter or a memo that Bart didn't sign; this piece of paper didn't even have his initials on it.

Edmonson had Paulie Denick sit in the room while I reviewed my file. He was visibly upset when I wrote a note on the letter of reprimand saying I had never seen it before. He tried to lunge across the table and grab the file but we were too far apart and he would have dropped the coffee cup in his hand. I don't think I ever saw him without a coffee cup in his hand. It's like his security blanket. He carries a cup of coffee everywhere he goes. I think it is very weird. He yelled out that I was not supposed to make any marks on anything in the file. I'm not supposed to make any marks on anything? They are not supposed to put lies in my file. Why is administration trying to ruin my reputation? I guess it is grievance time again.

May 5, 2006

Edmonson gave Miranda a copy of a very insulting letter. It accused me of drinking and acting weird with Miranda during both the award dinner and at the conference. The letter accused me of getting drunk at the awards dinner and trying to kiss Miranda in front of the kids when we got back. I didn't have one drink at the dinner. The state trooper who sat with us could vouch for me. And although I think the world of Miranda, woman on woman action is just not for me.

Miranda said Edmonson was furious that she gave me a copy of the letter. He said he didn't share it with me because Miranda was in charge. I asked exactly what she was in charge of. He just kept yelling she was in charge, she was in charge! Hello! We are co-advisors and the letter was about me as much as it was about Miranda. He also said he was going to have to share it with the board although he was fairly certain that the letter had already been sent to them. An unsigned letter telling outrageous lies and he feels like he has to share it with the board. Why doesn't he share anything about Pierce with the board? Oh yes, he wants to protect Pierce and he wants to fry me. There is something really fishy about the letter. It is too perfectly fake. It was signed *A Concerned Parent* and said how terrified their child was of me and Miranda during the trip. There were only six students that went with us to the conference and we didn't have any problems with any of them. They had a great time. I'm going to have to investigate this a little bit more. Maybe we will call the parents.

Edmonson gave Miranda a copy of some notes he wrote up to give the board about the situation. He said he tried to call her cell phone over a dozen times during the conference and that her phone wasn't working. He said that he had absolutely no other way to get in touch with her. Bull! Her phone worked fine. And if he had any issues why wouldn't he have called my phone? He never tried to call me once. He also had several other contact numbers for the hotel and the people who were in charge of the conference. They never received any phone calls from him. He tells so many lies. I wonder if anyone on the board will have enough sense to see through this.

May 18, 2006

The staff wrote a letter to Mancini voicing concerns about Edmonson's leadership. It was basically a letter of no confidence. Fifteen out of twenty two teachers signed it. Edmonson's behavior toward the staff is uncaring, antagonistic and rude. He deliberately withholds information we need to do our jobs properly. There have been new policies made and passed at board meetings. They were voted on and passed based on a number. At one board meeting they passed seventy policies. No one ever said what those policies were and we never got copies of them. But you better not violate any of them. How can you be sure if you have violated something that you don't know about?

I know this school year is almost over but I hope the letter of no confidence helps make things better for next year. I don't know that the board will ever see it since the letter went to Mancini. I don't think I will keep my fingers crossed. I haven't heard a word about any kind of help from Mancini since I received his roses. I saw him twice and he seemed really pissed at me. I guess because I didn't call him up and swoon over him and the roses and go to dinner with him. They have names for men like him. Very bad names.

May 22, 2006

A state conflict mediator from PSEA called me to set up a meeting with Pierce. She also called Miranda and Daniels. I was more than willing to sit down and try to talk about how we can all get past this situation with Pierce and move forward. Daniels told me Pierce said under the advice of legal counsel he should not be party to any mediation with me or Miranda. What kind of attorney would tell you not to try to work out any problems by sitting down and talking? Pierce could have brought his attorney with him. We wouldn't have cared. We just want to see the problems resolved. Miranda called the mediator and requested that she still come. She told Miranda it would be a waste of time since Pierce would not participate and they had more important things to do with their time. What is more important than helping the people who pay union dues and who are in trouble? I am so disappointed in the regional and state teachers union. What do my dues go for?

May 24, 2006

The Penn student awards banquet is still a wonderful thing but over the past few years Wanda has been the chair and her focus has been more on the style of the event rather than making the students and their families feel comfortable. She wanted to have the dinner at Nemacolin. She said we could get a real deal with dinners at only $55 a plate. This is a high school banquet in a county where families are struggling to provide the basics for their families. You cannot ask families to pay that kind of money for this event and we certainly don't have the money to cover the costs. What is she thinking? I haven't been involved much over the past few years so I don't have much input. My name is no longer on the checking account and the only thing I really have to do with the banquet is writing the opening for the program. I enjoy that. Putting thoughts together that will hopefully have an inspirational message for the students and their families. I don't sign my name to the message. I look at it as a message from the entire teaching staff. A very nice guidance counselor from the Mountain District called me. Someone had given her a copy of the program; she wanted me to know that she found out that I wrote it and found the first two paragraphs so inspirational that she got permission from their school principal to photocopy it and distribute it their school mailboxes. I was truly touched.

PASSION, PURPOSE AND POSSIBILITIES

When you think about what it is you want to do with your life, ask yourself what makes you come alive. Trust the inner voice in your head; the voice that inspires you, motivates you, and drives you. It is your passion that is resonating to you.

Trust in your passion to guide you to your purpose. Do not stop and ask yourself what the world needs; if you do this, your world just becomes about working at a job that you can't wait to leave at the end of the day. This can leave you unfulfilled and stagnate. But when you couple your passion with your purpose and involve the two in your career choices, it will not only have a positive impact on your life, but on your community as well. You create an opportunity to assist in the advancement of our town and cities.

Tonight is an evening to celebrate the young men and women who, at this young age, have started the process of connecting their passion with their purpose. They have worked hard at developing their skills and gaining experience in their chosen fields. They have demonstrated that they have what it takes to become leaders in society. They will be better off for following this path and more importantly, the people and the communities with whom they work will benefit from their insight.

We are extremely proud to showcase their accomplishments and we hope they never lose sight of their passion. Simply by doing what you are passionate about leads to the potential for success and happiness in life, something that is beyond measure. The possibilities for a rewarding future are endless.

Congratulations to all of the honorees and their families.

MAY 27, 2006
The end of the year school party wasn't a big blowout like it normally is. It rained most of the day yesterday so we just had a DJ in the cafeteria and some teachers had movies in their rooms. Everyone is packing up their rooms for the summer. Edmonson wants us to have everything packed up

by the last day of school. I asked my niece Jo to come by and help me pack up because of the continued pain in my shoulder. She said she would be glad to help me out. Lots of teachers have had people come in to help them in the past with things. I was counting the minutes till she got there so I could actually get something done. I am very limited in how much I can use my arm and shoulder. I don't have a lot of mobility. Life has become a series of doctor appointments, physical therapy and chiropractor visits. It is very draining.

Jo was supposed to come around 11:00. When she got there, Edmonson was standing in the front hall as usual. When he heard she was there to help me he wouldn't let her sign in. He told her she had to leave because he couldn't allow visitors in the school on party day. He also wouldn't let her call my room to tell me that she had to leave. I just happened to be on my way to the restroom and ran into her upstairs. I had been wondering where she was. I don't know how to describe what I was feeling. Obviously I was upset; more so because she felt humiliated and that she had let me down. I didn't want to upset her more so I hugged her, thanked her for coming and told her just to go ahead home and I would deal with the room.

How strongly can I say this? EDMONSON IS AN ASS AND A LIAR! There were *many, many, many* visitors in the building yesterday. They were all given visitor passes except for Jo. She said Edmonson had talked down to her and even had the gall to talk very slowly like she was stupid. I have seen him do it to students before and it is disgusting. The thought of him doing it to Jo makes my blood boil. She is one of the brightest and most beautiful young women I know. She is also a very physically strong person. Boy do I wish I had her strength! I bet if she smacked him on the head he would have gone down through the floor tile. I like the image of that in my head. It plays out like a cartoon. Down, down through the earth to a place that he would never been seen from again. I wish I could have that dream every night.

Edmonson conveniently wasn't available for me to talk to after Jo left so I immediately wrote him a letter and took it to the office and asked that it be given it to him right away because I was so upset about the situation. Messing with me is bad enough but when you deliberately try to hurt someone I love or try to make them look like an idiot it's worse than doing something to me. He crossed a line today. I will never forget this and I will never be able to forgive him. I always tell everyone that forgiveness frees the forgiver but I don't think I will ever be able to forgive him. So how am I ever going to be free of him?

At the end of the day I was signing out and he walked past me not saying a word. He went out the office door and then came back in. He walked over to me, grabbed my arm, squeezed it hard and said that he was very hurt by my letter. He said I should know better; that he wasn't like that. I couldn't keep it in. I said, **No**! I did not know that he was not like that. In fact I thought he was exactly like that and I thought he did it just because it was me she was coming to help. He just kept saying how could you hurt me like that, how could you hurt me like that? Is he off his rocker? I pulled my arm out of his bony grip and left as quickly as I could. I had to leave because I was either going to say something that would get me fired or I was going to cry. I cry when I get very angry. I think my body has to release the anger or I will do something I shouldn't so it comes out in the form of tears. Why did he have to grab my left arm? My shoulder is killing me. I have to do all this packing by myself. He is a tiny, vicious evil man with what seems to be an unbalanced emotional state.

MAY 30, 2006

Edmonson issued a memo today stating that teacher evaluations will be completed in September after he has had an opportunity to review all notes, etc. from the information he has collected throughout the year. I can understand why it would take so long. He had a year to complete a little over twenty evaluations, sarcastically speaking. Things like this enrage me. I would get my head chewed off if I was late on an assignment.

I guess he thinks that he is above the Department of Education regulations. He is supposed to come in to the classroom, do an observation and the evaluation is supposed to be reviewed with the teacher by the end of the school year. He never observed me. The last time I was observed was three years ago by Bart and Edmonson. Edmonson stopped my lesson to tell me that he wasn't getting that warm fuzzy feeling from me. It was so inappropriate and Bart didn't say a thing. I think trying to give anyone a warm fuzzy feeling in the classroom could land me in jail! I think Edmonson is afraid to go into the shops alone and he can't take Peter in with him to do an observation. How can you be a director if you are afraid of the people you are supposed to be directing?

This latest missed deadline doesn't surprise me. Edmonson and Bart have consistently missed deadline after deadline. Some of the missed deadlines have caused the school to be fined but it was just all buried and the board was never told. I wonder if the board or Mancini knows that he hasn't done the evaluations; I wonder if they would even care.

So far nothing has been addressed with the staff over the letter of no confidence that was sent to Mancini. We were hopeful but I have a feeling it is going to get swept under the rug.

Edmonson also asked the PHRC for a month's extension on the Fact Finding Conference. There was no need for the delay; he's just trying to control the situation again. He has the right to request one delay without giving a reason.

I have always told my students to look for the lesson in every situation. If it is not obvious at first, then you need to look deeper. I didn't have to look deep with my PHRC case. I got several big lessons dumped right in my lap. The first thing I learned was how naïve I was. I believed once the school received the joint complaint from the PHRC and the EEOC the harassment at work would stop. It did not. It continued heavily at work and it spread to my home. There were so many nasty phone calls made to my mother about me and gun fire outside of my home. It was annoying when my mailbox, post and all was stolen but it was terrifying when my front yard was set on fire. I think that Edmonson stayed awake at night strategizing ways to make me look like a paranoid woman who was just coming unglued.

JULY 30, 2006

We had the Fact Finding Conference with the PHRC two weeks ago. I learned another lesson when I saw the responses that Edmonson had submitted to the PHRC. It was a real eye opener into Edmonson's true character or lack of it. I really thought that he would actually be afraid to lie to a state/federal official. I guess he thought because he didn't bother to show up at the conference and just sent in paperwork that he could lie or talk in circles all he wanted. He kept repeating comments like, "We did all we could," "Our hands were tied," or my personal favorite, "I don't remember saying that but if I did I misunderstood your question or comment." I like that one the best because it was actually a line I gave him. A former boss used that line and I thought it was genius. Used properly it can get you out of any situation. Edmonson apparently thought he would test that theory.

Things seemed to go really well. Edmonson sent copies of Pierce's and Rick's interview transcripts about the assault. The funny thing is that neither gave their permission to be recorded but Edmonson had someone take dictation and then transcribe everything that was said. Isn't that really the same thing as recording the interview? In the transcripts Pierce said that he didn't do it, then he didn't remember doing it and finally he said well, if he did it then he didn't mean to do it. Denny Kirkward, the PHRC Rep assured me that based on all of the information everything would be made right. When you file a complaint with the PHRC they ask you what you are looking for in the way of a resolution to the problem. I was not asking for money. I asked that harassment training be held for the staff, consequences be established for violating the harassment policy and that I would be able to work in a safe, hostile free work environment. Kirkwood said he was going to make calls and see about a lateral transfer to one of the sending districts so I would be in a safer environment. I really don't want to leave Penn but it would be a good thing to get out of a potentially dangerous situation. He said I should hear something formal in the next six weeks. I had taken my mother to the PHRC hearing. After all she has gone through all of this with me. She seemed so happy. It was nice to see her smiling so big. We drove home feeling on top of the world. We stopped for lunch and could not stop smiling. We smiled so hard that my face hurt. Life was going to get better. I was somehow going to be able to work in peace.

AUGUST 1, 2006
Well, I gave it a shot. My mother and I discussed it and even though I love the students at Penn we agreed that I needed to try and remove myself from a dangerous situation for Alonna's sake as well as my own. She said that if I was proactive it might help speed things along with the PHRC/EEOC transfer. There was a position open at The Unity District so I applied for the job. I realized I may have to take a cut in pay until the PHRC stepped in but I want to be around to watch Alonna grow up and although some people may feel I am being dramatic, I am actually that afraid that something really bad might happen to me if I stay. The month after I graduated from Washington University I subbed for Unity and I taught summer school for them over the past several years. I have worked

in their Life Skills classroom before and I found it to be a very rewarding experience. The Life Skills position was the one that was open. It would be a perfect job for me.

I was very excited when Mancini's assistant called to schedule an interview. I don't know why I even bother to get excited about anything anymore. My interview lasted for under ten minutes. I don't know how to describe what kind of an interview it really was; if you can call it that. Most of the board members looked like they were bored. One board member actually fell asleep and not one of them asked me any questions. None at all! I thought an interview was an exchange of information through a question and answer process and if all goes well it should just seem more like a conversation. Bryson did ask me a few questions. Nothing, however, that would give anyone insight into my background or skill level. Bryson was very snippy and in my opinion the board members were very, very rude. They never gave me a chance to talk about my background or discuss my references. I had put effort into the process. I sent in a huge portfolio to Mancini but I don't even know if any of the board members ever saw it. My portfolio wasn't there. All they had was a copy of my resume which they never even glanced at.

I can't help but wonder if the rose incident with Bryson had anything to do with the way the interview went. The Unity District typically relies on what Bryson's recommendations are. Bryson is good friends with Dan Gathey who also works for Unity. They are an unlikely pair of friends. Mancini always has his jet black hair and eyebrows perfectly groomed and his suits tailor made. Gathey looks more like a much older version of the original Spanky from the Little Rascals. Gathey spends a lot of time in the local bars and likes to talk. He seems to have a need to feel important. He told dozens of people I would never be hired at Unity because of all the trouble I had caused at Penn. I don't know why I was surprised but I was. I am a good teacher; I had subbed for Unity but that was under the former, female superintendent, and I taught summer school but the principals in each of the buildings chose their own staff so it all came down to Bryson's recommendation which I obviously didn't have.

Did Bryson tell people I caused trouble because he felt rejected and wanted to pay me back? He can't possibly believe that I caused any trouble. I was the victim. I asked for help and I was ignored. What am I supposed to do? I feel trapped. I have to provide for my daughter. Needless to say I did not get the job. Unity hired a young woman who had just graduated six months ago. I heard she cried at her interview while she told a story of how teaching the severely disabled was her lifelong dream. She had no teaching experience but felt she had enough enthusiasm to make up for that. That might make a more cynical person wonder what she had experience in. Am I becoming a more cynical person? Or am I finally seeing the system for what it truly is?

AUGUST 10, 2006

How does the saying go about counting your chickens before they are hatched? Yes, I left the PHRC Fact Finding Conference feeling on top of the world, but, wait for it. I got a form letter from them; being overloaded the PHRC made an administrative move. They passed the case along. Final Conclusion: Harassment – Possibly/Unknown. The PHRC has now washed their hands of the situation but left the door open for me to pursue it at the next level. This means there is no lateral transfer coming and I have no choice but to return to Penn for the upcoming school year if I want to be able to support my child. I met with Garcia and the next step was to file a civil lawsuit. I was left with no other options. If I don't file a lawsuit than I know deep inside that the harassment at Penn will continue and things will get very, very ugly. To file the federal lawsuit we just have to wait for the confirmation opinion letter from the EEOC. It could come in a week; it could come in six months. There is no way to tell. It just has to get to us before the end of August of next year. I can't believe this. We may have to wait a whole extra year to receive one little piece of paper. But it is a very important piece of paper. It gives us the right to file the lawsuit in federal court, not just on a state level. I pray that I can hang on for another year.

AUGUST 14, 2006

It appears I am still on the federal funds email list. I got an email from Harrisburg that said the federal grant had not been submitted yet. Look at the date; August 14th! Nikki should have submitted the grant last month. What happened to Bart telling me that he wanted the performance report submitted by August 1st and Edmonson telling me that he would be freaking on me if he was in charge instead of Bart. The performance report gets submitted *after* the grant is done so I doubt that the performance report was submitted on August 1st. Is Nikki going to get a letter of reprimand in her personnel file? Probably not. Hmmm. I wonder if he just got freaky with her instead. Oh my! What a visual; I think I might vomit!

AUGUST 15, 2006

Unity made a very wise decision hiring the young woman for the special education job and not me. Yes, I am just being a smart ass here! A job came open in a regular education classroom in their district before school started due to a last minute retirement. She called Bryson to see if she could bump out of her job into the regular ed classroom. I could see that they hired her because of her lifelong dream to work with special needs students. The board flipped. They are talking about putting a new clause into the next contract that locks you into staying in special ed for three years if you are hired in that position. Needless to say she was not allowed to bump out. Until she steps into the classroom she technically is not covered under the contract. I don't know who I feel worse for, me or the students. I do feel happy for Charlotte though. She is getting away from Penn. Unity hired her for the regular education position that the crier wanted. I am going to miss her very much. I know everyone says that they will always stay in touch but life gets in the way. I hope she knows that I will always be around if she needs me for anything.

AUGUST 17, 2006

The new school year is going to be starting soon. I sent a letter to Edmonson, the superintendents and the board today asking for a safe and hostile free working environment. I don't want to go to school and be assaulted on the first or second day again. I am still hoping that someone will do something to make the working conditions at Penn safe. I gave them all my contact information so they could call me and talk about the situation. I am hoping that I will hear from someone on the board.

AUGUST 18, 2006

Lonnie called me today. She used to be the assistant in Brian's shop until the big layoff. She told me she had gone in last week to see Edmonson. She was applying for the new position of Student Recruiter. As a furloughed employee who had worked at Penn for eight years you would think she would be valued. She knows all the programs, is very personable and would have made an excellent recruiter. While Lonnie was talking to Edmonson she asked him what he had to do to get where he was. His reply was cold and matter of fact, "It's not what you know. It's who you know. It just takes a little bit of cash and a little know bit of know how." I don't know about his know how, but I think the cash part would explain a lot of things. I don't understand how the whole exchange of money thing happens. How could someone have the gall to offer money for a job? It's not the first time I've heard of that happening around here. I hear $10,000 has been a going rate for some jobs. Is it true? I don't know, but why would you say it if it wasn't true. I guess I am stuck where I am for the time being. I don't have that kind of money to buy a job somewhere else and I am not having sex with any of these people. I think I would rather lick a toilet bowl.

AUGUST 24, 2006

Another year; another nightmare. Paulie gave a rather mundane presentation to the staff about how to complete a seven step justification for purchase orders. Of course he had his coffee cup in his hand. Pierce just sat there reading the newspaper. How rude! Edmonson did not say a word to him. I believe I'm not the only one who is afraid of Pierce. I think Edmonson is a scaredy cat too.

I was in shock as to what was said next. Pat Simon told the staff, with Edmonson sitting there nodding his head, that the school's Middle States approval plan was one year late and that Edmonson was requesting an additional year's extension. To top things off, the extension letter was due on June 2, 2006. Pat proudly told everyone he sent the extension letter by FedEx on June 1, 2006. That is just a bunch of bullshit. I couldn't believe my ears. It was a year late and Edmonson is asking for another year to get it done. It was almost like Edmonson was taunting me as he sat there nodding and smiling at me. What a bastard.

Edmonson took over the conversation then and really started rambling. He wasn't making any sense at all. I don't know how the thoughts were organized in his head but they just spilled out of his mouth without any sense of rhyme or reason. He talked about placing an emphasis on *health* this year. Health in general? The Health program here? My health? His health? He also talked about getting out more into the community and to the schools to talk to students and answer their questions before they come here. Isn't that what he wouldn't let me, Charlotte and Amy do last year? He did say that last year Pierce and Stacey Smith went to one of the elementary schools to talk to a group of fifth grade students and he praised them for how well they represented Penn. He never mentioned any of the work that Miranda had done. Pierce was still reading the paper and didn't bother to look up. I guess when you are too cool for school you don't have to look up.

Edmonson also told us about a *top secret* study to have a $25 million dollar county, comprehensive tech school. He said he couldn't talk about any of the details and the information wasn't to leave the room. Then out of the blue he said, "Are we our brother's keepers? I don't know." Where did that come from? Was he talking about me? He said he had to spoon feed the superintendents and the board information because it's hard for them to comprehend things. Wow! Did he just call the superintendents and the board members stupid?

August 25, 2006

Mike Greene is the River District bus driver and also does work around Penn. When I saw him, he looked surprised and asked me what I was doing at school? What did he mean? He said Nikki was telling everyone that I wouldn't be back for the school year under any circumstances. Did she get that feeling from pillow talk? Was Pierce that sure he had scared me enough that I would just leave? I guess it is a good thing that my blood pressure runs on the low side so when I get aggravated, which happens a lot with Edmonson and some of his groupies at the school like Nikki, my blood pressure rises up; sometimes more than it should though.

Toward the end of the day Edmonson found himself trapped with questions from the staff that he had a hard time answering. I guess he didn't know what to do so he just said the first thing that popped in his head. He said just last week he was at his parents' home where he is now staying and he had to use the restroom. He sat down on the toilet and when he went to get up found that he was stuck to the seat because his father had varnished the toilet seat. He was very animated as he told us how he tried and tried to pull away from the seat and in the process he lost a lot of skin and hair. He said he is still a little sore but he was able to take care of his wounds without going to the hospital. That was just one disgusting story. It couldn't possibly be true. Wouldn't you need to go to the hospital after something like that? But I guess if you don't have to go to the hospital for hawk talons embedded in your head then you don't need to go to the hospital for a de-skinned ass. Oh my stars; please get that vision out of my head!

The room was stone silent for the longest time. Finally Sam tried to get him back on track and asked if we were going to get a guidance counselor. Miranda had resigned. I am sad for us but happy for her. Just as she had reached her breaking point she had a wonderful opportunity to join Administration at another Vo-Tech. Man do I wish I could go with her.

Edmonson said that Holly had called and begged to come back to Penn to take Miranda's job but he told her he was revamping the position so it would be a 12 month position. I don't know if he talked to Holly but it would have been a great asset for the school to get her back.

Edmonson closed the day by saying that he had run into a set of parents in Ohio when he was on vacation this summer and they told him what a difference Pierce and Stacey had made in the lives of their children. Come on? What are the odds of a sister and brother in Stacey and Pierce's shop and Edmonson running into the parents in Ohio and striking up a conversation? I don't buy it. Then he started to cry, clenched his fist to his heart, and in a broken voice said, "And they have made an impact on me." Exit—stage left!!!!!! I don't think he could have flown out of the room any faster. Has he absolutely lost his mind? What kind of a school year is this going to be?

AUGUST 28, 2006

Miranda appeared before the Penn Operating Board in Executive Session at the August JOC meeting. She wanted to talk to the Board openly since she was no longer an employee. She talked to them for twenty minutes. She told me they all just sat there looking at her not saying a word; not caring. She told the Board that if they had questions about the truthfulness of her remarks that they could talk to any of the teachers still working at Penn. She told the board that many of the teachers were afraid to come forward because they didn't want to jeopardize their jobs but if they were approached by the board they would tell the truth. They all still sat there like rocks. They didn't even thank her for her twenty years of service to Penn.

I don't understand it. If you run for an elected position such as school board, then shouldn't you care about what happens in the school? Is it just a power trip for them? Does it have something to do with the kick back situation everyone keeps talking about? Seriously, I want to know. I have always had a hard time believing things like that happened but I am beginning to change my mind. What other reason could there be for their lack of concern?

AUGUST 30, 2006

Edmonson made a crack today about the fact that I am not doing my fair share of work at Penn. The special ed staff is down to just me and Amy and we sat down together and divided up the shops. We didn't just look at the number of shops; we looked how many students in each shop would need our help. We split the shops based on student numbers and the size of the districts. I'm trying to let comments like that roll off of my back but it's hard when he keeps implying I'm not doing my job or I'm doing less than I should. I work very hard. I don't stand in the front hall all day. I have the feeling that this school year is going to be one of my difficult years here yet. Edmonson also would have received the PHRC findings and he would look at it like he won. He won't see any further than that piece of paper. He won't think that there is a possibility that it can still go to trial. He is an idiot.

SEPTEMBER 6, 2006
Nikki used to walk every day during her lunch time last year. This year she has started walking during the school day. She will take a couple of students walking with her a few laps around the building. She says it is part of the health effort that Edmonson was talking about. Nobody says anything to her about this and it doesn't affect my job performance, but the amount of time involved is enormous. She changes into a track suit before she goes walking, walks for twenty or thirty minutes and then changes back into her working clothes. I'd like to see what would be said to me if I changed my clothes and went walking during the work day. Walking is a great way to exercise but we only have a 30 minute lunch. She is taking her lunch as scheduled, plus twice that time for her daily walk. I will say that she has lost weight but does that mean her skirts have to get shorter and her clothes tighter? I don't want to see that. From what I have heard, I don't think anyone does.

SEPTEMBER 7, 2006
We had a teacher's meeting after school today. Edmonson was talking about releasing a Department of Education report to the staff, but he made the comment, "It's public information, but sometimes you just don't want the public to know. They can see something and make an issue of it. Why bring it up if you are not going to show it to anyone? He makes less and less sense as each day passes.

Jim asked what we were supposed to do about students who had problems and needed to see a counselor. Edmonson said he was a counselor and he would see the students. We should refer students with problems to Lindsay our office manager to make an appointment to see him. Why don't we just send them to the front hall? They would be more apt to run into him there. Personally I would be afraid to send a student to him for counseling.

Edmonson also distributed a list of committees that he put together for the 2006-07 school year. It boggles my mind that not only does Edmonson continue to reward Pierce and Nikki with conference getaways that they never have to report on, he has now made Pierce and Nikki Co-chairs to oversee all of the committees. Of course they will both get an additional $2,000.00 stipend for their extra effort.

SEPTEMBER 9, 2006
I received a letter today from the Unity District that I was not selected as a volunteer for the Local Tax Study Commission. There was to be a cross section of taxpayers chosen to represent the Tax Study Commission and I live in the Unity District. I was not contacted to discuss the commission; I was just rejected. I don't think Unity likes me very much. Or would that be Bryson? I don't get it. You try to be a good citizen and volunteer for a project and get rejected. I'm going to try and not let it bother me but I know it will.

SEPTEMBER 14, 2006
Jim made another request to Edmonson to receive minutes from the board meetings and attachments. He said Edmonson has been ignoring his requests for the information for almost a year. I told Jim it reminded me that before Bart left he advised Edmonson to never give information to anyone until they ask several times and then only give them the bare minimum of information. Bart said that if you give people too much information they will start asking questions. I guess that he has taken that advice to heart because Edmonson won't give up any information without a fight. It is at times so much more than ridiculous. I understand his frustration. I have to fight to get copies of discipline write ups for the students so I know if they have any behavior problems when I got to an Education Plan meeting at the home schools. I think Edmonson wants me to look incompetent at the meetings.

SEPTEMBER 25, 2006
Edmonson made the decision, without interviews or board approval, to appoint Nikki as Head Teacher and be in charge of the building in his absence. She now has three or four extra duties that she gets paid stipends for. There were five other people who submitted letters of interest for the

position, but were not interviewed, nor informed of his decision. Jim later told me that Edmonson said Nikki would be appointed because she has what it takes. I don't even want to think about what he really meant.

Edmonson also took the Information Technology Coordinator position away from Patty, our IT teacher, and gave the extra duty to Peter, our Security Guard, and increased the stipend. This means that Peter now has access to our computer passwords. Will Edmonson plant unauthorized information on our computers; or just my computer? Peter seems to be Edmonson's top groupie. The majority of the staff thinks that Peter would do anything that Edmonson asked him to do. I'm sure he would be well compensated. I used to trust everyone, know I find myself wondering if there are that many people who are honest.

Betty Rolla stopped down to talk to Amy this afternoon. She was very upset. A student in her program had deliberately slammed into her while she was bent down at the snack machine. Betty fell forward and to the left and she received quite a jolt. She told Amy that the girl went running to Edmonson and said Ms. Rolla was going to try and get her in trouble but she didn't mean to do it. Edmonson put his arm around her and told her that he knew she didn't mean to do whatever it was; she just wasn't that kind of a girl. After Mrs. Rolla pushed the issue, the girl received a two day in-school suspension, which is exactly what the girl suggested she should receive. This is a bad sign. Students learn from example. When you let teachers get away with assault it is a natural next step for students to think they can get away with assault as well.

Daniels told me that Edmonson instructed Brenda to find out what information he wanted from the board packets and charge the union .10 per page for making copies. This is just part of his big stall tactic. He knows the union president is supposed to get a copy of the board packet prior to each monthly meeting. Edmonson is very good at putting off giving people what they request. But if he asks you for something, no matter how ridiculous or how complicated, you better get it up to him right away or he gets really upset.

SEPTEMBER 26, 2006
It is starting to get cold early this year and my room still has no heat. I have been filling out maintenance requests for several years to check my heating system. I had made a notation on every form that I do not have any heat in

my room. Sometimes it gets so cold in the room it is almost unbearable. I have actually had to wear a coat on some days and I brought a blanket to put across my lap or wrap around me. This room can be absolutely freezing and the little heaters don't seem to do much to help the problem. Isn't it funny that it's just my room that has had this problem for six years?

OCTOBER 1, 2006

I have heat in my room! Cory, our new HVAC teacher, gave me heat. I cannot thank him enough. He told me that the office gave him a hard time about ordering supplies he needed because he didn't submit the purchase order thru email. Cory doesn't know a lot about computers and there hasn't been proper PO training. He had handwritten the purchase order before. He didn't understand why this time it was a problem. I could tell him why; it's because it is heat for my room. I found out later that Cory ended up buying the supplies himself. I hope the office reimburses him. If they don't I need to pay him for what he spent. He is a very nice man. We are lucky to have him at Penn.

SEPTEMBER 27, 2006

During the union meeting today I made a motion to become a sponsor of the National Park Association for $100.00. The motion was seconded. Pierce wanted to ask a question on the motion. In a very hostile voice he said, "What do we get out of it?" I explained that it was an opportunity to make a lot of good political contacts. And as Public Relations Chair for the union I am always looking for ways to highlight the school and our union in a positive way. He became very argumentative, but a vote was taken and the motion passed.

Later in the meeting Pierce brought up the fact that the Agenda was not done according to Roberts' Rules. Jim Daniels said he had been using the same agenda format that Pierce did when he was president. Pierce picked up the information I had given out on the National Park Association and said to use an example, I had not properly placed the information on the agenda and the information should have been skipped over, then he threw it across the room. He went on for over five minutes about "Maria's motion." When Pierce was president he spent over $300.00 on lunch for the union without a vote but he doesn't want to support the National Parks. I got the feeling he was trying to goad me into a fight but I kept my mouth shut. I was afraid that he would either start throwing things at me or hit me again.

OCTOBER 3, 2006

Edmonson told me the Unity School District thinks I am incompetent but he wouldn't give me a reason why. I am really upset. I have always done more than what is required of me. I take tremendous pride in the work I do. I don't know whether to believe him or not, but just in case I emailed one of the administrators at Unity. I'd really like to talk to him but I'm not going to hold my breath. It seems like Edmonson can lie about anything he wants to and no one cares.

OCTOBER 5, 2006

There was a staff meeting today. They are becoming more frequent and more pointless. Edmonson told the staff, "I got a call **at home** from a former, furloughed employee who said, *Why didn't you hire me. I was disappointed because I was qualified.*" He said they are getting misinformation. He said whoever is giving out the information to please stop it. He said it's very disheartening when you've worked hard all day and you get someone calling with misinformation. He said, "Get the facts. Call me. They were not qualified."

He never took his eyes off me. Boy, if looks could kill I would have been chopped up into little bits. Yes, a job was posted for the Math Academy. Yes, I told Andie about the job. Yes, she called Edmonson but he wasn't in his office so she left him a message. He emailed her and gave her his cell number to call him back. How was she supposed to know that he was at home when she called his cell? During his conversation with Andie he told her that there were people talking who did not know "their ass from a hole in the ground….and if it's Maria who is telling you, then she doesn't know what she is talking about and she has no right to discuss any open positions with you." She is a furloughed employee. Doesn't she have the right to inquire about an open position she is qualified for? He doesn't care about anyone's rights!

OCTOBER 13, 2006

I put in a purchase request for supplies, which included a flashdrive and a planner with a simple PDA. I work on school business and I had plenty of money in my department budget. It was a justifiable expense. My PO was denied. When I called Paulie about the rejected PO he told me he was sure I could just find a calendar at the 99 cent store. I know that everyone needs to tighten their belts but these were items that would make my program run more efficiently. It wouldn't bother me so much that I was denied these items if Paulie hadn't gotten an entire office filled with Cherry furniture. That was an outrageous expense! Some of the staff refers to him as *Cherrywood*. Administration has no problem spending money on themselves but not on school programs. It isn't right.

OCTOBER 16, 2006

Nikki was acting as head teacher last week and she said she smelled a gas odor in the building. She had the gas company come to the school to check it out. She told them it was an emergency and she called 911 to have the gas company escorted with a fire truck; sirens and all! The next day Edmonson told Jim the gas company said it had simply been fumes from an engine running in the Diesel shop. He told Jim that he was not to turn on any engines without first notifying the office that he would be doing so. This didn't make any sense. Working on engines is an ongoing event. Kevin Klein was going to meet with Edmonson about this ridiculous rule. I am glad for Jim that someone from Regional will step up and help him but I've never been able to get any help from them when I've had a problem at school unless it involves other people as well. I don't understand why they don't want to help me. In my opinion Nikki really overreacted. There is no doubt in my mind that Nikki would just make an absolutely wonderful administrator! Her intellect ranks right up there with Edmonson.

OCTOBER 22, 2006

During the October Operating Committee meeting, another fifty polices were approved for addition into the school's policy manual. One of the board members asked Edmonson if he went over the policies with the teachers and staff. Edmonson said that there was a continual review of all the policies with the staff. There is no other way to say this—this was an out and out lie. He has never gone over any policies with us. I have no idea what any of the policies are in the policy manual. I may have seen some of them but I would have no way of knowing. Shouldn't we have to sign something saying that we have reviewed them? How did we end up with over five hundred policies? I wonder what they say.

OCTOBER 23, 2006

Our Fall Open House is coming up in a couple of weeks. All the teachers received full color flyers to post in their rooms and around the community. The flyers cost $1.00 each. Edmonson had 500 flyers printed. He also had 100 full color posters printed. The flashdrive and planner that I was wanted cost less than $100.00. Maybe I should have asked Wanda to put in the order for me. She doesn't seem to have any problem getting anything she wants.

October 24, 2006

The only little bit of security I had for my car was taken away. Stan told me Edmonson said I was no longer allowed to park in the area with the cameras. I know exactly why he is doing this. Edmonson is a car freak. He has an interest in a used car business. He buys flashy cars, drives them for a little while and then sells them. I have never had what he would consider being a car of his standards. Well, last week my car broke down. My brother loaned me an old van that he had. It may be old but it ran great. I drove it to school for a few days and parked where I had been parking, right next to Dr. Edmonson. I imagine that seeing the old van next to his flashy car of the week sent him into a tail spin.

I called Edmonson to ask him about it but got his voice mail. He sent me an email instead of calling me back. He said according to the security tapes there was no proof of my allegations regarding damage to my car. How do I know this is true? I haven't been allowed to see any of the tapes. I don't believe they watched them at all. Peter told me that you had to watch the tapes in *real time* using the special machine at school. He said there are many cameras that capture different views of an area and to watch all the tapes, even of one area, would take many man hours. So when did anyone sit down and watch the tapes?

October 25, 2006

At this month's union meeting, Nikki felt the need to try and stir up trouble again. Out of the blue she said she could not understand why anyone would allow themselves to be audio taped. Someone asked if that ever happened? She said, "Well, there was an incident last year." Seriously; *an incident last year.* Why does she really feel she needs to bring up something that happened a year ago?

I said it was regarding the incident where I had been injured and everyone who was spoken to was asked if they could be audio taped. I also said those who did not want to be audio taped were aware that Edmonson's secretary, Brenda, was taking shorthand during the interviews in essence to record the conversations on paper. The conversations were transcribed and were entered as evidence into the PHRC claim.

Nikki crossed her arms real tight, curled up her nose and threw her head back as she said she thought the whole thing was ridiculous. That has become her signature move. I did not respond to her. I didn't know what the hell she was talking about. What was ridiculous? The tape recordings? The assault? How ridiculous would it have been if she would have been assaulted? What I don't understand is why would she bring this up after a year? I guess she couldn't think of anything else to bring up and since she is joining forces with Pierce to try and make me uncomfortable she had to say something. She has after all joined with him in every other way.

OCTOBER 26, 2006
Tracy, a former Penn student, came back to visit. A lot of grads do. She stopped to see me. She said she was really upset because Pierce had just accused her of stealing a brochure from his desk last year and giving it to me. Tracy had no idea what he was talking about. The students in Pierce's shop told her that I was trying to blackmail him, and was looking for any information I could get to try to get him in trouble. What the hell is wrong with Nikki and Pierce? Did they both just fall into a time warp? Why are they bringing things up from a year ago? And what is Pierce doing telling students I am trying to blackmail him. No matter what Pierce has done to me I have never said anything about him to any of the students. This man has no sense of decency.

NOVEMBER 3, 2006
Checking the mail every day has become an experience that gets my emotions all wound up. It has been months and there still has not been any word from the EEOC. There is just nothing I can do but hang on and wait for that letter and try to keep the faith!

Jake Myers is coming to work at Penn with me and Amy. Edmonson told Amy he is sure that Jake will be assuming a great leadership role at Penn. Why? Because he is a man? I do not know Jake but Amy says he is a nice guy. He is married to her best friend. It will be good to have another person in the department. We will finally be able to give the students more individual attention.

NOVEMBER 6, 2006
Amy and I went to the office to sign out and look for Jake. His first day was today and he should have signed in by this time. Lindsay said he was in the back with Edmonson, Peter and Chuck. She went back to Edmonson's

office to get him. He came out fifteen minutes later. We had to be at the IA by 8:30 a.m. It takes a good 40 minutes to get there. We didn't have any time to waste. I hate to walk in late to meetings. I introduced myself as we were heading out the door.

Jake said Edmonson was angry that he was going to the training today. Edmonson was the one that signed us up for it though. How can he not remember what decisions he makes? He is becoming more and more forgetful. I don't mean for this to come out as just a wise crack, but I seriously think something is wrong with him, aside from the whole pathological liar issue. He doesn't seem to be able to focus on things and he has been forgetting basic things like people's name even when the people are in the same room with him.

While we were waiting for the training to begin Jake told me and Amy that Edmonson told him this morning that he wanted him to be the department head. He told Jake that I liked to think I was in charge but I didn't know what I was doing and that if someone with some intelligence didn't take over, the school could be ruined. What a liar! What a drama queen.

Jake does seem like a very nice person and I feel bad he was placed in an awkward situation with Edmonson. But it doesn't surprise me. It is a classic Edmonson move to try and poison the minds of his new hires.

NOVEMBER 7, 2006

There were no students today. It was a teacher's in-service day. Pat came up to talk to me after the morning session. Edmonson stopped by his room yesterday with a Behavior Chart for a student. He said the chart needed to be completed every day and turned into him. Pat was not sure how he was supposed to fill it out. The chart was for a Mountain District student. I was surprised that the Case Manager bypassed me since I am the liaison for the district and I thought we had a pretty good working relationship. I told Pat I would check into and get back to him. I left a message for Ted Zemko, the Case Manager and he called me back within an hour. Ted has been teaching for over 20 years and he is one of the most organized people I know. Not only that; he does everything by the book. He told me that he had mailed the information, first class mail, to me. He even had a note in the file on which day he mailed it. That was over a month ago. It does not take a month for the mail to make its way across town. Ted wondered why he hadn't heard from me. I wanted to tell him it was because Edmonson is an ass, but I was raised better than to bad mouth my boss like that no matter how much he deserves it. I told Ted that the chart was misplaced internally. The chart was supposed to be filled everyday for a week and then mailed back to him so he could write a behavior plan for the student. Ted also said he had mailed another chart for another student about a week after the first one. Damn! It sounded bad to tell him that the second form had also been misplaced internally. I just told him I would get things straightened out. I checked with Tyler, the other student's instructor, to see if he had received anything to fill out from Edmonson. Tyler said he had received something in his mailbox from Edmonson, but he didn't know how he was supposed to fill it out or what he was supposed to do with it when it was done. There was just a blank form in his mailbox with the student's name. It's going to take another week to get the information to Ted that he needed almost a month ago. Damn Edmonson!

I feel so violated. What gives him the right to take my mail and open it? I don't even open Alonna's mail at home or read notes from her friends. I have no idea what else he has taken from me. I think a man who steals a woman's mail is capable of doing anything. It seems like he was trying to sabotage my relationship with Ted Zemko by taking my mail and holding onto it for a month. Did he think I wouldn't find out? By the way, is it legal for him to open and keep mail that is addressed to me? I will have to check into that.

During the afternoon session, Edmonson announced that Hank is taking a medical leave for the rest of the year and then will retire. Then he pointed at me and said although I had approached him and volunteered to take over the Work Release job, he was pleased to announce that as of the previous Friday, Nikki had obtained an Emergency Certification for the position and she would be taking over immediately. He said he will just get a substitute to fill in for her. He pointed at me again and said he was sorry he couldn't give "the other woman" the job but he had to go with the most qualified person. My blood began to boil. First of all, I never wanted the job or asked him for the job. Secondly, I am not saying that Nikki isn't capable of doing the job but when Edmonson pointed that bony little finger at me so people would think I wanted the job and I would look like an ass it just made me want to snap it off like a twig and poke it in Nikki's eye.

Not to toot my own horn, but I think I will... my business background could easily kick Nikki's butt. She is a nurse. I have great admiration for nurses but nursing and business are two entirely different things. Before I became a teacher I learned every area of business and worked my way up the ladder. I had been a secretary, and a fiscal assistant, and a sales rep for a large manufacturing company and dealt with major companies all over the east coast. I became the marketing manager for a large cable company and supervised a staff of twenty-five in my department. I had free reign to hire and fire. I served on many county committees and negotiated million dollar deals on a regular basis. I was great in the business world. I think I inherited a strong business sense from my father. In college my Business Law professor said I knew more about business than he did. I definitely know more about business than Nikki and Edmonson combined! I just have to try and let this wash over me and stay focused on the fact that I never wanted the job. I like what I am doing. It would be so much easier if Edmonson would just stop telling lies.

NOVEMBER 8, 2006

Why, why, why? Why is Edmonson hell bent on showing me that he can make life difficult for me? I have spent the last six years as The Mountain District liaison. I have a great rapport with everyone in the district; well, no one could have a good relationship with Kurt, the superintendent. How can you have any kind of a relationship with someone who gives off the impression that the world was meant to revolve around them? It has worked out okay though because I don't have very much contact with him. I don't have to kiss his ring.

When Jake was hired to replace Charlotte he should have just become the Unity District liaison. But today Edmonson had to throw some more upheaval into my life. He left me a voice mail and said he was assigning Jake to the Mountain District because Jake lived in the area and I lived twenty minutes from the school. Plain craziness! We all start our work day at Penn. Where we live should not have anything to do with what district we are assigned to. He said it would be good for the district assignments to change. He did not change Amy's assignment though; he only changed mine. I have no doubt that I can work just as well with the staff at Unity, it just doesn't make any sense to create confusion when there doesn't have to be. Edmonson thrives on chaos and confusion though. Jerk.

NOVEMBER 20, 2006

I got some information from the Post Office. It seems that in a business situation, even though the mail is addressed to me, the person in charge of the facility can open and distribute the mail as he or she sees fit. So once again, even though it is morally and ethically wrong he can get away with it. No wonder people call him Teflon Ed—nothing ever seems to stick to him.

DECEMBER 5, 2006

Today is my 47th birthday. I always wake up in a good mood on my birthday. Somehow this day gives my spirit a renewed sense of hope and a feeling that it is the beginning of a brand new year; a chance to wipe the slate clean and start again with a fresh new outlook on life. I know that most people feel this way on New Year's Day, but for me it has always been my birthday. It was a fantastic morning. I couldn't stop smiling. And then I heard the page for me to report to Edmonson's office immediately. Not today! Not on my birthday! Couldn't I have just one peaceful day at Penn? I guess that would just be too much to hope for. So I headed to the office.

I felt sick when he shut the door. I do not like being alone with him. He said he just wanted to wish me a happy birthday and he then placed a five pound chocolate bar on the desk in front of me. And then another, and another, and another, and another! He did this another five times. I could feel my jaw starting to drop. I felt like I was in a cartoon. And then he said, "Fifty pounds of chocolate for your fiftieth birthday!" He looked so pleased with himself. Now I am not a vain woman, but no one in their right mind tells a woman that he thinks she is fifty unless he is absolutely sure; and then that is not always a great idea. Did he think I was really fifty? And what the hell am I going to do with fifty pounds of chocolate? I told him I didn't quite know what to say. He said I didn't have to say anything; he could tell how excited I was about the chocolate. Then he said that was all he wanted, I could leave. I opened the door and stood there for a minute wondering how I was going to manage to pick up the chocolate. He came around the desk and told me to hold out my arms. He started to pile the chocolate up in my arms for me to carry. Let me tell you what! A dislocated clavicle sternum joint and fifty pounds of chocolate do not go well together. I just hoped to make it out of his office before I dropped them. I was almost out of the door when he called me back. He asked me if I had plans for dinner. Was he just making conversation or was he asking me out to dinner? I couldn't tell. My mind was fixated on the pain that was started to radiate along my shoulder. I told him I was having dinner with my daughter and mother and kept walking.

He must have been asking me out to dinner because that's when evil Geoffrey popped out. His voice changed as he called me back into his office again. He told me that he needed me to put together a month's worth of lesson plans for the Reading Academy program. What? That isn't my job. He had hired Helena Maven as the Resource Instructor; shouldn't she do her own lesson plans? He said he wanted them by the end of the week then he literally pushed me out of the doorway and slammed the door behind me. I made it to the outer office and had to put the chocolate down. There was no way I could carry it all the way to my room. I got a cart from the storage room and loaded up my chocolate bars. It dawned on me as I was walking down the hall just how much money it would cost to buy that much chocolate. Did Edmonson actually pay for it himself? If he did, why would he do that? I couldn't think about it at the moment, I had to go see Helena to find out what was going on with these lesson plans.

Wow! My birthday just went downhill. Helena seems like a nice person but she also seems to be scared. Her fear seems amplified because she is such a petite woman. I am a small woman but I have picked up some extra weight since turning forty. Either I have picked up more weight than I thought or she is just really, really tiny! I felt huge standing next to her. I told her that Edmonson wanted me to write her lesson plans and I didn't understand why. She told me that she had never written lesson plans before and wasn't sure how to do it. Edmonson told her it was a simple job and anyone could do it. He said he would take care of it for her. I asked her how she got through college without writing a lesson plan. Well, she didn't go to school for teaching. Her degree is in Communications. She said Edmonson knew this before she was hired, but he told her not to worry about it. You can't hire someone without a teaching certificate to teach; at least not legally. No wonder Helena seems so afraid; high school students can sense fear and they will eat you up and spit you out. I guess I am going to be writing lesson plans for her; but not today, today is my birthday and I am going out to celebrate with two of my favorite people in the world. I wonder if I would have to write lesson plans for Helena if I would have gone out to dinner with Edmonson?

DECEMBER 12, 2006

Good Lord! Another meaningless teacher's meeting today. I guess Edmonson was feeling the need to show how important he thought he was because he started talking crazier than usual. He proudly told us that he had the superintendents on his side and they loved all of his ideas. He said he had them and the board members eating out of his hands.

He is also either getting very forgetful or is just mean because he then said Hank was going to retire and Nikki would officially be taking over as Work Release Liaison. Then he said, "Sorry Maria, I know how much you wanted the job." Why does he say things like this? I didn't want the job. I think if Nikki wants the job then she should be able to bump into it. Why does he say things like that? Why does he get away with saying things like that? He dropped a file on his way out the door. I was going to leave it there but I thought the right thing to do was to pick it up and drop it off to Lindsay in the front office. When I picked it up I was stunned. Pictures fell out of the folder. They were pictures of me. And they just weren't pictures of me at school. There were pictures of me having dinner with Alonna and my mother for my birthday. And there were pictures of my home and pictures of me getting out of my car at the mall. What! Is he spying on me? I felt violated yet again. What am I supposed to do about this? Who would I even talk to about something like this? What a perv!

DECEMBER 22, 2006

I received a Christmas card from Edmonson. When we're in meetings with other schools and even in front of students he calls me Maria but on a Christmas card he calls me Ms. Martin. Did he send everyone a card? A few years ago when we were in a discipline meeting for a student he told Ted Zemko that he was Jewish and practiced his faith religiously. On the front was a drawing of Santa working on his Naughty and Nice list. The card was signed, "With warmest thoughts, Geoffrey."

Was it a coincidence that I received the card on the same day that the local newspaper published the Santa's Naughty and Nice list? The paper does it do to raise money for a local charity. Someone put my name on the naughty list. They paid to do it. I would have thought maybe it was a friend or relative but Andie's name is also on it. And then there is the card from Edmonson. It was definitely his handwriting. I called the paper and they won't tell me who put it in. Andie is really upset about it. I'm really not thrilled either. I'm probably being a little too sensitive. Oh well. Hope someone got a nice chuckle from the money they spent on adding our names to the Naughty List. I'm going to try and not think of anything connected with Edmonson right now. I'm just going to try and enjoy the Christmas break with my family.

JANUARY 4, 2007

We are almost half way through this school year. There should have been at least one Federal Grant Participatory Planning Committee meeting held so far this year. A minimum of two meetings need to be held each year. It is customary for the special education teachers to be included in the PPC meetings to offer input and so we know where our job focus should be. I have asked Nikki several times about meeting dates but she continues to ignore me. She seems to want to keep everything she is doing with the grant a secret. It sickens me to think that she is handling the money that pays my salary.

JANUARY 10, 2007

I was summoned to a meeting with Edmonson. He wanted me to bring an outline of the work I have done so far this year and a list of what I planned on doing for the remainder of the year. That wouldn't be a problem; I keep really good records. He told me that my presentation of information was perfect like me. He said he was going to give a copy of my information to Jake and Amy so they could use the same format when they had their meetings with him. Why is he being so nice to me? It makes me nervous when he is sweet like maple syrup. After finding the pictures he had of me it actually makes me feel sick. I did give the folder back to Lindsay in the office but I kept all of the pictures. I wonder if he noticed they were missing.

JANUARY 24, 2007

There was an association meeting after school today. There are less and less people that come every month. Our contract is up next year and we need to put together a team to prepare for contract negotiations. The team that was selected was Daniels, Amy, Jeff Snyder, Pierce and me. Nikki had volunteered, but she was not on the list. Pierce started pounding his fist on his chest saying he didn't have a problem with the men on the team but instead of me and Amy they needed people with business experience like the Work Release Coordinator. What a pig! He knows nothing about my background. Could his motives be any more obvious?

JANUARY 25, 2007

Pierce took it upon himself to send an email to the staff today offering guidelines for conducting union elections. They will be coming up in April. Honest to goodness! There are less than thirty union members at Penn. We aren't putting someone in the White House. We don't need his forty-five step procedure. Why does he think anyone cares what he has to say?

JANUARY 26, 2007

Jake Myers had his review meeting today with Edmonson. He didn't share the outline I had done with Jake instead he told Jake that he really didn't need to see anything from him because he knew as Department Head Jake was very busy and probably didn't have time to keep records. Jake is really a team player and he told Edmonson that we all worked hard with the students. Edmonson said he knew that Jake worked hard and that he felt Amy did her fair share but he believed the students just liked to come and hang out with me. That pissed me off. I work as hard as anyone with the students; we don't hang out. And by the way, Jake is not the Department Head. He is my co worker, not my supervisor.

Jake asked me not to say anything because he has not obtained tenure yet in Pennsylvania and he was worried about receiving a bad evaluation if Edmonson got upset with him. I know how vindictive Edmonson can be so I'll just keep my mouth shut. I like Jake and don't want to see him put in a bad situation but I still get filled with a sense of rage when Edmonson bad mouths me like he does. It makes me even sadder that there isn't anything I can do about it at the moment.

JANUARY 27, 2007

I thought for sure we would have a two hour delay yesterday because of the snow but we didn't. The front inside entrance had water all over the floor from the melting snow. I slipped and lost my footing. I hit the ground pretty hard. Peter Griffin came rushing over, reached down and grabbed me by my left arm and jerked me up to my feet. Spasms started shooting up my back into my shoulder and neck. I don't think that is the way you are supposed to help someone up and certainly not on the side where they have a dislocated joint. I felt like I was right back to the pain of the day that Pierce hit me. I sent Edmonson an email and told him I was going to go for follow up medical treatment. I have a feeling I am going to be spending more time in physical therapy. It feels like I just got done with therapy. That was one of the worst parts about getting hit by Pierce; the amount of time it took away from my life going to doctors and physical therapy. There is no easy comeback from an injury like the one I had. The doctors all told me that it was one of the worst possible joints to injury. There is just no way to keep it secure in the socket once it has popped out. I don't think that anyone understands how severe the injury is. I still say that I believe Pierce didn't mean to give me a lifelong injury but he did and I don't think he is the least bit sorry about it.

JANUARY 29, 2007

Today is my second favorite day of the year; it is Alonna's birthday and my birth – day! I can't imagine what my life would be like if she hadn't pulled through when she was a newborn. The two days that she spent in NICU were two of the scariest days of my life. Every birthday she has is a glorious reason to celebrate. We always go shopping together and we each get a new outfit; a new birthday suit! I took a personal day today so we could go shopping during the day. That is the nice thing about Alonna being homeschooled; we can take an occasional weekday to do things and make up school work on the weekends.

JANUARY 30, 2007

I got an email from Pierce today. He sent it to the entire staff. It read: "Mrs. Martin: It has come to my attention that yesterday you tried to devise a scheme by sending me an email suggesting that I chair the election committee for the upcoming Association elections. I find it curious that you thought you could get away with something so thinly veiled. What exactly was your purpose for this course of action except to hopefully eliminate any opportunity for me to run for office as Section 28 of the election guide that I created prohibits the election committee chair from running for office while serving on the committee? Mr. Pierce."

Woooah! Before he decides to try to stir up trouble saying that I sent him an email yesterday he should have checked to see if I was even in the building yesterday. I usually keep my mouth shut about things like this but either Pierce is just trying to cause trouble by sending that half brained email to everyone or I am being set up. Edmonson would have access to my computer password. He could log on to any computer in the building with my code then Peter could give him remote access to my email. It seems like something out of a crime drama but it is very possible. Since Pierce sent the email to everyone in the building, not just everyone in the union,

I thought I had to do something to clear my name. I emailed Pierce and sent a copy to everyone he has sent his email to. I said it must have been someone playing a sick joke because I wasn't even at school yesterday. I could have said a lot more but I just left it at that.

JANUARY 31, 2007

I received another email from Pierce today. Of course he sent a copy of the email to everyone. It read, "Mrs. Martin: Please have your computer checked. I don't receive all of the delightful emails that you send out about me. I have to hear about them second hand." I really don't know what he is talking about. I don't send out any emails about him, delightful or otherwise. I have no intention of responding to an email like this. He just tries to goad me into back and forth banter and he tries to make me angry. I'm not playing his games. I wonder if it really is Edmonson though sending out emails from my account. I would not put it past Edmonson to try and push Pierce so far that he actually snaps and puts me in the hospital.

FEBRUARY 6, 2007

Sometimes you just have to do something to lighten the tension a little bit. We play a game at work to pass the time during some of the outrageous staff meetings we have. The way Edmonson talks in circles you can't really understand what he is saying but he always throws in a few key phrases. We came up with a game called Executive Bingo. You just draw a Tic Tac Toe board then randomly write in some of his favorite sayings. When you hear him say one you put an X through it until you get three in a row and then you have our version of Executive Bingo. Some of his favorites are: Au Contraire, It's Slippery, True Story, Now That's What I'm Talking About, and my favorite, I Will Check Into That. I wonder if Edmonson has any idea how ridiculous he sounds at our meetings? Brian won BINGO today. There are no prizes but it sure does make the meetings much more tolerable.

FEBRUARY 26, 2007

I was off work on Friday because of a doctor's appointment. I had to get two cortisone injections deep into my shoulder joint. Oh my stars! I actually did see stars; those injections hurt! Since I slipped in the front hall and Peter jerked me up my shoulder has become very inflamed. I can't lift my arm over my head or pick up anything heavier than a plate. The doctor said with the combination of the old injury and the new aggravation I could end up with a frozen shoulder to the point where they would have to put me under to be able to manipulate my arm. I am going to try injections first and start another round of intensive therapy and daily exercises at home.

When I came back to school on Monday, Jake and Amy told me Edmonson had a conversation with Jake "in confidence." Edmonson told Jake that he wanted him to come up with an idea for the special education teachers to do that no other vo-tech was doing. Jake asked Edmonson if he would like him to discuss it with me and Amy and kick some ideas around. Edmonson told him No, No, No! He wanted him to come up with something on his own because anything that Edmonson told me to do I would argue about. Jake said he didn't think that was true. Jake is right; it's a big lie. If I am given an order by my boss, not matter how big of an idiot he is, I have to do it or I could get fired. Jake told Edmonson that I knew I was a school employee, he was my boss and I would do what I was told to do. Jake said the same applied to both him and Amy. Edmonson said he knew that about Amy and Jake, but it was not true with me. He told Jake that I was not a team player, I didn't care about the kids or the school, and that I was all I ever thought about. I think Edmonson has me confused with himself.

Jake is still worried that since he does not have tenure, if Edmonson knew he discussed this information with me there would be some type of retaliation against him. Jake is in a tough spot. I want to confront Edmonson but I understand Jake's concern. He has a family to support. It just makes me so angry because I have always done my job very well no matter what was going on with Edmonson or Pierce because I care very deeply about the students. What gives Edmonson the right to try and destroy my reputation? I don't believe that Edmonson has ever cared about anyone in his life. One of the former office staff told me that Edmonson has two children, all local, who he never sees and certainly never talks about. The only reason the existence of the children is known is because he carries them on his school health insurance; not life insurance though. Of course he wouldn't want to share something like that with his children. My heart actually does ache for his children. I'm sure that they have always wondered about him. I hope they are strong enough as they grow up to realize that his lack of feeling doesn't have anything to do with them; for whatever reason he lacks the ability to feel for anyone other than himself. He is going to end up very lonely in his elderly years.

FEBRUARY 28, 2007

During the union meeting today Jim Daniels asked if I would chair the election committee for the upcoming union election. Before I could answer Pierce began to grunt and snicker. I just ignored him. It was a little hard to do though. He sounded like a cross between a sick goat and a dying hyena. We hadn't even settled anything about the election committee when Nikki began complaining that she was not selected to serve on the negotiation team and that as Work Release Coordinator she had valuable expertise in negotiations. PLEASE! Patty said that she felt that if someone wanted to volunteer they probably should be given the opportunity to do so. Pierce cut Patty off and said that while he was president if anyone at anytime wanted to volunteer he embraced them with open arms and let them serve on whatever committee they wanted to volunteer for. I raised my hand to speak and when I was acknowledge by Jim Daniels, the president, I said that when Pierce had formed the last negotiation team, I called him and said that I would like to serve on the team and he told me no, saying he had already selected the team that he wanted. Pierce started to raise his voice very loudly and he said it was not true. He said that he had called me and begged me and begged me to serve on the team and I refused. I know I should have kept my mouth shut but I felt like was going to explode. I said, "Pierce, you are a liar." He reiterated that it was he who called me and again he said that he BEGGED ME to serve on the negotiation team and represent my area and the new people in the building. I said, in a little louder voice, "Pierce, you are a liar!" He said that he was tired of being slandered and being called a tyrant and a dictator and a fornicator and now a liar. I said I had no idea what he was talking about. I don't know who has called him a fornicator. Sure he is a fornicator but I have never called him that. Jim Daniels said that he felt this wasn't the place for this. Patty interjected and said to Jim that if there was some particular reason why Jim felt that Nikki shouldn't serve on the negotiation team maybe he could talk to her one-on-one in private. Jim said that he had already done that. Patty looked very surprised and embarrassed. It seemed like Nikki had prompted her to speak up about her being on the negotiation team. In my opinion, Nikki sets a lot of people up like that.

As far as Pierce calling me, it most certainly is a lie because Andie was sitting next to me when I made the phone call to Pierce about being on the negotiation team. Nikki also made a fuss about me not being able to serve as election chair or any of the negotiation team members being able to serve until the executive committee approved the appointments. It is in the by-laws, I guess, but the stamp by the exec committee has never been done for committees. When Jim said that he was just following past practice and if he made a mistake it could be corrected. Pierce started raising his voice wanting to know if Jim was implying that he had done things illegally as president. It was just drama, drama, drama. I'm getting sick of union meetings but if I don't go I'll never know what is going on at school; it's the same with board meetings. I sometimes wonder if it would be better to stick my head in the sand and not look up and around to see what is actually going on around me at school. I can't do that. It's not in my blood. My blood line stood up to a King, put their name on the Declaration of Independence and fought for this country so I would have these unalienable rights; Life, Liberty, and the pursuit of Happiness. I am not a very political person. I don't have any aspirations to hold office or lead a group but I do hope that I can make my own kind of a difference in the world. If I can make a difference in the life of a student who knows what kind of a difference in the world they will make. My happiness lies with my family and my work. I cannot just put my head in the sand. It's not in my blood. I am still very afraid but I think that my ancestors must have been afraid too and they still stood up to defend themselves and fight for others. If they could stand up to the English King, I can stand up to a couple of wannabes.

MARCH 5, 2007

There was an executive committee meeting today right after school. The exec committee was to meet to vote on approving me as election committee chair and to approve the negotiation team – me, Amy, Jim, Jeff, and Pierce. Jim started talking about who would serve on the election committee but Pierce cut him off and started yelling that the people on the negotiation team didn't understand what negotiations were like and were under the impression that Kevin Klein was going to be there to do all of the negotiating and that just wasn't the case. Then he said that no one knew the background of people on the team and he jumped up knocking over his chair, pointed at me and screamed, "Mrs. Martin, why don't you tell us what kind of a background, if any, that you have in negotiations."

My heart almost stopped. I thought he was going to attack me. He has absolutely no idea of my background and what my negotiation skills are. I am a hell of a lot more tactful than he is though; I don't bully people. As marketing manager of a large cable corporation I helped negotiate higher end deals in a month than he could dream about negotiating in a lifetime. How dare he presume to know anything about me?

Someone asked him why he was talking about the negotiation team at this point and he replied that it was being discussed for me to be the negotiation chair. Andrew told him the executive committee was talking about me being election chair. Pierce snickered and said, "Oh, well, that's different; anyone can do that." What an ass. Mister 220 IQ can't even seem to follow a simple conversation.

The election chair was approved but then the executive committee decided that they should put together guidelines for the election committee to follow. I said that I believed the election committee should put together its own guidelines; no other committee has had guidelines set down for them and I believed the executive committee was giving the impression they were taking power away from the committees.

The committee voted to have Jeff work on putting together guidelines. Then they asked me if I felt I could work with Jeff. I said I could work with anyone that I needed to. I was extremely offended that this governing body, who are supposed to be my colleagues and who I have worked with and done many things for more than six years, did not feel they could trust me to put together guidelines to run a simple union election. I think it wasn't so much a slap against me as it was just a way to shut up Pierce and Nikki. I can guarantee you that there is no way in hell that I am using Pierce's suggestions.

The executive committee voted to table the approval of the negotiation team until the end of the year. I think everyone felt there was just too much tension in the room and they wanted to get out of there. Pierce began to grandstand again and said that the efforts of the negotiation team would not be fruitless over the next couple of months. He did his usual pounding on his chest and said that through his contacts with the county association, he could get anything that was needed. The vote to table the negotiation team was passed.

Jim Daniels left me a message at home asking me to call him. He wanted to make sure that I wasn't mad. I'm not mad; I've very offended. But maybe I should be mad. I didn't go looking to chair the election committee. I was asked to do it and now Pierce is trying to shove his guidelines down my throat. How is it that the committee I chair is the only committee that the executive committee is going to regulate? And why do so many people feel the need to placate Pierce? Do they do it just so he will shut up? Don't they realize that it just makes things worse?

MARCH 6, 2007

Edmonson sent me, Amy and Jake to Tri Valley Vo-Tech and River High School to tour both schools and to see the A Plus Computerized program they're using. I'm not sure what it has to do with my job. A Plus is a nice system for a math class but Edmonson got rid of our Math classes. It was just a wasted day!

When we got back to Penn, Jake was checking his school email. Pierce had sent to another email to all the union members about his suggestions for election guidelines. He attached another copy of the guidelines he wrote; they were now up to fifty-six steps. He is not on the election committee and I did not ask for his help. He also included the non-union staff members and administration in the email. Communications that involve the union should never be sent to anyone outside of the union. As a former president, and someone who claims to have a 220 IQ, you think he would know that. Pierce is just trying to make me upset. I'll ignore him as usual. He can play whatever game this is by himself.

APRIL 9, 2007

Edmonson decided he was going to have a meeting with the students today to talk to them about math and reading to pump them up for the state assessment tests. I'm not sure why he felt they he should do this. The home schools handle the state assessment tests for academics. We handle vocational assessments. He stuck a microphone in front of a shy student's face and asked her why the state academic assessment tests were so important. The student was quiet for a moment and before she could say anything Edmonson said, Duhhhhhhhhhhhhhhhhhh! What a great pep talk that was.

APRIL 17, 2007

A school solicitor came from Greensburg to talk about after school activities and how they affect teachers' jobs. We were told if an off campus action causes a disruption in the educational process it is cause for dismissal. That is about as clear as mud. They also talked about evaluations from administration. No need for us to worry about evaluations. Edmonson hasn't done a teacher's evaluation in two years. I thought it was a PDE regulation that evaluations had to be done every year. It doesn't matter to me though; if he doesn't do them it's just an automatic satisfactory. I wonder what you say if you apply for another job and they want to see copies of your prior evaluations. Would they believe that your boss never did them?

APRIL 28, 2007

Another Student Leadership conference is done. There was a minor issue and one of the girls made the decision to go home. She was a senior, eighteen years old and she smokes. I couldn't allow her to smoke at the conference. We were in a non-smoking facility and that was that. I couldn't give her permission to go off somewhere in the city of Pittsburgh so she could smoke. She made the choice to go home because she felt she could not go two days without smoking. She told me that she is so addicted to smoking that she and her mother even leave church services to go outside and smoke. She has been smoking since she was twelve.

I talked to the girl, her parents, and her grandparents; they all agreed she should go home. The problem with the situation was that no one in her family could come and get her. I called Edmonson and Peter but neither answered my calls. I left them both messages. I decided to call Brian who is her shop teacher. He just happened to be at a Pittsburgh Pirates' game so he called her mother, got permission to drive her the 60 miles home, left the ball game and came and got her. The world would be so much better if there were more teachers like him.

Since Miranda left, I am the only advisor for the club. I miss working with her but I handled all the meetings and projects just fine. When it came time for the conference Edmonson wanted me take Chuck as another chaperone. I thought it was a good idea but I'm not sure if he was sent as a chaperone or a spy? He was on the phone back and forth with the school constantly. He would always walk away from me when he was talking to them. Funny how I had left a message for Edmonson to call me but he never did, he called Chuck. I asked Chuck if Edmonson had asked to talk to me and he told me no that he had handled things. How exactly did he handle things? He didn't do anything when it came to dealing with the smoking situation. I will have to remember for next year to make sure everyone is clear that if they smoke they cannot smoke for two days.

APRIL 30, 2007

Pat told me today that Edmonson said he was going to abolish the special education jobs at the end of the year and replace us with paraprofessionals under the federal grant. That would be a form of supplanting. That's illegal. Amy and Jake and I need to talk to someone about this. I have my doubts that the regional union will be much help; they never helped me with the Pierce situation but there are other people involved in this so maybe, we'll see. Now I understand why Nikki would never tell me when there was a Perkins PPC meeting; she didn't want me to know that she and Edmonson were planning to eliminate my job.

I also found out when I got back from the Student Leadership conference that Edmonson suspended the girl who came home from the conference. For what possible reason? She didn't cause a problem. I took care of it. I felt sorry for her that she missed a wonderful opportunity because she couldn't go two days without a cigarette but I didn't look at it as a problem for me; it is just one of those things you have to deal with when you teach on a high school level. Edmonson said she was an embarrassment to the school. She was an embarrassment? In my opinion Edmonson is an embarrassment!

MAY 1, 2007

Brian was going to be out of town for two days and he has a very small class this semester. He asked me if his kids could come to my room while he was gone because Edmonson said there were no subs available and he was going to deny Brian his personal days. Brian's been a good friend and I like his kids and I am the support teacher for his shop so I said yes. On the 30th I took the kids for a walk to look at landscape items for a design technique that I learned at Fallingwater. The next morning Edmonson told the kids that they didn't have to do "arts and crafts" with me, and if they wanted to walk around the campus and get lost for the day they could pick up debris. He said they could take anyone they wanted. They wanted to do it but I told them they could only do it by themselves; they weren't going to interrupt other shops and upset the teachers. I gave them a pass to get garbage bags and pick up debris. Edmonson stopped them and told them I had to go with them to pick up garbage. He completely contradicted what he had said, but that is a daily occurrence. Needless to say, we did not go out and pick up garbage. He can pick it up himself.

MAY 4, 2007

Kevin Klein met with the union officers and me, Amy and Jake today about our jobs being cut. Klein said well, "It is illegal, but we will just sit back and wait to see if he does it and if he does then we're going to push for a transfer of entities." He also said he advised us, strongly advised us not to do anything…do not contact any board members or administrators or parents. He said if we did talk to any board members we could be considered insubordinate and be terminated. What the hell kind of advice is that? He did not mention one word about trying to save our jobs at Penn. What he said didn't make any sense. Why would we sit back and watch Edmonson do something illegal *again?* Well, I guess it makes sense if you think about the fact that Klein and Pierce are close friends and Nikki and Pierce are having an affair and Nikki is the one who is writing the grant with Edmonson to abolish my job. Neither one would care that they would have to kick Amy and Jake to the curb to get to me.

Amy called me after she got home. Her husband, Ted, was furious. Ted said Edmonson wasn't his boss and he could do anything he damn well pleased. He called our board president who said he didn't know anything about our jobs being cut. It seems like Edmonson does whatever he wants and the board says they don't know anything about it, but they don't do anything about him. No one on the board has ever contacted me about the problems I've had at Penn and I've written to them and given them my contact information for both at work and at home many times. I could make a book out of the letters, memos and emails that I have sent to Edmonson, the superintendents and the board. We'll see what happens next.

MAY 21, 2007

Pierce has become more openly hostile toward me. He leers at me during meetings and he has started lunging toward me more frequently in the hallways. I sent Klein, Bryson and Daniels another letter about my safety concerns. I emailed it yesterday. A few minutes after I left the school today Edmonson called me on my cell phone. I don't know why he waited until I left school to call me on my cell. I was in the same school building with him all day. Maybe he wanted me to know that he had my cell phone number. I guess talking to him by phone is better than standing by him and having him putting his hands on me all of the time.

He said he just got my "note" and was going to talk to Bryson about setting up a meeting with me for the next morning. He said Bryson would be in the building for something else anyway. We'll see if he talks to me tomorrow. He cancels a lot of meetings.

May 22, 2007

I wasn't sure what was going on today before the meeting because Pierce was meeting with Edmonson and Bryson and the solicitor. He stormed out of the conference room and went straight out the front door. I found out later that Pierce had been suspended for three days because he allegedly had become verbally volatile with a student. He didn't hit the student, but allegedly was cussing at him and lunged at him. The boy's father called board members about it. It is strange. Board members don't care what teachers have to say but if a parent calls them they start to get nervous. They should remember that parents aren't the only ones who vote.

I don't know if they were trying to appease me or taunt me. The solicitor gave me a song and dance about due process and how they just can't fire Pierce for what he's done to me. He also said that he would have handled things differently because he's a man. I couldn't believe my ears. He actually tried to explain it so I clearly understood. In a very slow manner like he thought I was stupid and would only be able to understand if he talked slowly he said, "You see, everyone has a different level of response-ability. And he, because he is a man, would have had the *ability* to have handled Pierce differently." I have to say it; I think that Pierce could take him. I don't see a lot of ability there.

Anyways. Once again, they told me that they would review the situation and get back to me. They always tell me that and they never get back to me. What exactly are they reviewing and with whom? I think they are just hoping I will eventually go away. In one of my behavior classes at Washington University I learned about a technique called Extinction. If you want to get rid of a behavior in someone you can sometimes just ignore them and they will eventually just go away. They cannot extinguish me. I am not going away. It is their responsibility to make sure I work in a safe, hostile free environment. Why do they look at me like I am the problem?

MAY 24, 2007

I had dinner with Hank and Katy. Hank told me he ran into Rick who said Edmonson had been down to his shop. Edmonson told him that I was happy about Pierce's suspension. Rick told Edmonson that he believed not even I was happy about how the suspension came about. I think that Edmonson knows Rick and Pierce are close friends. Edmonson must be hoping that Rick will tell Pierce how happy I supposedly am so there will be trouble from the minute he gets back.

MAY 25, 2007

Last night I went to the Regional Economic Development Council's Annual Dinner at Nemacolin Woodlands as the guest of a friend. Governor Ridge was there for a brief presentation before dinner.

I was standing in the arrival area when Edmonson came in. He looked stunned to see me there. I was equally stunned when he came up to me, told me that I looked absolutely beautiful, grabbed me, hugged me and dove in for a kiss. I turned my head quickly and he caught my cheek. Judas! Send me a potential lay-off notice and kiss me on the cheek. I couldn't do anything though but stand there. I had a drink in one hand and my clutch in the other hand. I thought about kneeing him in the groin, knocking him down and throwing my drink on him but I did not think it was wise to make a scene at an event where the Governor of Pennsylvania was the Keynote Speaker. I did pull back hard and walked away from him as fast as I could without breaking into a run. Edmonson didn't speak to me for the rest of the night. It made my night a lot nicer. I saw a lot of people I've known for years who now hold what Edmonson would consider influential positions. He tried to suck up to as many of them as he could as fast as he could. He kept gushing over a lot of the women and then would glare at me. Did he think I might be jealous? Not a chance in the world!

I think Edmonson wanted to punish me today for last night. He called me himself first thing this morning and said we don't have money left for subs. He told me to spend the day in Computer Tech as a sub. It's not that I mind so much because the kids are great; it's just that I can't get any of my own work done when I am not in my room and I don't understand why there is no sub money. There was plenty of sub money to have paid people this year to do security work and work on special projects for him and work on print work and vinyl lettering work for the office. I don't understand where that man's priorities lie. Certainly not with the students!

May 29, 2007

Amy and I went to Daniel's room this afternoon right after school to look at the tentative school budget. Our jobs aren't included in the budget. I guess that is a very good indication of how serious Edmonson is about cutting our jobs. Amy was going to call Jake later. It is never the kind of news that you want to tell someone.

When we were going back to our classrooms we could hear my phone ringing. It was close to 3:00. It was an outside line ringing but I couldn't get to it in time. I didn't want to run for it and take a chance on falling again. It went into voice mail and they left a message. It was the same woman who had called me last week about Nikki. When she called last week she said she overhead Nikki talking to someone and laughing about how she wrote the letter to the board about me and Miranda last year from a concerned parent. This time the woman said I should keep an eye on Nikki and Pierce because they were planning on writing another letter about me. I wonder who this woman is and how she knows what they are doing. It has to be someone close to one of them? I have a strange feeling that the woman is Pierce's wife.

I believe this woman. It doesn't surprise me but it does make me sick. I told Edmonson but he didn't seem to care at all. A thought then occurred to me. If Nikki wrote the letter, the only way she would know the things that happened would be if Edmonson told her. Is that why he doesn't care? Does he know about it? Did he put her up to it? There were only six students at the conference with us. Anyone smart would have to know it wouldn't be hard to figure out which parent wrote the letter, and after talking to the kids I didn't think any of the parents wrote the letter.

I forwarded the message to Edmonson, Pierce, Nikki, Jim and Liv. I wanted Pierce and Nikki to know that I knew what they had done. I forwarded it to Jim and Liv since they are union officers. I didn't hear anything from Edmonson before the board meeting but I saw him in the hall. He grabbed my arm and asked me what I was implying with that message? He asked me if I knew that woman. I told him I didn't know the woman but it was the same woman who called last week. Edmonson said he talked to the solicitor and they would check into it. Of course they will.

After the board meeting I asked the solicitor if Edmonson had talked to him about the phone calls. He said that he had mentioned something about it. He seemed very unsure about the whole situation though. I wonder what Edmonson had really told him. Thank goodness I was able to tape record the phone message. Hank is going to ask Katy to put it on a CD for me. It is so frustrating. If Nikki and Pierce wrote that letter trying to trash my reputation who knows what they are really capable of. In hind sight I probably should not have forwarded the message the woman left me to Pierce and Nikki. If it is Pierce's wife did I just put her in danger or does she have enough on Pierce to keep herself safe?

Amy and I were supposed to meet with the board tonight. Jake wasn't able to be there. He is a good man and he has been under so much stress lately. In the past year he has lost his mother and he and his wife just had a new baby. Now he was having chest pains and ended up in the hospital. Edmonson is putting so much unnecessary stress on him by threatening to eliminate our jobs and take away our livelihoods. Edmonson knows he has to cut all three of our jobs to get to me because of seniority. He has done it before. He and Bart told me when they laid off all of the aides that it was a shame they had to cut so many people to get to one. Edmonson told us that we were not permitted to talk to the board. He said anything we had to say would need to go through the union.

Jim said Pierce is taking the rest of the year of due to high blood pressure because of all the stress that he is under. Right!! He is under pressure? It's only two weeks but it works for me though. I feel much more at ease knowing that he will not be in the building for the rest of the year.

JULY 1, 2007
I'm not sure what happened with our jobs but the board didn't cut any of our jobs. Jake resigned though and they are not going to fill his position. He was hired at the Mountain District. He said he couldn't work for a man that he couldn't trust. I'm sure he didn't tell the board that. He just needed to feel secure in being able to provide for his family.

AUGUST 6, 2007
I got a call early this morning from the school. Lindsay, our office manager, said Edmonson wanted to see me at noon about a room change. When I got there the office staff was at lunch so I called his extension and he told me to come back to his office. He told me that a nearby community college was going to be coming into our school to teach classes for an associate degree in Electricity *hopefully* in the near future and they needed my classroom

and Amy's classroom immediately. He wants to move one of us upstairs and one of us downstairs. I don't understand why he is taking our rooms now. I don't think the community college is going to be coming in at all. It will probably be another one of his great plans that goes nowhere.

Edmonson wants me to talk to Amy to see who will take the upper office and who will take the lower office. It's not even a classroom. How are we supposed to work with students? We'll have to see about the split in the districts too. Edmonson also said that Brian is only going to have kids the first semester and that he's going to have to close him second semester. That wasn't approved at the board meeting. I wonder if they know about this. I asked him if he had told Brian. He said no but that Brian was a free spirit and he would probably just want to do something else. There is something seriously wrong with Edmonson's ability to deal with people. He just causes major upheaval in people's lives without so much as a ten second thought. He thrives on all of this drama. My head was spinning. And then he told me that he talked to Pierce and he wasn't going to be returning to Penn when school started. He said he was just waiting on his retirement letter. Oh my God, that would be fantastic! My happiness was short lived when his true nature came out. He came around to the back of my chair and put his hands on my shoulders and squeezed. He told me that I had the power to control what happened. I wasn't sure what he was talking about but I decided to take control of the moment. I pushed the chair back as hard as I could. It went a little faster and a little harder than I thought it would. I guess that was because the chair was on wheels and I pushed off with my hands on the table. He staggered back a bit and doubled over. I didn't stop to see if he was alright, I just bolted out the door. There was no one there to help me and if I called anyone would they believe me? Is that why he had me come at noon; so everyone would be at lunch?

AUGUST 7, 2007
I talked to Amy. Edmonson had already called her yesterday afternoon. He told her that he wanted her to take the lower level office and the lower level shops because he felt that she had a better rapport with the staff on the lower level. That isn't exactly true. I get along well with everyone on the lower level except Pierce. Oh well, I guess I'm going upstairs, close to Edmonson. I wonder if he made that decision before or after I ran him over with the chair. I still don't understand how I am supposed to teach without a classroom. The students we mostly work with have it written in

their education plans that they are supposed to have a separate place to go to be able to study and get academic help. I guess with an office we will only be able to see one student at a time.

AUGUST 10, 2007

There was a small fire at Penn this morning. From what I heard it started as an electrical fire in the maintenance room. It took about an hour to get the fire put out. It won't affect the start of school or most of the shops but of course my classroom was close enough that it a majority of books and supplies had severe smoke and water damage. I guess I won't have that much to move. I really won't know until school starts. I don't want to set foot in that building unless it is absolutely necessary.

AUGUST 17, 2007

The clock is ticking on the EEOC letter. The law states that civil suits must be filed within two years of the date of the incident. The specific incident date we were looking at was August 26, 2005; the date I was injured. To file in federal court we needed the green light letter from the EEOC. Checking the mail every day has been torture! My mother is an amazing woman! She was a wonderful social worker and she knew that waiting would not get you anywhere. She counseled me to call Senator Spector's office to see how they could help expedite the letter. His staff was nice but they still live in the world of bureaucracy. They requested that I write a letter detailing the information which I could fax to them and they would pass along to the Senator. I wrote the letter and before I even faxed it a light bulb went off in my head. Why didn't I call the EEOC? We live in a world of email and faxes and forms, but there are still people; *real* people who work there. I'm a real person. Why couldn't I just call them and talk to someone? After a handful of transfers I talked to a staff member who found the green light decision letter in a stack waiting to be typed. There was no way to tell how long it would take. I explained the situation and asked her to please help me. She promised me that she would pull the letter, type it herself and get it in the mail that very same day. She even called me back to tell me that she had done it. The woman whose name I don't even know completely restored my faith in people going out of their way to help each other. She was a God send.

AUGUST 20, 2007

I went to the Student Leadership Advisors Meeting today. It was a pretty good meeting. There are around twenty schools in the Pittsburgh region that participate. I'm looking forward to working with the group again. The student projects will focus on mentoring younger students this year. Edmonson hasn't signed the contract yet. Hopefully he'll do that soon. The program is completely cost free to the school. We even get funding for the students to do their projects and then we can take as many as fifteen students to the Leadership Conference in Pittsburgh for two days. It's such a great experience for everyone involved. Some of the students have never stayed in a hotel before let alone some place as nice as the Downtown Marriott. You would think that it would be a no brainer but since I am involved he is dragging his feet.

AUGUST 21, 2007

My Garcia was relieved but still worried about getting the EEOC documentation in time to meet the deadline. We trusted this unknown woman but what about the postal service? Would it get lost in a bag somewhere? I once owned a third class mailing business and I used to find all kinds of mail in the bottom of empty bags the post office gave me to put the bulk mail in. This was too important to leave to the postal service. The decision was made to file in the Commonwealth of Pennsylvania Court and then petition to move to federal court when the EEOC letter came.

AUGUST 23, 2007

So much for that retirement letter from Pierce that Edmonson was waiting on. He showed up for the first day of in-service. Helena Maven didn't come back. I don't think she had any idea of the preparation it takes to actually become a teacher. We were meeting in the large conference room. Edmonson had placed our teacher binders where we were supposed to sit. They were divided into four groups. Edmonson apparently wanted to prove to me that he could still mess with me all he wanted; I was placed in a group with Pierce and a few others. Luckily Rick picked up his and Pierce's books and moved to another table. Edmonson just looked at him like he wanted to say something to him but he just didn't have the guts. This is a great way to start the day. Why would Edmonson sit me and Pierce together?

Edmonson told us that he had a big announcement; he was going to have Chuck named as Principal of the building. Why do we need a Principal at Penn? We don't offer any kind of academics any more, not since the math department was dissolved. Even if we did, the job would have to be posted and awarded. And what about a guidance counselor? Nothing against

Chuck but there is a legal process that needs to be followed; you just don't appoint people to positions. I don't know what is the matter with me? I keep forgetting that Edmonson can do anything he wants to and gets away with it. The law be damned!

AUGUST 24, 2007

Edmonson is still telling people that next year there won't be any special education people in the building. It's the beginning of a new school year and he is already making plans to get rid of me. Maybe because I plowed him down with the chair. He is just lucky that I haven't snapped so far and plowed him over with my car in the parking lot. I think about it. It scares me to think that I don't believe I would feel the least little bit bad about it. I can't imagine that I would ever actually do it but sometimes I do dream about it.

Usually on the second day of in-service in the afternoon Edmonson lets us have a union meeting and then get our rooms ready. Today he called us all together for one more meeting. It was actually quite funny. He strutted around the room and told everyone that *many* people have sued him and even called PDE in Harrisburg and told them he was crazy and shouldn't be working at the school. He looked directly at me and said, "You know what? I've beat them all! I've beat every lawsuit that anybody has tried to bring against me." He pointed his finger at me and said a little bit louder, "I have beaten them all!"

I don't think he's ever been sued. But even if he has I thought it was just a touch ironic that at that very moment the paperwork was being filed at the County Courthouse; by my mother who not only was my strength but who had become an active member of the Garcia team. It made me smile; and smile big. Edmonson looked very confused. What could I possibly be smiling about?

AUGUST 26, 2007

I got a phone call at home from a friend who works at the newspaper. The story was hitting the local newspaper the next day about the lawsuit; only the story said the lawsuit was filed in federal court. I talked to my Garcia. A last minute feeling told him to take the gamble and file in federal court before the deadline, knowing that the EEOC letter was on its way. We were doubly covered.

My boss, the bully, the superintendents, solicitor, and school board members would all be reading about the federal lawsuit in the morning's newspaper. What a way to find out you have been sued. I wondered how things would be now. I wondered if they would take this seriously. I wondered if by involving the federal court I was finally on my journey to justice.

AUGUST 27, 2007

As I drove to school I knew that the next few years would be a test of my convictions but I was ready; I held my head up high and walked through the doors.